Pink

Stephanie Powell

ISBN: 098961221X
ISBN 13: 9780989612210
Library of Congress Control Number: 2013909785
KickStart Press

Dedication

To my teen first readers—Tasneem Ahsanullah, Claire Herlin, Celina McPhail, and Ashley Pancho—who shared with me their insightful and heartfelt feedback.

I

Cassie opened her locker and rifled through the remains of last semester: a biology project, volleyball kneepads, old English papers. From the bottom, she pulled out *United States History: The American Experience*. To Cassie, the book was as heavy as it was dull. Out of the corner of her eye, she spied Ashley threading her way through the crisscrossing students.

"Cassie!"

Oh no, Cassie groaned to herself. *Just because we were friends in the first grade doesn't make us besties for life.* She hoisted her backpack and slinked off, hoping Ashley would see another person she knew. No such luck.

"Hey, wait up! Didn't you hear me calling you?"

"I've got to get to history. Mrs. Watson is strict about tardies."

Ashley had the irritating habit of not taking a hint. "That's what I want to talk to you about. You're not going to believe it." She paused, reveling in the drama: "Mrs. Watson turned."

"No way," Cassie shot back. "She'd never do that." Cassie thought of her history teacher as tough yet fair with a dry sense of humor that made sleeping pills like the Articles of the Confederation go down a little easier.

"Kristen had her in first period," Ashley said. "She told me." The second bell rang.

"Ashley, I've got to go," Cassie declared as she took off down the crowded hallway. She wanted to unload Ashley as much as get to class on time, which now wasn't going to happen. For Cassie, punctuality was still a work in progress.

Slipping into the classroom, Cassie took her usual seat near the wilting ficus tree. Mrs. Watson wrote an assignment on the whiteboard—at least Cassie thought it was Mrs. Watson. The Mrs. Watson she remembered before winter break was tall with wavy blonde hair past her shoulders and a figure that could best be described as voluptuous.

Well, she's still tall, Cassie thought.

Mrs. Watson wore grey trousers and a white button-down shirt, a far cry from her usual splashy print dresses. Her hair, now dark brown, was cropped close, her body straight where it had once curved. The look of shock on Cassie's face matched every student in the classroom.

It wasn't that the girls hadn't seen a turned male before—more and more students had a mec in the family: a mother who was now a father, an uncle who had once been an aunt. The name—from the French word for *guy*—came from the scores of women in Paris who had started the trend of having surgery to become male.

Mrs. Watson took a deep breath. "I guess I don't have to tell you what I did over the holidays," she noted, the droll quip lost on the dumbfounded girls. She pressed on. "As you can see, I underwent gender reassignment surgery. I know this is a surprise, but I'm still your teacher. In time, the strangeness will fade."

Mrs. Watson put the marker back on the whiteboard holder. "And considering the world we live in, it's actually not so strange. But for now, we have the aftermath of the Great War to contend with." She punctuated her statement by pulling down a pre-World War II map of Europe.

Even her voice is different, Cassie remarked to herself as she raised her hand. *It's all raspy and deep like she's got a cold.*

"Yes, Cassie?"

"What should we call you?"

"Mr. Watson would be appropriate," she—who was now a he—answered. The students pulled out their notebooks, knowing they wouldn't be able to concentrate on anything but the familiar stranger before them.

***

The cafeteria buzzed as students seesawed between the excitement of seeing friends and the depressing realization that winter break was over. George Washington was the largest high school in the area that had once been Washington, D.C. When the school was built, its turrets and towers lent the air of a venerable university. With the passage of time, however, the deteriorating buildings and neglected grounds looked less like a college and more like a mental institution.

Cassie, Ashley, and Terry, Cassie's best friend since the fifth grade, grabbed a table near the soda fountain.

"Why would she do that?" Cassie asked as she took a turkey sandwich from a brown paper bag. "What would make a normal person—a normal *woman*—want to turn male?"

Terry pushed her short auburn hair behind her ears, her angular face showing indifference. "Personally, I don't see what the big deal is—if Mrs. Watson wants to be a mec, that's her business."

Ashley leaned in. "I wonder if she did the downstairs part, too," she said, raising her eyebrows.

Cassie put down her sandwich. "I don't want to think about it." She tore open a bag of pretzels, grabbed one, and popped it into her mouth.

"Of course, she did," Terry answered. "I mean, why stop at the top?"

"Yeah," Ashley continued, pushing her tortoiseshell glasses up her nose as if to take a better look at the image in her head. "They take your pink and turn it inside out—"

"Yeah, we know," Cassie said, glowering at Ashley. "It's just so permanent. Why would anyone want to do that?"

"Maybe she did it for her, I mean his, wife," Terry offered.

Mr. Watson's screensaver materialized in Cassie's mind: it was a photograph of the female Mr. Watson with her arm around a woman with cinnamon-colored hair. Their smiles beamed happiness.

"I just don't get it," Cassie said with finality.

Terry spoke only when Cassie's eyes met hers: "I guess she did it for love."

"Love?" Cassie snapped. "Is that what love is? You have to com-pletely change who you are so the other person will *love* you?" Heat fanned across her face.

I don't know much—well, anything, really—about love, she admit-ted to herself. *But having to turn into a different person for it just seems wrong.*

"Or maybe changing for someone is the way you *show* love," Terry responded.

The conversation made Cassie's head hurt. She took a bite of her sandwich as if to end the subject, then rose and stuffed her half-eaten lunch into the brown paper bag.

"If I'm late for economics again," Cassie mumbled through the mouthful, "Duncan will give me Saturday school. I'll see you two later." She crossed the cafeteria, tossed the paper bag into the trash, and then pushed through the double doors into the commons.

"Cassie, wait up!" Terry called out, hustling after her.

"I really need to get to class," Cassie said, striding forward. During the winter break, Terry had dropped a bombshell—*I want to be more than friends*, she'd told Cassie. *I think it just makes sense to, you know, take our friendship to the next level.* Blindsided, Cassie had been barely able to reply. She'd never considered her best friend as any-thing more than that.

"About what I said before—" Terry began.

"I told you," Cassie responded, her words clipped with impa-tience. "I want to be *friends*—that's all." Cassie knew she sounded mad—in reality, she was terrified.

Will this thing *ever go away?* she sighed in despair. *Or will it ruin our friendship?* The last question made her stomach feel like a cement mixer, heavy and churning. Despite her rumbling innards, Cassie was sure of two things: she loved her best friend—and Terry as a *love interest* was as weird a concept as Christmas in July.

Terry matched Cassie's pace. "I'm just asking you to keep an open mind," she said as she pulled out a small gift-wrapped box from her pocket. "Didn't think I'd forget, did you? Happy birthday."

Cassie stopped, her face softening as she eyed the gift. "Thanks," she responded, putting the present into her backpack. "I'll open it tonight." As Cassie walked off, Terry added, "Cake and ice cream sound really great . . ."

The hopeful look on Terry's face made Cassie flinch. *It'll be weird not having Terry at my birthday celebration*, she thought, *but this whole* next level *thing is so awkward—I don't want it to ruin my birthday.*

"Yeah, about that," Cassie began with a hint of apology, "my birthday's going to be really low key this year, just me and my mom. I'll see you tomorrow." And with that, Cassie disappeared into the current of girls in the hallway.

2

Cassie sat at the kitchen table in the dark as her mother, Amanda, carried a red velvet cake, stepping slowly so as not to fan the lit candles. After a wobbly rendition of the birthday song, Amanda set down the cake, bathing Cassie's face in a warm glow. Luka, a husky with silver and black fur, positioned herself for cake crumbs at Cassie's side.

"Go on, make a wish," Amanda said.

Every year, Cassie wished for the same thing—that her mother would find the cure for SN-146, the virus that had killed every male on the planet.

Ten years ago, virologist Amanda O'Connell had been on the front lines to find a cure. None was found. Even after the epidemic and ensuing Black Years, the dark aftermath of chaos and starvation, male babies created by artificial insemination still died within days of birth. XY, as it was more commonly known, picked them off like a sniper.

As the years stretched on, the cure remained elusive. Amanda knew that, even with sperm banks around the world, artificial insemination was not the long-term answer—one day that supply would run out. To Amanda, finding a cure was no less than saving the human race.

Cassie blew the candle flames into curls of smoke. "You know what I always wish for, Mom, and it's going to come true . . . someday."

"Yes," her mother replied as she turned on the light, "someday soon, I hope."

Cassie looked at the cake: *Happy Birthday Cassie & Cody* was written on top in loopy red frosting. "Happy birthday, Cody," she whispered. "I miss you." After letting a swell of anguish subside in her chest, Cassie slid a knife into the cake, then flopped a slightly mangled wedge onto a plate.

"What do you think Cody would look like today?" Cassie asked.

"He'd look like you, only the boy version, complete with wavy chestnut hair and hazel eyes. When you were toddlers, people thought you were identical twins."

Cassie enjoyed listening to her mother talk about Cody and her father, mostly because she did it so rarely. "I'm scared I'm forgetting them both," Cassie said, her voice drifting. "Last night, I remembered Cody's thing for waffles with Marshmallow Fluff, then I realized I hadn't thought about that in years."

The concerned look on Cassie's face melted into a smile as she thought of her brother smeared with sticky white. "He always hated it when I told him I was his big sister. But I *am* fifteen minutes older than him . . . or was, anyway." Cassie licked icing from her fingers. "I wish I could remember him at the end."

"Maybe that's a good thing," her mother commented. "Some memories are better left forgotten."

"No, I want to remember them all," Cassie shot back, "even the bad ones." An uneasy stillness stretched across the kitchen table. "It was really cold and windy the day they took Dad away. He was wrapped in an old sheet. They threw him in the back of that truck like he was a log. All those bodies . . ."

Although she could see her mother's eyes glisten, Cassie pressed on. "But the last thing I remember about Cody is playing Guess Who? with him. And he was cheating because somehow he knew who my person was before we even got started. The next morning, he was gone."

"After losing Dad, I thought the sight of your brother would be too much."

Cassie noticed something in her mother's tone. Sadness was always there when she talked about Cody. Yet beneath the sorrow was a whisper of guilt. Before Cassie could let the idea sink in, Amanda nodded toward a small present tucked behind a clump of giftwrap. "Is that from Terry? I'm surprised she's not here tonight."

"I didn't invite her."

"Did you two have a fight?"

"Not exactly . . . it's hard to describe." Cassie tore off the wrapping paper and opened the box—inside was a ring made of interlocking silver bands. "She's my best friend. She always will be."

One of Amanda's eyebrows crept upward. "But she wants more?"

Even though she was close to her mother, Cassie squirmed at the turn in the conversation. "I know girls are pairing up . . . that's the way it is now. I just don't know how I'm supposed to feel."

Amanda sighed. "It's tough growing up in this new world. I don't envy you." She regretted the words the moment she saw her daughter's face fall. "You'll find your way, Cassie. Don't let Terry or anyone pressure you. You'll know when the time is right."

Cassie took the opportunity to let the subject drop even though there was still more on her mind. *All those old movies, where the guy takes the girl in his arms and kisses her—will I ever know what that feels like?*

At school, Cassie had noticed girls holding hands in the hallways and had witnessed Marcy Stone and Sue Ming getting popped for PDA in the cafeteria—their lip-lock left little to the imagination.

Yet Cassie had never felt that way about anyone—*if Terry, my closest friend, doesn't make me feel like that, then who will?*

She stared at the ring in the box and then snapped the lid shut.

3

The boy crouched behind a thicket of brambles watching two rabbits nuzzle through the snow. They worked their jaws, chewing what brown grass was left under the white crust.

Killing the first rabbit would be easy—placing the arrow in its head so as not to damage the soft fur was a skill well ingrained in the boy's muscles. He raised a second arrow in his quiver; he would need to replace the first in order to hit the rabbit that would soon be running for its life. The boy drew back the bow, held his breath, and released.

Fzzt!

The arrow found its mark just below the rabbit's ears. The other rabbit leapt into the air and then hit the ground, tearing between the trees. The boy gave chase, his legs pounding the earth as he took aim at the zigzagging target. He let go of the bowstring just as the rabbit jumped over a rock.

The fleeing animal slammed into a tree, pinned by the arrow. The boy approached, then firmly grasped the kicking mass of fur by the scruff of the neck. The rabbit snapped at the air. When the boy was ten, a rabbit had sunk its teeth into his forearm; the bite had left behind two scars—the raised white line in his skin and the memory of the pain etched into his brain.

The boy tightened his hold on the writhing animal and pulled the arrow from the tree, being careful to avoid gnashing teeth. Then he twisted his grip, producing a faint *snap*—the rabbit fell limp. After attaching the drooping animal to his belt, the boy retraced his steps to retrieve his first kill.

***

The lake's edge was rocky and steep. The boy set down his bow, quiver, hunting knife, and rabbits. Shielding his eyes from the sun, he watched as a hawk rose on an updraft.

The boy stripped off his jacket, shirt, and pants. After kicking off his boots, he scrambled to the top of a boulder that jutted over the water. Glints of light flashed on the lake's surface. A crisp breeze played over his skin. He dove.

Freezing daggers pierced his body as he swam down. He opened his eyes to the darkness. The deeper he swam, the blacker the water became. His lungs burned.

Suddenly, the boy felt as though someone had grabbed him by the ankle. He searched in the dark with his hands, discovering that his foot had become wedged in the branches of a sunken limb. The boy tried to free himself, but the snare held tight. He fought the tree, the cold, the darkness.

As his consciousness slipped away, the boy felt a strange sensation wash over him. Slowly, he realized that he was no longer in the lake but in another place, a black one of unfathomable size. Pinpricks of light appeared—they began to swirl, filling the boy with fear and wonder. The lights whirled until they became a brilliant blur. The vortex pulled at the boy—some unknown sense told him to let the radiant spiral take him. Instead, his will to live reared like a wild animal.

The shock of cold water brought the boy's consciousness back to the depths of the lake. He wrestled himself from the snare and then flailed his numb arms toward the surface. The boy broke through the water just as his breath was spent. He took in and blew out ragged breaths, trying to quell his need for air. When his panting subsided, the boy swam to the shore. He pulled himself from the lake and fell on his back, splaying arms and legs on the ground.

The winter sun radiated on the boy's wet gooseflesh. His chest heaved. As his mind drifted back to his brush with death, the boy recalled a memory, one that surfaced from deep within his past.

The lights, the fear, the awe ... I've felt all that before, a long time ago.

***

From the slope overlooking the lake, the tracker watched the figure through a telephoto lens. As the silhouette undressed, the camera whirred through several exposures. The tracker continued to shoot even though the angle wasn't right. When the form dove into the lake, she thought *Fool! No one in their right mind swims in a mountain lake in winter.* The tracker rested the camera on her knee. *This can't last long.*

After a time, the figure broke the surface, treaded water, and then swam toward the shore. As the form emerged from the lake, the tracker clicked the shutter; once again, she could only see the person's back.

Damn. Turn around.

And the figure did just that, sprawling spread-eagled on the ground. The tracker looked through the lens, zooming in as close as possible. She caught her breath, almost forgetting to shoot. The naked figure lay in full view.

It's been a long time since I've seen the likes of that!

His testicles were drawn up by the cold, something that didn't happen with those who had undergone surgery.

He's an authentic!

The tracker's heart beat fast enough to jostle the camera. *I've found one! I'm going to be rich!* She sat back on her haunches, realizing that her years of hunting down every rumor, false lead, and lunatic raving on the existence of a live male had finally paid off.

The tracker watched as the male dressed, gathered his belongings, and then vanished into the woods. After taking a moment to absorb what she'd just witnessed, the woman packed up her equipment and headed down the mountainside.

4

The boy entered the cabin. "Mom? Emily?"

He leaned the bow and quiver against the split log wall and scanned the room. A black pot-bellied stove squatted in a corner. Three beds, covered with quilts, stood against the walls. A rough-hewn table with wooden chairs took up the center.

The boy swung open the back door to an expanse of land that ended at the tree line. He stood in the doorway, admiring the hazy outline of mountains in the distance.

Near a massive stack of cordwood, the boy's mother, Jane, placed a log upright on a tree stump. She was dressed in a wool coat, tan shirt, and faded jeans, her short hair sprinkled with wood chips. In a smooth arc, Jane came down on the log with an ax; the wood split in two and fell to the ground. She looked up at her son.

"Good, rabbit stew for dinner," Jane said, wiping her forehead with the back of her hand. "We still have carrots and onions in the larder." A ten-year-old girl with messy braids picked up the pieces of wood and placed them on the stack. As Sam approached, Jane noticed the dark patches on his jacket left by his shoulder-length wet hair.

"Sam, I told you not to go swimming—someone could see you."

"Like who, the squirrels?"

"No, the wolves," Emily chimed, "not that they'd be interested in your bag of bones." She spotted the rabbits hanging from her brother's belt. "Would you make me some mittens?"

"Bag of bones, eh?"

Emily smiled oh-so-sweetly. "What I meant to say was 'bag of bones that could feed a pack for a week.' "

Jane was not amused. "Sam, you never know who's in the woods—hunters, rangers—it's dangerous for you to swim, especially because you insist on doing it without clothes on. I've told you time and again not to do that."

"No kidding," Sam responded. He'd already decided not to tell his mother about his close call with the sunken tree. He also knew the danger she referred to had nothing to do with drowning.

During the Black Years, Jane had kept her family on the move. It took Sam a while to figure out that he was the reason they never stayed in one place. Sam had asked his mother why he hadn't ended up like the bloated corpses that littered the streets during the worst of the epidemic—she had no answer.

When Sam was nine and Emily, three, Jane found the cabin outside of Sutter's Creek in the Canadian Rockies. No plumbing, no electricity, no neighbors. A decrepit outhouse stood forty yards too far in the winter and forty yards too close in the summer. The family settled in to make a home. Jane liked that the local folk kept to themselves. Emily made pets out of the chipmunks that lived under the cabin. And Sam scouted the wilderness, turning it into his own personal playground.

"I haven't been to town in two years, and now I can't go swimming?"

Sam recalled the last time he'd been to Sutter's Creek: an old woman had pointed a gnarled finger at him, staring wide-eyed and speechless. Jane gathered up their supplies and hustled Sam and Emily out the door. They rode home to the sound of creaking wood and thudding hooves as their horse Bailey pulled the wagon over the rutted dirt road. Jane's furrowed brow had spoken well enough. Now Sam saw that same expression on his mother's face.

"You need to wear clothing when you swim," Jane said, searching her son's face for any sign of common sense.

"I tried that—it just weighs me down."

Jane shook her head and then placed another log on the tree stump. She wondered how long she would be able to keep her son safe. At 16, she had little control over him. *What will happen when he's twenty? Twenty-five? Will he be content to live at the cabin making mittens for his little sister?*

"Those rabbits aren't going to skin themselves," Jane stated, hoping her stern tone would mask her fear. She swung down on the wood. "What are you waiting for?"

***

The aroma of baking cornbread filled the cabin. Jane stood in front of the black stove, stirring a large pot of rabbit stew. She brought a ladleful to her mouth, and upon tasting it, nodded with satisfaction. It never failed to amaze her that such simple ingredients—rabbit, onion, carrots, spices, and a little flour—could yield something so satisfying.

"Sam, Emily, dinner's ready!"

Emily put plates on the table while Sam pulled the cornbread from the inside of the stove. He placed the pan on a folded towel; before he could pick at a corner, Jane slapped his hand.

"Don't tear up the cornbread. Let it cool."

Sam grimaced while Emily snickered. He made a face at her, squinting his eyes and flopping out his tongue. Emily responded with a face of her own, her eyes rolled up, her nose scrunched.

"Okay you two, settle down," Jane said wearily, as if she'd said the phrase too many times before. She placed the steaming pot on the table and then ladled stew into bowls. Sam cut into the cornbread and placed crumbly yellow squares onto plates. Emily held up a small plate with the remains of a stick of butter.

"This is all we have," she announced, glaring at Sam, "so don't hog it all."

"What? Me, a butter hog? I'm offended."

Jane cut what was left of the stick into thirds. "There, butter crisis solved." They dove into their meal. In time, Emily looked up from her bowl.

"We need to go to town, Mom. We're out of butter and almost out of flour and sugar. And I want to get some new books—I've read all the ones we have at least ten times."

Jane glanced at Sam who was intent on his cornbread. "We'll talk about that later. Let's just relax and eat."

Sam scraped the last of the stew from his bowl. "Which means 'don't talk about it in front of Sam because, oh, that's right, he can't go to town because some old bag pointed at him.' What do you think, Mom, she had x-ray eyes and could see my wanker through my clothing?"

"Sam, it was easier when you were little. Now that you're older, it's harder to hide your . . . condition."

"Yeah, well, you've been hiding my *condition* for most of my life—and it's getting old."

"I don't think you fully understand what could happen to you," Jane responded, her voice on edge. "If you were discovered—"

"I know," Sam said, cutting her off. "You've told me a thousand times—they'd take me away, a lot of bad stuff would happen. Maybe it wouldn't be like that. Maybe I should be found out. I'd be famous, right? *Step right up, ladies and, well, just ladies—feast your eyes on the last guy on earth!* We could make a lot of money, then live in a real house like we used to, one with those chairs with the swirling water. What were they called?"

"Toilets," Jane answered with annoyance.

"That's it. I've had it with the outhouse. I'm tired of getting splinters in my—"

"That's enough, Sam," Jane snapped, all trace of composure evaporating like the steam off the stew. "This isn't a game. I've kept you hidden for a reason: to keep you safe. But I can't do that if you go and do stupid things that put yourself in danger."

Jane stared at her son as if the intense gaze could drill her words into his skull: "If you don't understand why it has to be this way, fine—some day you will. I know you don't like it, but that's too bad. You follow my rules."

"Or else?"

"There is no 'or else.' "

A cold silence descended on the dinner table. Emily buttered the last of her cornbread and handed it to Sam. "Here, I'm stuffed."

Sam didn't take it—he was too angry to accept anything.

"Go on. You know you want it," Emily said, looking at Sam as if to say *Sorry I brought it up!*

Sam took the cornbread and stuffed it into his mouth. He loved his mother and sister and was, for the most part, happy living at the cabin, spending his days in the woods. He also knew there was a world beyond those woods, one he barely remembered.

You can't keep me here forever, Mom, Sam thought, glancing at his mother's stony expression. *Someday I'm going to go out into that world again, with or without your permission.*

5

The mec wiped steam off the bathroom mirror in wide circles. He assessed his reflection through the mist—it had been only three months since his surgery, yet the scars on his chest had already faded into his pale skin. He touched the place where his right breast had been.

The mec opened the medicine cabinet and took out a syringe and an unmarked vial. He inserted the needle into the neoprene top and drew back on the syringe; clear fluid filled the chamber. After cleaning a patch of skin with an alcohol wipe, the mec stuck the needle into his thigh, slowly injecting the testosterone. The doctor—if she'd been that or not—told him 1 cc four times a day for the rest of his life. More testosterone, she'd warned, would make him aggressive. Yet the mec's thigh muscle was now absorbing double the recommended dose. The doctor failed to understand that aggressive was the point.

The mec exited the bathroom and pulled a grey silk shirt and pair of black pants from the closet. After dressing, he slipped on his watch—it was a Rolex, a real one, not some cheap knockoff from the deadbeats down on E Street.

A short knock came across the airy loft. The mec crossed the hardwood floor and opened the door. A young woman dressed in drab green pants and a camo jacket entered; she had wiry black hair and would have been considered pretty if not for the dark circles under her eyes and the scar that ran from her left temple to her cheek. The woman looked the mec up and down.

"It's a business meeting, Brandon, not a date."

Brandon smirked as he straightened his collar. "And that's why you're the hired help, Dana, and not the big dog. Here's a free piece of advice: it never hurts to look good."

The woman shook her head and surveyed the loft. Exercise equipment filled one corner while a small kitchen, clean from lack of use, not tidiness, took up another. A folding chair and card table stood next to a twin bed.

"I don't think this woman's going to become your testosterone supplier because she thinks you look good in Armani," Dana noted as she crossed the wide space. "And maybe if you spent less on clothes, you could spring for some furniture."

Brandon threaded his arms into the sleeves of a black leather jacket and then grabbed a set of car keys. "And what would I do with furniture?"

***

Brandon hit his fist on the steering wheel as a row of brake lights flashed before him—the double dose of testosterone was kicking in. "Half of the world's population is gone, and there's still traffic?"

"Take it easy, Brandon," Dana said. She took a deep breath, knowing the only way to broach the difficult subject was head-on: "This is a bad idea." She looked at Brandon, trying to gauge his expression—his square jaw and protruding brow were more set in stone than usual. "The outfit that's supplying your testosterone will cut you off if they find out you've been talking to another manufacturer."

"Let them," Brandon muttered. "When they hiked the price, they cut into my profits. It's bullshit that the cost of materials has gone up. They think they can put the squeeze on me." After turning right on a red light, Brandon cruised past the white tower of the Washington Monument.

"I checked it out," Dana responded. "What they said was true—the chemicals have gotten more expensive. You've got a good thing going with your supplier. Why screw that up?"

"Profits need to go up, not down. I think this new outfit can make that happen."

"But we don't know anything about them. And their T could be cut with all kinds of crap." Dana's brow tightened as she gazed out into traffic. "I don't like it."

Brandon turned down Avenue F and parked in front of an abandoned warehouse. The dingy grey of the building mirrored the cloud cover that hung over the city. Mottled grime covered the few windows that had not been blown out by rocks or gunfire. Brandon shoved the car into park and turned to Dana.

"First of all, there is no *we*. Like I said, when you're in charge, you can do what you want." He opened the door, got out, and then leaned back into the car. "Are you ready?"

Dana pulled back her jacket to reveal a .357 revolver stuck in her belt. She swung open the car door and followed the mec to the entrance.

The supply of testosterone was the least of Brandon's problems. The real threat came from the Sisterhood, the New York crime syndicate. As the country emerged from the Black Years, politicians decided local control was the only way to fuel the recovery. They divided the United States into independently governed regions called sectors.

The wealthiest sectors were the Northeast—the area formerly known as New England—and the Pacific, the stretch of land that had once been California, Oregon, and Washington. The Coastal, Southwest, and Mountain Sectors had made great strides in recent years—only the Appalachian and Plains Sectors still struggled with the hardships of the Black Years.

The Sisterhood was spreading throughout the Northeast Sector like a fungus. When it laid siege to Baltimore, Brandon knew it was only a matter of time before the syndicate would set its sights on Columbia, the smallest sector that had once been Washington, D.C. After years of eliminating every skank punk who tried to sell black market testosterone on his turf, Brandon wouldn't just hand over his hard-won territory to the Sisterhood—not without a fight.

Brandon's phone rang as he approached the warehouse door. "Make it quick, Margaret," he barked into the phone.

"The tracker's found one."

"She's thought that before."

"I've seen the photos."

"They're doctored, or he's a mec."

As soon as Brandon and Dana entered the cavernous building, two women emerged from the shadows. Dana stiffened when she saw the larger of the two carrying a semi-automatic assault rifle. The other woman, wearing square glasses and a matronly bun, looked like a high school chemistry teacher. She carried a small black briefcase.

"He lives outside Sutter's Creek," Margaret said through the garbled connection, "some hick mountain town up in western Canada."

"I'll send Dana to investigate," Brandon responded as he approached the two figures. "If he's really an authentic, she'll bring him to me."

"The tracker wants her money."

With profits down and too many losing bets at the track, Brandon didn't want to waste precious funds on the tracker. "She's a loose end—Dana will take care of her, too." Brandon ended the call, then looked at the women, flashing his most charming smile.

"Ladies, is the firepower really necessary?"

6

The clock on the night table read 3:02 AM. Cassie lay in bed, trying to will herself to sleep. The more she fluffed pillows, rolled from side to side, and silently listed her teachers' names since kindergarten—Cassie's version of counting sheep—the more sleep eluded her.

I'm going to be so wiped out at school tomorrow, she thought. *Good thing it's Friday and a half-day.* It had been six weeks since the start of spring semester, the half-day dedicated to progress reports and conferences.

Okay, time for a different strategy, Cassie decided as she snapped on the light. She sat up, leaned her pillow against the headboard, and took a book from the nightstand drawer, hoping a little light reading would make her drowsy.

Luka lay curled up on a braided rug at the end of Cassie's bed. After twelve pages, Cassie shut the book, though it wasn't fatigue that made her return the book to the drawer—it was boredom. Trapped in an attic, the heroine had spent the last five pages describing a dusty couch, broken birdcage, and wavy mirror in excruciating detail.

Cassie rose and grabbed a scrapbook from her desk. After nestling back into bed, she opened the album on her lap. A photograph of her and Cody in a red wagon shared a page with their first baby picture. Bundled in hospital blankets, Cassie and Cody looked like squishy-faced old men in little knitted hats. Her mom and dad were also in the photo—they were smiling yet seemed worn out, like they'd just crossed the Alps on their hands and knees.

A Halloween snapshot showed Cassie as a goblin with green skin and a warty rubber nose. Cody was at her side, wrapped in aluminum foil. He was supposed to be an astronaut but looked more like a baked potato. Another picture showed Cassie's father, Matt, kissing Cassie on her forehead—she could almost feel the sandpaper of his cheek. Flipping through the pages, Cassie studied the photographs, trying to pull her fuzzy memories into focus.

Yet the family photos took up only the first seven pages of the scrapbook. To fill the rest, Cassie collected pictures of men. Cut out from old magazines, the images showed men in business suits, boys wearing grass-stained football uniforms, gentlemen decked out in tuxedoes, soldiers in faded fatigues.

Were they so different from us? she wondered, examining the pictures as if they were artifacts unearthed from an archeological dig.

Cassie had asked several women, among them the then Mrs. Watson, the librarian at the downtown branch and her mother, what men had been like. Their answers had been vague and unsatisfying. With the cure nowhere in sight, Cassie knew she would never be able to answer that question for herself, a notion she found depressing.

Her feeling down, however, had an upside—suddenly, Cassie wanted only to close her eyes and escape into the oblivion of sleep. She took one last look at the photos of Cody and her father, shut the scrapbook, and then placed it on the night table. Snapping off the light, she said good night to Luka and all but disappeared under the covers.

***

The vast empty space held no dimension, no time, no matter, only Cassie's mind and the endless dark void. A prickling sensation came over the body she didn't have. It built slowly until fire and ice permeated every atom of her being. A voice called out:

Open the door.

She understood the words in a way that was unknown to her.

Open the door!

Cassie sensed something moving toward her, something frightening. A sinister shadow engulfed her—she tried to scream but had no mouth. The darkness began to consume her, reducing her slowly, deliberately, as if it were savoring her annihilation. Having no body to fight with, Cassie resisted the destruction with her mind. Yet the terror was overwhelming—she gave in as the darkness devoured all that she was.

Cassie shot her eyes open. She caught her breath and sat up in bed, wiping damp hair from her forehead. Clicking on the light, Cassie saw the comforting sight of her bedroom—jeans draped over a chair, laptop and books on the desk, shoes scattered like debris after a storm. Luka woke up and padded to the bedside, her clear blue eyes asking in dog speak *Are you okay?*

"I'm fine," Cassie said, stroking the husky's thick fur. "It was just the dream again." She entered the bathroom, splashed cold water on her face, and then drank from cupped hands to ease her dry throat. After toweling off, she returned to bed.

"Once again, good night," Cassie said softly. Luka returned to her spot, circled, then landed, her tail hiding the black button of her nose. Cassie snapped off the light and settled under the covers. As soon as she closed her eyes, a lingering fear echoed in her mind.

Who am I kidding? Cassie thought as she reached to turn on the light. She sat up and took the novel from the night table. *Okay, so what else is in that attic? Better to be bored than scared.*

It had always taken Cassie a while to fall back to sleep after the dream—this time would be no different.

7

To the ladies of the local historical society, the Taft Building was an excellent example of the art deco architectural style that had been popular in the 1930's; to Amanda, the granite structure was a drafty old monstrosity with temperamental plumbing. Originally built as a hospital, The Taft was twelve stories high with rounded corners and ornate carvings above the windows. In the fifties, it had been converted to a governmental facility—at present, the building housed various research and development departments, including Amanda's team that continued to search for the cure to SN-146.

Cassie took the elevator to the basement. A sharp whiff of disinfectant pricked her nose as she entered the lab. Jennifer, her mother's lab assistant, stood over a sink pouring a blue-tinged liquid into a beaker. She looked up.

"Hi, stranger. Long time, no see."

"Hi, Jennifer," Cassie responded. "Yeah, it has been a while." She looked around, hoping her mother wasn't in a meeting.

"She'll be back in a minute," Jennifer said, answering Cassie's unspoken question.

Cassie nodded and took a seat on a stool. Beakers and test tubes of all shapes and sizes covered the workstation that took up the center of the room. Small machines hummed and whirled. A refrigerator stood in one corner, the sign "specimens only, no food allowed" taped to its drab front.

A large whiteboard on a stand took up half of one wall. Formulas, equations, and notes scribbled in her mother's angular handwriting covered the board, threatening to turn it black. As Cassie tried to decipher the hieroglyphics, Amanda walked in carrying a cardboard box of Petri dishes.

"Hey, sweetheart, what brings you here?" she asked as she set the box on the counter. "I thought you and Terry were going to try out that new burger joint on Florida Avenue."

"We are," Cassie replied. "I just had some time to kill, so I thought I'd stop by." She nodded toward the whiteboard. "Any luck?"

Amanda shook her head. "I thought we were onto something with the nucleic acid extraction reagent, but it was another dead end."

Cassie frowned in solidarity with her mother's disappointment and then looked at the whiteboard. "There's still something I don't understand."

"What's that?"

"Why do male babies still die? I mean, if all the men are gone, and they gave the virus to each other, then there aren't any men left to infect the boy babies."

Amanda's mouth curved into something between a grimace and a smile. "And that's just one of the crazy-making mysteries of SN-146. It's like the air became saturated with the virus even though we can no longer find any in our atmospheric samples."

Cassie looked at a picture taped to the whiteboard—it was a dark, fuzzy circle filled with edgy lines. "What's that?"

"It's a photo of the virus taken with an electron microscope. I like to keep it up there so I never lose sight of my goal—to obliterate the menace from the face of the earth."

Feeling herself veering into obsessive territory, Amanda switched gears. "You look tired. Did you sleep okay last night?" That morning, Amanda had left the house at dawn, missing the opportunity to give her daughter the customary maternal once-over.

"I couldn't get to sleep," Cassie said, welcoming yet still inwardly grumbling at the fact that she was transparent to her mother. "And when I did, I had the dream again."

"Was it any different this time?"

Cassie shook her head.

"And you don't recognize the voice?"

"It's not like I hear a voice—I just feel the words. Anyway, that's not what creeps me out." Cassie held back, shuddering at the thought of her nightmare. "It's this *thing* that comes over me. It's really scary."

"Well, it was just a dream," her mother responded as she unpacked the rest of the Petri dishes. "And as scary as it seems, a dream can't hurt you."

Just then, Cassie's cell phone chimed. She dug into her backpack's front pocket and pulled out the device; a text from Terry came up on the screen: waiting for you.

Cassie texted back: omw.

A crash of glass startled Cassie as she returned the phone to her backpack—Jennifer had dropped a test tube, leaving a puddle of blue liquid on the floor. Cassie headed for the door as her mother and Jennifer put on gloves like oven mitts to clean up the spill.

"Bye, Jennifer. See you later, Mom."

***

Cassie rose on tiptoes to see above the throng of waiting customers. She spied Terry waving her hand from a small table in a back corner. Pushing her way through the crowd, Cassie wondered if trying out a restaurant on opening day was such a good idea. "It's like a mosh pit in here!" she exclaimed as she landed on the seat.

"I know! Five women tried to take your chair." Terry grabbed the squirt bottle of ketchup and held it up like it was a machine gun. "I was ready to let 'em have it!"

A harried waitress dropped off two menus and two glasses of water, promising to return shortly. Cassie opened her menu and scanned the choices. Whatever she ordered, she would make sure it was free of tomatoes.

When she was five, Cassie had eaten some tomato soup—almost immediately, the red liquid had charged up her throat and splattered onto the table. Dry heaves turned her stomach inside out for several miserable hours. A blood test later confirmed the allergy.

After that, Cassie decided tomatoes were neither fruit nor vegetable but pure evil.

Cassie noticed that Terry wasn't reading her menu. "Have you already decided?"

"Yeah, while I was waiting." A somber look shrouded Terry's face. "Cassie, I need to talk with you."

"Sure, what's up?"

"It's kind of an important topic."

Cassie gave a lighthearted snort. "So that's why you picked such a quiet place?"

Terry couldn't even manage a polite laugh. "I've stopped trying to find a time for us to have a private conversation. Ever since winter break, we never seem to be just by ourselves anymore. I get the feeling you don't want to be alone with me."

Terry hadn't brought up the topic of becoming more than friends since Cassie's birthday, giving Cassie hope that the idea had faded away for good. "Terry, you're my best friend," she stated, as if there was nothing more to say on the subject.

Terry smiled. She reached her hands across the table just as Cassie slid hers into her lap. "Your birthday present," Terry said, noticing that Cassie wasn't wearing the ring, "don't you like it?"

"Yeah, I do," Cassie replied, fidgeting in her chair. "It's just that I'm not too sure what it means."

"It just means happy birthday," Terry said, working for a breezy delivery. Then she gave up trying to be casual. "It also means I care about you"—she hesitated as if searching for the best way to continue—"in a special way."

Cassie felt her body tighten. She knew she had to deal with the subject once and for all. "Terry, I love you . . . you know that. But I just don't feel *that way* about you." Cassie closed her menu. "I guess I'm not a lesbian."

A wan smile crept onto Terry's face. "Cassie, we're all lesbians now—XY took care of that." Before Cassie could utter a word, Terry forged ahead: "Which is what I wanted to talk with you about. I know some girls have a harder time with the whole girl-on-girl thing . . . so I was thinking of turning."

Cassie stared in stunned silence. After a long moment, she pulled herself together enough to grunt her response: "Tell me you're joking."

"Listen, if you want a guy, I can be a guy," Terry said with a shrug. "Well, as close as you're ever going to get."

Cassie leaned back in her chair as if to distance herself from the disturbing conversation. "First of all—"

"Just hear me out," Terry interrupted. "I know someone who knows a doctor who can do the surgery and get the hormones for—"

"Haven't you seen those pictures on the Internet, the ones of the botched surgeries? Those *doctors* are butchers, women who are only in it for the money. You bleed out on the table, no problem—they get their money up front. And, anyway, it's illegal. They catch you, they throw you in some juvy prison."

"I can hide the change until I'm twenty-one," Terry said. "But I'm sure I won't have to wait that long. Cassie, things are changing. Soon it'll be legal for girls our age to turn. I know you're part of the old guard because of your mom—"

"What does my *mom* have to do with this?" Cassie blared.

"She's trying to bring back men. But it's been ten years—even if your mom finds the cure, the world will never be like it was."

"I know that," Cassie insisted. "And maybe someday I'll feel differently. But for right now, all I know is, you're my best friend, and I just want to keep things the way they are." Cassie glowered at Terry, wanting to yank the idea of turning male out of her head. "Promise me you won't do anything stupid."

"I'm not going to promise you anything," Terry responded. "I want to do this because I think it's the only way we can be together. I love you and *not* just as a friend."

Cassie felt her anger dissolve into despair. Just then, the waitress appeared at the table, frazzled but smiling.

"Sorry about the wait. Ready to order?"

***

As they ate their burgers, the girls' conversation—when there had been any—deteriorated into discussions about regular versus crinkle-cut fries and the various levels of tart in sour pickles. Walking out of the restaurant, Cassie suggested a movie as it was something that didn't involve talking. They headed over to the Pentagon City Mall, the local hangout for high school kids.

The mall parking lot was full. Cassie and Terry parked their cars at the furthest corner, then hiked toward the stores. At the theater, Cassie bought popcorn and a large drink for them to share, part peace offering, part movie-going habit. She was stuffed from lunch, but a movie wasn't complete without greasy popcorn and a fizzy drink. The caper flick about two teachers who rob a bank and save an orphanage was just corny enough to lighten both their moods.

After the movie, Cassie and Terry walked back to their cars. With the sun down, a chill permeated the air; Cassie drew her jacket close around her.

"My favorite part was when the pigeons attacked the corporate boss," Terry said, making dive-bombing motions at Cassie's face. She added zooming sound effects for good measure.

Cassie recoiled, laughing. "You're so demented!"

They reached their cars, Terry's, a Honda Civic and Cassie's, a vintage Mini Cooper. The next day was Saturday—the girls made plans to meet at the mall at noon for a marathon of shopping, junk food, and all-around time-wasting.

As Terry opened her car door, Cassie rooted around in the front pocket of her backpack, knowing it was time for the routine mother/daughter check-in. Cassie felt her wallet, a couple of pens, a lip balm, and some wadded-up tissues—but no cell phone. She searched the main part of her backpack.

Terry rolled down her window. "Lose something?"

"My phone."

"Did you use it at the movie?"

"No."

"How about at the restaurant?"

Cassie continued to shove things around in the compartment. "No, not there either." She replayed the afternoon in her head. "I must have dropped it at my mom's lab. Can I use yours?"

Terry pulled out her phone and handed it to Cassie who then tapped the screen.

"Hi, Mom. I left my phone at the lab. I'm at the mall, so I'm pretty close." After a short silence, Cassie responded with an eye roll for Terry's benefit. "Yes, Mom, I'll come straight home afterwards."

Cassie pressed the End button and handed the phone back to Terry. "My mom's lab assistant is working late—I'm going to head over there now." She got into her car, turned on the ignition, and rolled down the window.

"I can't live without my phone. See you tomorrow, Terry."

8

Unlike the afternoon, the parking lot at the Taft Building was empty except for a few cars scattered at random. Cassie pulled up close to the building and parked under a light. As she got out of her car, she spotted a familiar figure hurrying toward a small truck.

"Jennifer!"

The young woman stopped to peer in Cassie's direction. "Who's there?"

Cassie started to make her way across the lot. "It's me, Cassie. I think I left my phone at the lab. My mom said you were working late."

Jennifer tried to hide her annoyance, her expression an odd mixture of sheepishness and determination. "I was planning to set up this experiment so it would be ready first thing tomorrow morning. But then this woman I've been wanting to hook up with said she was free tonight. I'll swipe you in at the front if you don't tell your mom that I left early."

"Don't worry—your secret is safe with me," Cassie commented, though she really wasn't interested in Jennifer's love life.

They walked up to the main doors. "I know I should play hard to get," Jennifer murmured as she passed a card in front of the reader. "Anyway, I'll come back early tomorrow morning to finish the prep. Do you know the code for the lab?"

Cassie shook her head, then pulled open the front door.

"It's 0115. I really have to go." And with that, Jennifer race-walked back to her truck and spun the tires out of the parking lot.

0115, Cassie thought as she paced through the half-lit lobby. *Figures. January 15th—Cody's and my birthday*. She pushed the elevator button for the basement. Outside the lab, Cassie entered the code on the keypad and opened the door. She turned on the lights and made a quick sweep of the room. Not finding her phone, she crouched down on all fours.

It has to be here, she thought as she moved around the workstation, hoping the linoleum had been recently mopped. *No telling what funky stuff is growing on* this *floor!*

Then she stopped and smiled.

There you are!

Cassie spied her phone tucked behind the whiteboard. She rose to her feet and dragged the stand across the floor. As she bent down, she noticed something on the wall. She moved in to get a better look. A small button, barely visible, blended into the textured surface. As if by reflex, Cassie moved her index finger toward the button. Then her mother's disapproving voice popped into her head, spouting a litany of maternal warnings.

It's tempting but . . . Cassie thought as she picked up the phone and slipped it into her jacket pocket. Then something else, something out of place, caught her eye. She leaned toward the wall—the faint line of a groove ran straight up from the floor. She traced the indentation with her fingertips; the line came to a right angle above her head, traversed the wall, then hit another right angle and descended to the floor.

Now her mother's scolding voice was drowned out by a curious one: *What the heck is that?* Once more, Cassie dropped to her knees and, holding her breath, pushed the button.

The muffled mechanical sound of a door sliding open took Cassie by surprise. When the quiet rumbling stopped, a dark, narrow passageway stretched before her.

"Hello?" Cassie called out, feeling half-relieved there was no reply. She strained her eyes into the receding darkness.

What I need to do is just go home and not get into trouble, Cassie told herself. She wasn't afraid to admit it—the dense black intimidated her. Then she thought of trying to get to sleep that night still baffled by the mystery of the hidden hallway.

Actually, what I need to do is find a flashlight, Cassie decided, knowing the light on her phone was on the fritz. She rummaged through shelves and drawers, finding test strips, funnels, pipettes, filter paper, glass slides—but no flashlight.

Again, Cassie looked down the mysterious corridor. She took a few hesitant steps, her heart beating against her ribs as she skimmed her hand along the cool wall.

For some reason, a short story she'd read in English class appeared unbidden in her head. It was this freaky Edgar Allan Poe tale about a guy screaming his head off while some villain walled him into a crypt. *What was it called*, Cassie wondered, trying to distract herself from her shaking knees, *The Cask of Armadillo?* She looked over her shoulder, making sure the sliding door hadn't decided to go Poe on her.

Seeing the faint light of the lab, Cassie continued to pace down the passageway, one hand still on the wall, the other outstretched in front of her, waving in the dark like a giant bug feeler. Then her fingertips brushed against a wall. She explored the surface and came upon something; her fingers outlined the object—a light switch. She flipped it up.

It took a few seconds for Cassie's eyes to adjust to the fluorescent glare. A small window appeared in front of her. She looked in. Behind the glass was a sparsely furnished room no bigger than a large closet. Cassie noticed a twin bed—a body rustled beneath the covers. A teenage boy woke up and swung his legs over the bed, his eyes squinting in the bright light.

"Mom?"

Cassie would hardly think, let alone speak. Finally, she managed to get out one word: "Cody?"

She stared at the boy, trying to force the image of her brother onto his face—like a wrong puzzle piece, the picture refused to snap into place. "Who are you?"

The boy rubbed his eyes. "Cassie!" he blurted, his voice muted through the glass. "It's me, Jamie!"

"I don't know any Jamie." Then her eyes widened as the thought of a young boy surfaced from her memory. "Jamie Burke?"

The boy brought his face to the window, examining Cassie like she was a rare flower. "It's really you!"

"How—?"

"See that button to your right? Press it!"

Too bewildered to speak, Cassie obeyed. A door slid open.

"Go inside and then wait for the light to turn green."

Cassie nodded and stepped into the chamber. After the door closed, air jets blew at her from all sides, making her hair fly up. She squeezed her eyes shut, hoping the wind tunnel effect would end soon. The light flashed green.

As the door opened, Cassie saw Jamie Burke dressed in a T-shirt and boxer shorts. Jamie had lived next door to Cassie before XY and the Black Years. From the time they were old enough to walk, Cassie, Cody, and Jamie had been inseparable. Cassie visualized the six-year-old Jamie with brown hair and freckles. The Jamie that stood before her was tall and thin with pale skin and short hair that still managed to look scruffy. He pulled on some pants, his face flushing with embarrassment.

"I'm not used to having guests," he mumbled, then looked her up and down. "You got big!"

"Yeah, well, you got *alive*—how'd that happen?"

Cassie looked around to see a bookshelf, a desk with a laptop, a sun lamp, a set of weights, and an oddly familiar-looking upholstered chair. The walls were decorated with black and white drawings. "What's going on here?"

Jamie sat on the bed. "This is where I live. My mom put me in here to keep me safe." He hesitated. "I mean *your* mom."

Cassie's stomach flipped. "You've been in this room since you were *six*?" The comment was more statement than question.

Jamie nodded. "Your mom takes blood from me and tests it. She says she's getting close to the cure and that I have to be patient."

"So you've been locked away in here for *ten years*?"

"Ten years, seven months, and twelve days."

Cassie ran her fingers through her hair. Everything she thought she knew about her mother came crashing down on her like a condemned building.

"I know it sounds bad," Jamie added, "but I have a computer that keeps me connected. I got my GED, and I'm now taking online classes at MIT. My screen name's Anne Frank—get it? And your mom gives me stuff to do, not that she's strict about it." He looked at the floor. "It gets lonely, but my, I mean *your* mom visits as much as she can."

Cassie's life with her mother pulled into focus. They never went out of town, and food, books, and toys would mysteriously vanish from their home. She glanced at the upholstered chair, suddenly realizing it was the one that had disappeared from their living room two years ago. Growing up, Cassie recalled nights when she had to stay with friends because her mother was working late.

All that time, Mom had been raising her own personal lab rat, Cassie thought as a familiar ringtone jingled from her jacket pocket; she made no attempt to retrieve the phone.

"Aren't you going to answer it?" Jamie asked.

"No. It's my mother . . . and I have no idea what to say to her."

Jamie stood up and pulled the phone out of Cassie's pocket just as it stopped ringing. "Can this one start your car?"

Cassie was in no mood for a cell phone tutorial. "Did my mom kidnap you and keep you down here to experiment on?" Saying the words made Cassie's hair stand on end.

"No, she saved me from XY, or she's going to, anyway."

"Where's *your* mother?" Cassie asked.

Jamie's face darkened. "She jumped off the roof of our house the night my father died." He sat back down on the bed. "I found her lying in the driveway. Your mom put me in here after that with Cody." Jamie took a deep breath as if to keep his haunting memories at bay.

"With Cody? What do you mean? Cody died when he was six . . ."

Jamie responded with only silence.

"Jamie, what are you talking about? What happened to my brother?"

Before Jamie could speak, the chamber door slid open. Amanda stood in the doorway, looking at Cassie with heartbreak in her eyes.

"Go on, Jamie," Amanda said, her voice solemn, "tell her about Cody."

9

Amanda entered the small room, her eyes now fixed on Jamie. "I can't," Jamie said in barely a whisper.

"Please."

Jamie paused and then dragged a large plastic box from under the bed. He set the box in his lap and lifted the lid, revealing a mess of toys, photos, and drawings. Cassie sat next to him, peering at the stuff.

"Hey, it's Robot Dude!" she exclaimed, holding up a beat-up action figure missing an arm. "This used to be Cody's favorite." Cassie raked through the box. "And Cody's bug collection . . ." A handful of plastic spiders, flies, and beetles tried to escape her grasp. A crumpled drawing of two stick figures with lollipop trees and a circle sun radiating yellow lines lay at the bottom of the box. The name "Cody" was scrawled at the top.

Cassie pulled out the piece of construction paper. "I don't remember Cody drawing this." She looked at her mother for some kind of response; when none came, Cassie continued to rummage through the box, eventually picking out a Polaroid photo of Jamie showing big teeth in a wide grin. The other boy in the picture was sticking out his tongue, making rabbit ears on Jamie.

"This is Cody!" Cassie exclaimed, not believing her own words. "But he must be at least nine years old here. How's that possible?" Cassie stared at her mother. "Mom?" Amanda crossed her arms in front of her chest.

"Mom!"

Amanda cleared her throat. "Eleven years ago, I moved to this lab to work on the Tachyon virus—that's when I found the secret chamber. I guess it was some kind of isolation room from the hospital days or maybe a retrofit bomb shelter from the fifties. Then

SN-146 hit. All research was converted to find a cure. I put Cody in the chamber to keep him safe. I thought he'd be in here no more than six months."

"Why didn't Dad go into the chamber?"

Amanda shook her head as she sat on the bed. "He was showing early signs of the virus."

"So where's Cody now?"

Amanda took Cassie by the hand. "He got appendicitis when he was twelve. If I hadn't taken him out for the surgery, his appendix would have ruptured, and he would have died. I put an oxygen mask on him, hoping to keep him from getting infected. Dr. Stanton, your pediatrician, did the surgery. She was the only other person who knew the boys were alive." Amanda stopped to collect herself.

"What happened?" Cassie asked. "Cody died during the surgery?"

"No, the surgery went well," Amanda replied, her voice starting to tremble. "We were so close . . ."

Cassie waited—after several seconds, she lost what little patience she had left. "Mom, tell me!"

Amanda let out a heavy breath. "When I was transporting Cody back to the chamber, his oxygen mask got knocked off. It was only for a minute, but I couldn't risk putting him back in the isolation room. If Cody was infected, he would have made Jamie sick, too."

Jamie lowered his head, then pushed the box of Cody's stuff back under the bed.

"I should have been more careful," Amanda said, blinking away tears before they fell. "Cody got sick the next day. He died in my arms." She looked at Cassie, her eyes pleading for forgiveness. "I couldn't tell you about Cody. You were six when I hid him away. It had to be kept secret!"

Cassie saw that her mother was suffering. She also realized that she'd been cheated out of six years of her brother's life. "I grew up, Mom! You could've told me when I got older. I would have understood!"

"I thought about that. It seemed better to leave things the way they were—just one slip, and the boys would have been found out. I was afraid for their lives."

Cassie knew what her mother meant: four years ago, a boy in Rio de Janeiro was discovered in a similar isolation chamber. The news spread like wildfire. A mob of crazed women just wanting to see a live male ended up trampling him to death.

"It was torture watching Cody—and your dad—get sick and not be able to do anything about it," Amanda said, her voice steeped in regret. "Maybe it was a mistake not telling you, but I did what I thought was right."

She stood up and walked toward the door. "I thought I was close to finding the cure so many times. I kept thinking how happy you'd be when I told you that Cody was still alive." Amanda stepped into the decontamination chamber. "But it didn't turn out like that."

Cassie's head throbbed. "I know, Mom. I just wish you would have trusted me!"

Amanda nodded in silence. "Stay as long as you like, Cassie. I know you two have a lot to talk about."

IO

Three hours had passed since Cassie found Jamie—the time on the computer read 1:15 AM. She eased back into the overstuffed chair while Jamie sat cross-legged on the bed, continuing to fire questions at her: What's high school like? Have you tried drugs? What music do you listen to? Why is there no more football? Jamie had learned about the outside world from the Internet and had figured out early on that not everything posted was reliable.

"Did you have to eat cat food during the Black Years?" Jamie asked. "I read that some girl survived on Kitty Kuisine for a year."

As long as Jamie didn't mention Cody, Cassie could push the strangeness of the night to the back of her mind. "I remember being hungry and cold and scared." She hesitated—thinking about those years made her stomach hurt. "It was dark all the time. The sun just disappeared." Then Cassie shook off the disturbing memory. "Whatever my mom found to eat, I ate. So, cat food? Maybe." She paused. "A year, huh? I bet that girl still has bad breath."

They laughed, the dark humor fitting the bleak time. After XY ravaged the planet, the problem of nearly four billion corpses overwhelmed the survivors. Women wanted to bury their dead; the rising body count, however, made the ritual a quaint relic of the past. Swollen remains floated down rivers or bobbed in lakes and bays until the waters turned green from the decaying muck. Eventually, the ground water became contaminated, making fresh water more valuable than gold.

Trucks rolled day and night, carrying the dead to incinerators. In time, the furnaces couldn't handle the staggering volume, forcing the survivors to make bonfires in parks, vacant lots, and school athletic fields. They stacked the dead like cordwood, the stench from the burning bodies casting a pall over the landscape.

The fires, thousands of them around the world, sent hundreds of tons of ash into the atmosphere, creating a dark cloud that enveloped the Earth. With the sun blocked out, crops failed. Governments—the few that remained—warned not to burn the dead, yet outbreaks of typhus and diphtheria left the women with no other choice.

"Okay, it's my turn," Cassie said, as much to rest her voice as to learn more about Jamie. "What do you do all day?"

"First of all, the concept of day and night doesn't exist here on planet Jamie," he began. "Your mom tried to keep me on a schedule because sometimes she'd show up, but I'd be too sleepy to stay awake. Eventually, she just gave up." Jamie held a beat, reveling in the fact that he was actually talking with Cassie. "And I liked the idea of not having a bedtime."

"There's that silver lining for being stuck in here," Cassie huffed, "other than the fact that you get to *live*."

After a brief chuckle, Jamie went on: "So when I'm awake, I'm either reading or on the Internet. I also like to draw." He rose from the bed and took down a pen and ink drawing of a circle with an intricate, repeating design.

"This one's my latest," Jamie said as he handed the picture to Cassie. "They're based on fractals, you know, the mathematical equations that make patterns, like snowflakes or seashells."

"Sure," Cassie responded, more interested in the design than the explanation. "These are really cool. When my mom finds the cure, you could be an artist."

Cassie returned the drawing to Jamie who then taped it back on the wall. "No, this is just for fun. I already know what I want to be when I get out of here."

"And that is . . . ?" Cassie asked, eyebrows raised.

"I'm going to be a physicist," Jamie stated. "All the greats—Einstein, Feynman, Bohr—made major breakthroughs with just math and thought experiments. I'm taking calculus online from MIT. It's tough, but I'm getting good grades." He clicked on his laptop. "Here, I'll show you."

"No, that's okay," Cassie said, deciding not to tell Jamie that she was squeaking by in algebra. "I believe you." She turned on the sun lamp and squinted. "That's bright!"

"I have to spend at least two hours every twenty-four hours under it, your mother's orders." He switched off the lamp. "Not that I do, but Sonny never tells."

"Who's Sonny?"

"The lamp, knucklehead."

"You named your sun lamp, and *I'm* the knucklehead?"

"I didn't just name the lamp. My bed is Jasper, and the computer is Rex." Jamie slapped his hand on the table. "This is Mortimer." Cassie sat up in the upholstered chair. "You're sitting in Manfred. He's pretty frayed, but he never complains."

Cassie wondered if the years of isolation had fried Jamie's brain; he read the thought in her expression.

"I know, you think I'm nuts. After Cody died, I was alone except for visits from your mom and check-ups from Dr. Stanton. I gave everything a name, and eventually they became my friends." He paused, rolling his eyes. "You're right, it does sound nuts."

Cassie settled back into Manfred. "No, I totally get it. It's like a crazy way to keep from going insane. I think I would have done the same thing." She stood up and inspected the furniture. "If I was living in here, I think I would have named the bed Ethel."

Jamie laughed. "Don't let Jasper hear you say that—he's very particular."

"And the computer would be Esmeralda."

"No way! Rex is hurling in cyberspace!"

They both giggled like little kids, Cassie relaxing enough to realize how exhausted she was. "If I don't go now, I'll snooze my car right into a tree on the way home."

When Jamie frowned, Cassie did her best to backpedal. "But I'll come and see you tomorrow, even though on planet Jamie, there really *isn't* a tomorrow." Then she stepped into the decontamination chamber, feeling guilty that she could leave.

Jamie pulled his latest drawing from the wall and handed it to her. "Here, take this . . . so you won't forget about me."

Cassie took the drawing. "I know exactly where I'm going to put it. And forget about you? Not a chance."

II

Although it had been a warm spring, the night air chilled Sam as he walked barefoot toward a small stand of maples up the slope from the cabin. The new moon made the sky a velvety black, shrouding the area in darkness. Sam wondered why it was called a new moon.

Why not call it what it was—no moon.

Still, he didn't need any light to find his way—every rock, bush, and tree around the cabin was as familiar to him as his own skin.

Sam hated to use the outhouse, much to his mother's chagrin. One summer day, she'd caught him taking a leak just outside the back door. His punishment had been a week's confinement in the cabin. For a boy raised on the expanse of the forest, the punishment had been more like torture. After his week of house arrest, Sam made sure he was well away from the cabin and, more importantly, the eyes of his vigilant mother before he did his business.

A nighthawk settled on a branch above Sam's head. When the bird spied him, it lifted into the air and flew toward the mountains. When Sam was done, he surveyed the seemingly tranquil scene, knowing nighttime was anything but peaceful. Bobcats and foxes hunted voles and possums; any field mouse daring enough to leave its burrow risked being swooped up by a great horned owl.

As Sam started back down the slope, a light flashed on inside the cabin, followed by a piercing scream. He raced down the hill, thinking a bear had nosed its way in looking for food. After leaping up the back stairs, Sam grabbed the doorknob yet halted before pulling open the door—an unfamiliar voice came from within:

"Where is he?"

Jane sputtered a frightened reply: "I don't know who you're talking about—it's just me and my daughter."

Sam peered through the window; a woman with a scar on her face pressed a gun to his mother's temple, gripping her in a chokehold.

"You've got one last chance before I pull the trigger," the intruder warned as she cocked the hammer. Emily whimpered in a corner, clutching her favorite doll.

Sam entered the cabin.

"No, get out of here!" his mother shouted.

"Let her go," Sam growled.

Jane struggled against the stranger's grip. The woman pistol-whipped her; a moan escaped from Jane's lips as a dark red line trickled down her forehead. The intruder glared at Sam.

"Drop your pants."

Sam was taken aback by the order, but he complied—he would have done anything to keep the woman from hurting his mother again. He shoved his pants to his knees.

"No, Sam!" Jane cried.

The intruder leaned forward and squinted. "Well, what do we have here? Thought you could hide him from the world, did you?"

Sam pulled up his pants. The woman took handcuffs from her back pocket and threw them at Sam's feet. "Put those on."

Sam picked up the metal rings, wondering what they were.

"Around your wrists, moron."

With a violent jerk, Jane pushed herself back on the woman; as soon as they hit the floor, the gun discharged with an ear-splitting blast. Although her breath had been knocked from her lungs, Jane still managed to scramble away from the dazed intruder.

Sam lunged. He landed on the woman and grabbed her by the wrist, pounding the gun to the floor. More shots fired. The intruder seized Sam by the throat; as he gasped for air, Sam slammed down the woman's hand—the weapon sprang from her grip and skidded across the floor.

The intruder butted Sam with her head, then shoved him off and rose to her feet. Fighting off his stupor, Sam grabbed the woman by the ankle and yanked, sending her down again with a thud. She kicked at his face, at the same time clawing for the gun that lay inches from her fingertips. As Sam dodged a boot, the woman seized the gun and pulled the trigger. He cried out as hot pain pierced his shoulder; a red splotch soaked into his T-shirt. He collapsed to the floor.

The woman picked up the handcuffs. "You're lucky he wants you alive," she grunted. "If it were up to me, I'd put a bullet in your head just for being a pain in the ass." She eyed Sam's bloody shoulder and scowled. "Now you're going to mess up my car."

Sam struggled to sit up. A glint caught his eye—his knife lay on the table mostly hidden beneath a rabbit pelt. The woman leaned over and raised her hand, ready to strike with the butt of the gun. Sam grabbed the knife and stuck it deep into her innards, then pulled up like he was gutting a deer. The woman dropped the gun and crumpled to the floor, her eyes wide with shock. She lay convulsing as shiny pink globs slid from the gash in her body. After several torturous seconds, she became still, her eyes staring at nothing.

Sam crawled over to his mother. She'd been shot in the neck but was still alive. He cradled her in his lap.

"Emily," she whispered, gurgling blood. Sam stumbled over to his sister who was slumped in the corner. He gathered her in his arms, then carried her to the bed. Her pajamas were drenched in red—she'd been shot in the chest. Sam heaved, torment twisting inside of him. He returned to his mother.

"She's fine," he uttered, hoping his voice wouldn't betray him. Sam put his hand on his mother's neck, trying to stop the flow; his fingers slipped in warm blood. "Mom, I'm sorry!" he cried, choking on the words. "I should have listened!"

Jane tried to speak but made only garbled sounds. She lifted her hand and touched her son's face. Looking into his eyes, she smiled faintly, shuttered, and then let go. Sam held his mother until the warmth faded from her body.

***

The sky was still dark when Sam splashed water onto his shoulder, washing off dried blood. He soaked a cloth with iodine, then pressed it to the bullet hole, gritting his teeth to keep himself from passing out. When the stabbing pain subsided, he taped layers of white gauze over the entry point, grateful that his mother, a former nurse, kept a well-stocked emergency kit.

Outside, Sam grabbed a shovel and started to dig. The hard ground and his throbbing shoulder would only permit a shallow grave. He laid his mother and sister on the cold earth, their arms entwined as if holding hands. Then Sam placed the blood-soaked fabric doll on Emily's front.

In time, the two figures disappeared under shovelfuls of dirt. When he was done, Sam placed two stones—one large, one small—on the pungent earth. He hesitated, unable to move from his family's final resting place. Before tears fell, he wiped his eyes and cleared his throat. Then Sam dragged out the intruder's body for the wolves and coyotes, regretting that she wouldn't feel the pain of the animals tearing at her flesh.

Sam dug into the woman's pockets and pulled out a wallet, a set of keys, and a vaguely familiar-looking thin black box. He tried to open it, but the box was sealed. The wallet contained $8 and several plastic cards, one with a picture of the woman on it. It read: Columbia Sector Driver's License. Below was a string of numbers, a name, and an address: Dana Roberts, 1302 Avenue B Apt. 4-C, Columbia Sector.

When he re-entered the cabin, Sam put the cards, money, and black box on the table. He looked at his bed. He was exhausted, but sleep was impossible.

What do I do now?

Sam's brain was too worn out for useful thought; all it could do was replay the night's horrors: his mother gushing blood, his sister small and limp, the attacker with his knife buried in her gut. He put his head in his hands, letting tears spill down his face. Strangled grunts, like those from a wounded animal, echoed in his ears—it took Sam several seconds to realize that the cries were coming from him. He rose to his feet and did the only thing that made any kind of sense to him: he ran.

Sam fled into the woods. Chest heaving, muscles aching, he pounded the terrain, hoping to outdistance his agony. Trees, silhouetted by the first rays of dawn, blurred past him.

Sam found himself at the lake. A scattering of sunrise sparkled on the inky surface. He stripped off his clothing, climbed the boulder, and flung himself into the dark water. Cold seized him. With sweeping arms, Sam swam down, welcoming the weight of the water. He didn't want to die—he just wanted the pain to end.

Plunging deeper than he had before, Sam fought against the pressure until he could no longer move his limbs. He floated in the dark depths, hoping for a sense of release.

Then a feeling seeped from his core. It was a strange sensation, one that burned in his chest despite the icy waters. Sam had never felt anything like it before. But he knew what it was:

Rage!

The anger pumped life into Sam's arms and legs; he worked them toward the surface.

The person who sent the killer is out there somewhere, Sam thought. His arms ached from the cold, his breath almost gone. Yet he had to make it to the surface. He knew what he had to do.

Sam broke through the water and swam to the lake's edge. He pulled himself onto the rocky shore just as the sun cleared the mountaintops.

***

At the cabin, Sam changed into dry clothes and stuffed the wallet, black box, and gun into his backpack along with the $94 he'd taken from his mother's cigar box. Then he grabbed a water bottle and their only family photo, the faded image of his mother with Emily slung on her hip and Sam at her side, holding her hand.

Sam entered the shed where he found Bailey munching hay. He climbed onto the horse's back and rode past the cabin. Down the road, he found the woman's car, a rusting maroon Cadillac. Sam hoped the cash and what he could get from selling Bailey would be enough to pay someone to drive him to the address on the plastic card.

As Bailey plodded down the road, Sam looked back at the cabin, thinking of the newly dug grave. The only thing that lessened the pressure in his chest was the thought of tracking down the person who had sent Dana Roberts and making him pay.

12

By one in the afternoon, the Pentagon City Mall was bustling with activity. Groups of girls swarmed, moms pushed strollers, elderly yet fit mall-walkers pumped their arms with focused strides. Terry stood in front of Cookie Mania, her and Cassie's usual meeting place and favorite mall treat. She glanced at the time on her phone. Cassie wasn't known for being punctual, but forty-five minutes late was pushing it even for her.

Terry passed the time by devouring a chocolate chunk cookie and watching the parade of mall-goers. After another time check, Terry pressed Cassie's phone number on speed dial for the third time. Once again, the ringing went to voice mail. Terry worked her thumbs on the keyboard: where r u?

Two girls around eleven years old hurried past; they talked and giggled, completely at ease in their bubble of friendship. Terry smiled as she thought of herself and Cassie at that age.

When Terry was in the fifth grade, her family had moved to the Columbia Sector in the middle of the school year. Terry remembered entering her new classroom, every student gawking at her like she was oozing slime—every student except one. A girl with chestnut hair looked up and smiled. Terry tried to return the kindness but couldn't force the corners of her mouth to turn up.

During recess that day, Terry wandered the outskirts of the playground, watching girls play four square, kickball, and tetherball. She saw the girl with chestnut hair narrowly escape being hit in a heated game of dodge ball.

"Hey you, new kid," the girl called out breathlessly, "wanna play?" Terry looked around as if she were in a crowd of new kids. Then she joined the girl on the field. Soon the two of them became inseparable.

Terry checked her phone one last time—there were no messages. She threw away the wax paper that came with the cookie and headed for the parking lot.

***

Terry slowly opened the door to Cassie's bedroom; she gazed at her sleeping friend who was no more than a lump under the covers. Luka trotted in, parked herself bedside, and then licked a hand that stuck out over the mattress.

"Cock-a-doodle-do," Terry said in singsong as she leaned over the mop of hair on the pillow.

"Huh?"

"Cassie, wake up."

Cassie opened her eyes to the blur of Terry's face. "What are you doing here?"

"We were supposed to meet at the mall," Terry replied as she landed on the bed. "I called and texted. When you didn't answer, I decided to come over."

"What time is it?" Cassie asked through a yawn.

Terry picked up the alarm clock and displayed it like it was a prize on a game show.

"One-fifteen? Sorry! I got to bed late, then didn't sleep very well."

Terry noticed Cassie's phone on the bedside table. "So you got your phone last night—then what?"

Cassie rolled out of bed. "Gotta pee . . ."

She entered the bathroom and closed the door. Cassie did have to pee. She also needed time to collect herself. The events of last night scrolled across her mind. Cassie couldn't tell Terry about Jamie—her mother had been clear on that point.

"My mom and I got a wild hair and decided to go to a midnight movie," Cassie said through the door. The lie had a better chance if it wasn't face-to-face. Cassie flushed and came out.

"Really? Doesn't sound like Amanda. What did you two see?"

"*Last Ninja Standing*," Cassie said, mentally crossing her fingers that the movie was still in the theaters.

Terry looked unconvinced. "You and your mom decided to see some lame chop-socky movie at midnight for grins?"

"It really wasn't that bad," Cassie answered. She pulled on jeans and a long-sleeved top, then slipped into and laced up black Converses. "I'm starving. C'mon."

Cassie fled the room, hoping a change of scene would make the conversation go away. Luka bounded down the stairs after her.

When she entered the kitchen, Cassie found her mother making a tuna fish sandwich. A news program blared from a small television on the countertop. "I was just telling Terry the martial arts movie we saw last night was pretty good."

Amanda nodded, acknowledging the setup. "Yes, I had no idea there could be so much raw emotion in a foot to the face." She looked at Terry. "Hi, Terry. Do you girls want some lunch? I've got enough tuna fish for everyone."

"No, thanks," Terry answered. "I ate at the mall, while I was waiting for Cassie."

"I'll make something for myself, Mom. My stomach is definitely still on morning time—and tuna fish isn't going to cut it as a breakfast food." Then Cassie took a carton of eggs from the refrigerator and slid two pieces of bread into the toaster oven, wanting only to quiet her rumbling stomach.

Amanda sat at the kitchen table and took a bite of her sandwich. She turned toward the TV screen.

"In other news, Sarah Murphy spoke at a rally in Boston, announcing her intention to run for the presidency this fall." The scene cut to a middle-aged woman in a navy suit in front of a podium.

"There are those who cling to the past, those who don't think the world is right without men," the woman asserted into a microphone. "I ask you, do you miss the war and violence, the rape and murder that came with a male-dominated world? Men had their time. And like the dinosaurs, their time has passed.

"We have the opportunity to re-invent our world, to make it a place based on cooperation and mutual benefit. The old world was riddled with competition—that competition, whether it was political, economic, or religious, bred corporations who stole from their workers, insurance companies who let people die rather than pay for needed care, and terrorists who bombed innocent victims into oblivion."

Cassie cracked an egg into a bowl. *Cheery breakfast topic*, she noted. Terry sat at the kitchen table.

"We are the United Sectors of America," the candidate continued, "but are we united? If I am elected president, I promise to make our country whole again. Our strength comes from our union. We will forge a new world in which to raise our daughters."

Murmurings of approval rippled through the audience. "Before the devastation of the plague, this great land of ours was divided, polarized by politicians who thought only of their own benefit. We had red states and blue states. Now we have sectors. But those sectors aren't red or blue."

Sarah Murphy paused to take a deep breath. "They are the color that represents us all—they are *pink!*"

The crowd erupted into applause, fists pumping in the air. "*Pink! Pink!*" the women shouted as Sarah Murphy raised her hands toward the electrified audience.

Amanda snapped off the set. "If she wins next fall, it's all over. Public funding for SN-146 research will dry up, and private funding is at an all-time low." Amanda shook her head and returned to her sandwich.

"Was it really like that with men around?" Cassie asked as she dug into her scrambled eggs. "She makes it sound so bad."

"The world had a lot of problems," Amanda replied, chewing as thoughtfully on the question as her sandwich. "And yes, men held most positions of power. But that's not the point. The point is male and female belong together—like day and night. It's about balance."

"If there was balance with both men and women," Cassie continued, "then why were things so messed up?"

Amanda hesitated. "The world's problems came from a way of life we couldn't sustain anymore but were incapable of changing—SN-146 changed it for us." Amanda finished the last of her sandwich and then placed her plate in the sink.

"But it wasn't just the men," she added, wiping her hands on a towel. "Trust me, all the old problems will come back. Just give it time—people are people."

13

Sutter's Creek hadn't changed in the years since Sam's last visit. The post office, Abe's Food Mart, and the Royal General Store made up the center of town. St. Mary's Church stood on the outskirts in need of a new roof; at the other end of town providing counterweight was The Dew Drop Inn, the town's only bar.

Sam rode down Main Street to the clip-clop of Bailey's hooves. He wore a scarf around his neck, hiding the lump neither his mother nor Emily had. An Adam's apple, his mother had called it.

Adam had an apple stuck in his throat? Sam wondered. It wasn't the only strange thing about being male. His mother told him he was lucky not to have facial hair. Sam was disturbed by the possibility of growing a thatch on his face. He feared waking up one morning looking like a grizzly.

Sam slid off Bailey and tied him to a cedar tree. Dread circled his stomach—he hadn't spoken to anyone outside of his family in years. He tried to recall his mother's warnings: don't talk unless you have to, don't look anyone in the eye, don't draw attention to yourself. When he was fourteen, Sam endured lessons from his mother on how to raise the pitch of his voice. His attempts produced squeaks that sent Emily into giggle fits. Now he wished he'd tried harder.

Taking in the scene, Sam was struck by how out of place he felt in the mountain town. He watched a car chug down Main Street, a woman talk excitedly as if to herself. Then Sam realized she was speaking into the same kind of black box that he'd found on Dana Roberts.

That's right, he thought, *I forgot about phones.* He scanned the area, wondering what other strange things would surface from his memory. *I know the forest like the back of my hand, but this world? It's just a jumble of hazy memories*. Sam headed for Royal's, deciding to start his search at the place he remembered most.

A bell tinkled as Sam swung open the door to the general store. Rows of fabric on bolts lined the walls. Hammers and screwdrivers, jars of nails and screws plus a variety of small machines Sam had never seen before filled up the hardware section. He inspected the items in the adjacent area: blankets, clocks, brooms, animal traps, pots and pans, dishes.

Yet Sam knew what he wanted couldn't be found on a shelf. He approached the counter where a woman with wire-rimmed glasses filed through receipts. She looked up.

"Can I help you?"

"I'm looking to hire someone to drive me somewhere."

The woman gave him a curious glance, then stiffened. "This isn't an information booth. You going to buy something or what?"

Sam grabbed a couple of chocolate bars from the counter and pushed them forward. He pulled out a fifty from his pocket. The woman frowned.

"It's $9.58. You got anything smaller?"

After fishing around in his pocket, Sam handed her a five-dollar bill.

"That's not enough. You got another five?"

Sam took out another bill and laid it on the counter. The woman scooped up the money and put it in the cash register. "Your best bet is the message board at the Dew Drop," she said, placing a few coins on the counter. "Just head down Main Street—you can't miss it."

Her decisive tone signaled the end of the conversation. Sam took the chocolate bars and change and headed for the door.

***

As soon as Sam stepped inside The Dew Drop Inn, he wanted to leave. The ramshackle building had no windows and was lit by only a few lamps, making it a tomb that smelled of beer and cigarettes.

Tucked away in a corner, the message board was a crumbling rectangle of cork covered by scraps of paper. Requests ranged from selling a goat to searching for a runaway daughter. Sam examined the papers—the dates on most were two to three months old.

I can't wait that long, he thought. *I need to find a driver now.*

Sam approached the bar. A few women sat at the counter, focused on their drinking. A figure half in shadow in the back lifted a beer mug. The bartender, a slight woman with a long nose, dried a glass with a grey rag. Her skin reminded Sam of the ghostly pale mushrooms that grew on dead trees.

"I need to see some ID," the bartender said.

Eyedee? What's that? Sam thought as he made a show out of checking his pockets. "I . . . I left it at home."

"Then I can't serve you. How old are you, anyway? Fourteen?"

"I'm sixteen," Sam retorted. "And I don't want a drink—I want to hire someone to drive me somewhere."

The bartender jerked her head in the direction of the message board. "Best leave a note."

"That'll take too long," Sam responded. He thanked the woman and headed out the door. Filling his lungs with fresh air, Sam made his way back to the center of town.

Maybe I should have started with the church, he considered as he paced down the sidewalk. The sound of shuffling footsteps came up from behind.

"Hang on," an old woman huffed as she pulled on a parka covered with duct tape patches. "I heard you want to hire someone to drive you somewhere. I got a license, but I ain't got no car. How much are you offering?"

Sam halted, taking stock of the woman's craggy face: the Black Years seemed to have been etched into every furrow. "I've got about $84 dollars and whatever I can get from the sale of my horse. And I have a car."

They resumed walking. "My name's Hilda," the old woman said as she drew a knitted hat over thinning hair. "Where's it you want to go?"

"The Columbia Sector," Sam replied—it was the only part of the address he remembered.

Hilda stopped. "The Columbia Sector? That's a long drive. You got enough money for gas? It ain't cheap, you know."

"Like I said, I've got $84 and whatever I can get from selling my horse." They came up to Bailey who was nosing the ground for anything edible.

"Well, you won't get much for that old nag," Hilda sniffed, scratching her head through the hat. "You barely got enough money for gas which means you ain't got nothing to pay me with." She turned and headed back toward the bar. "Sorry girlie, but you're on your own. Good luck."

Sam brought out the wallet from his backpack. "I have these," he said, fanning out the plastic cards. Hilda returned and inspected each one.

"Who's Dana Roberts?"

"A woman."

"Yeah, I got that part. And where is she?"

"In the forest."

Hilda paused as if weighing the consequences of knowing too much. "And when is she planning on *leaving* the forest?"

"Not any time soon."

A satisfied look settled on Hilda's face. "If I can keep the credit card and driver's license, I'll take you to Columbia."

Sam wasn't sure which one was the credit card, but he understood the rest. "When you drop me off at this address," he said, holding the card with the picture, "I'll give you all of these cards."

"You've got yourself a deal, girlie. We can use the credit card to get gas. You got a passport to get into the Northeast Sector?"

Whatever it was, Sam knew he didn't have it. He shook his head.

Hilda shrugged off his silent reply. "I know where we can cross where there aren't any border guards."

"Border guards?"

"You've got to drive through Northeast to get to Columbia," Hilda stated. She then squinted at Sam. "Are you high? You're acting kind of strange. And your voice sounds—"

"Just getting over a cold," he said, letting out a fake, barking cough.

Hilda continued to look askance at Sam. Then she peered just as dubiously at Bailey. "My neighbor might give you ten bucks for the horse. Or he might ask for ten bucks just to take him off your hands." Sam untied Bailey, and they walked down the street. "You got a name?" Hilda asked.

Sam didn't look at her. "Sam—it's short for Samantha." His shoulder began to pulse with pain, dots and dashes that signaled more suffering to come. The sooner he reached his destination, the sooner he could take care of business. "We need to leave right away."

***

By the second night on the road, the twinges in Sam's shoulder had transformed into a throbbing agony. Only two things eased his misery: the white pills Hilda had found in the glove compartment and the stupor of sleep.

"What's wrong with you," Hilda asked. "You sick?"

Sam shrugged and then grimaced at the hot poker that seemed to have been jammed into the bullet hole. "I've got a headache," he replied. It was true—his head did hurt. Still, his pounding temples paled in comparison to the relentless burning that seared deep into his muscle. Sam, however, had no intention of explaining to Hilda about his confrontation with the intruder. He unscrewed the top of the plastic bottle and tapped two white tablets into his palm. Then he popped them into his mouth and chewed, tasting bitter chalk. After taking a swig from his water bottle, Sam settled back into the seat.

Hilda glanced at him and then stared down the empty highway. "Those aren't candy, you know," she said, nodding at the bottle of aspirin. "The instructions say take every six hours."

"I'm not much for following a schedule."

Hilda shook her head disapprovingly. A sign read Dalton Next Right. "There's our exit."

"For Columbia?"

Hilda smirked. "We're not even at the border yet. Immigration doesn't take kindly to people without passports, so we're taking an alternate route."

Hilda turned down the exit ramp, following the route that threaded into the woods. Pine trees, as thick as blades of grass, loomed on both sides of the road. In time, the asphalt gave way to packed dirt. Reflections from the eyes of various critters gleamed in the dark.

"You sure you know where you're going?" Sam asked.

Hilda nodded. "This used to be an old logging road. It crosses the border, then meets up with County Road 17 on the Northeast side."

"Good," Sam said. He closed his eyes, looking forward to the relief of a nice long nap.

"You've got to stay awake in case we hit trouble."

"Trouble? I thought you said this was an alternate route?"

"It is, but border patrol could be working the area—or there might be a bigger bear in these woods."

Sam was too worn out from his hurting shoulder to decipher the old woman's comment. She continued: "Robbers hold up people crossing the border."

"In that case, we're okay because we don't have anything to steal."

Hilda arched an eyebrow, wondering when she would reach the bottom of this strange girl's cluelessness. "They'll take the car."

Sam paused. *Not having a car would be a problem.*

"Then they'll kill us," she added. "They don't like to leave witnesses."

As he digested Hilda's last statement, Sam stared at the road ahead. "When do we know if we're out of danger?"

"When we hit County Road 17."

"And how long will that take?"

"I have no idea."

***

Twenty minutes had passed since Hilda turned off the highway. She drove slowly as the road became little more than a rugged path.

"I think we're okay," Sam said, half asking, half telling.

"Like I said, when we hit County Road—"

Two headlights flashed behind them, appearing as if from nowhere. Hilda looked in the rear view mirror. "Damn, so close," she muttered just before shoving her foot on the gas pedal.

Sam spun around only to be blinded by the glare. "They're coming up fast!"

Hilda gripped the steering wheel as the Cadillac careened down the bumpy road. The car, a Land Rover, was huge. It rammed them from behind, jerking Sam and Hilda from the hit.

"We stop, we die!" Hilda yelled.

The Land Rover zoomed alongside the Cadillac; Sam saw two women in front, their faces obscured by the dark. The driver slammed the vehicle into the Cadillac, colliding the cars to the screech of metal on metal.

In a flash, Sam remembered the gun in his backpack. He grabbed it, wishing he'd taken the time to look it over. Hilda stared at the gun.

"What the—!"

"Just stay ahead of them!"

"I'm trying!"

Sam rolled down the window and crawled halfway out. He tucked his feet under the seat in a desperate attempt to keep himself from flying out.

If this doesn't work, it's all over!

Sam stretched his arms across the roof of the car. The Cadillac lurched over the grooved road, making aiming impossible. He pointed the gun in the general direction of the Land Rover and pulled the trigger.

A loud crack exploded above the cars' roaring engines—the Land Rover's windshield shattered into pieces. The vehicle hit a deep rut, swerved, and then rolled before smashing into a large pine. Hilda witnessed the scene in the rearview mirror.

"Hoowee, girlie!" she yelped, letting up on the gas. "I don't know what you're doing with that gun, and I don't care! You just saved our necks!"

Sam wiped the sweat from his face with his jacket sleeve, then put the gun back into his backpack. Adrenaline coursed through him, making him feel better than he had in days. After taking a long pull from the water bottle, he asked, "How much longer till we get to Columbia?"

14

After Cassie had left that first night, Jamie brought up a website that marked time. He typed in 16 hours and hit the Enter key—numbers whizzed by down to the millisecond. He figured he would have to wait at least that amount of time—until 6 or 7 p. m. in the outside world—for Cassie's return. Then Jamie stretched out on his bed, happy to have a reason to start a countdown.

The next evening, Cassie showed up, waving her hand through the small window. She was dressed in jeans and her favorite sweater, a purple V-neck that was soft from wear and washings. Cassie stepped out of the decontamination chamber carrying a white plastic bag with *Chinatown* scrawled across it in red script.

"I hope you like Moo Goo Gai Pan," she chimed. "If not, you can have some of my Kung Pao Chicken." She put the bag on the table and pulled out two Styrofoam boxes. "And if you don't like either, I also brought eggrolls and wonton soup."

"It all smells great," Jamie said as he watched Cassie set up the feast on the table. "Most of the time, dinner is either cold cereal or granola bars. And what's with your mom and granola bars? She brings me boxes and boxes, but I don't have the heart to tell her I'm sick of them."

Cassie chuckled. "Yeah, it's a thing with her. She gets the cheap kind—they're so hard, you could pave your driveway with them."

"If I had a driveway . . ." Jamie noted with a wry smile.

Cassie returned the grin and then placed a container in front of him. "She tries to get me to take them to school, you know, for a mid-morning snack like I'm in kindergarten—which reminds me: I have something to show you later."

Jamie's eyebrows went up. "A mystery . . . I'm intrigued."

"It's no big deal, really. I'll show you after our fortune cookies." Cassie searched the white plastic bag and frowned. "They forgot to put in the forks. Do you have any? I'm pretty terrible at chopsticks."

Jamie pulled out one fork from a plastic box. "This is all I have . . . no sense in having a bunch when it's just me. We'll have to share."

"No problem," Cassie said as she opened the containers, letting a tangy aroma fill the room. "So what's new in the, um, ten hours since I last saw you?"

"It's more like 17 hours," Jamie replied, immediately giving himself a mental thump on the head. He forgot to minimize the countdown on his computer—he didn't want to have to explain to Cassie that she was the zero point.

"I've been reading something your mom gave me," Jamie continued, "*The Count of Monte Cristo*. It's pretty good for an old book. This guy is wrongly imprisoned, escapes, finds an outrageous treasure, and plots revenge. I especially liked the way he gets out of prison, in a coffin with a dead body in it."

"Whatever it takes, I guess."

"Personally, I plan to walk out of here—corpse and coffin-free."

"It's going to happen," Cassie said just before she bit into an eggroll. "It's just a question of *when*. Mom's been working really hard." A silence followed. "How's the Moo Goo?"

"It's amazing. Do you eat like this every night?"

"I wish. Mom isn't big on home cooking—other than making really good Sloppy Joes, she's pretty useless in the kitchen, which isn't a bad thing because she gets take-out several times a week." Cassie stabbed a piece of chicken with the one fork. "You should tell her you want more interesting stuff to eat."

Jamie opened a container of soup and grabbed a spoon from the bag. "I don't like asking her for stuff. She's pretty busy, what with trying to save my life and, oh yeah, resurrect the male of the species."

"No, you've got it all wrong," Cassie countered. "If you think of her as your mom, it's your duty to get on her nerves every so often . . . you know, piss her off. It's a basic part of the parent/child relationship."

"Well, at the risk of stating the obvious," Jamie said dryly, "our situation is a little different. But you have a point—I'll at least confront her about the granola bars."

After eating their fill, Cassie and Jamie stuffed the empty containers into the plastic bag. Then Cassie tossed a fortune cookie to Jamie. Before she could unwrap hers, Jamie said, "The mystery first, then the fortune cookies. It'll give us a chance to digest before we eat this huge dessert." He held up the cookie as if it were Exhibit A.

Cassie pulled a large photograph from her backpack and sat on the bed; Jamie parked himself next to her. The caption at the bottom read: Adams Elementary Mrs. Rhodes Kindergarten Class. Three rows of students, all dressed in their picture-day best, beamed with kid-toothed smiles. Mrs. Rhodes, grandmotherly plump with glasses on a chain around her neck, stood at the back looking proud of her brood.

"I haven't seen this picture in years," Jamie said, huffing a laugh at his freckles and big ears. "My mom made me wear that stupid vest—it itched like crazy." He scanned the photo. "Where are you?"

"C'mon, you mean you can't pick me out? I'll give you a hint: electroshock therapy."

Jamie searched until he found a girl with unruly locks that looked like they were sprouting from her head. "I don't remember your hair being that wild."

"I do. I'm glad it toned down as I got older. My mom put my hair in a ponytail, but I pulled it out as soon as I got to school."

Jamie found Cody in the back row. His mouth was drawn up in a dopey grin, his hair a shorter version of Cassie's untamed mane. "Look at him," Jamie said, managing to smile and frown at the same time, "what a doofus." He put down the photograph. "Thanks for the picture. It's cool . . . a little sad maybe, but still cool."

Cassie thought about the time before the Black Years, before XY, when life was normal. From Jamie's expression, she knew he was thinking the same thing. But Cassie had promised herself not to become morose. She was happy just to have dinner with an old friend who just happened to be a boy. It was almost like having Cody back.

Almost.

Cassie looked at her fortune cookie as if she were gazing into a crystal ball, one that didn't reveal the future but uncovered the past. "My dad used to say if you open your cookie at exactly the same time as someone you care about, the fortune will come true."

The comment gave Jamie a slight flush. "Can I see what the fortune is first? What if it says 'you will be eaten by a rabid panda'?"

Cassie snickered, bringing her thoughts back to the present. "No, it's going to be a good fortune," she replied as she tore the wrapping off the folded treat. "I can feel it."

"Well, that's enough scientific evidence for me," Jamie responded with ironic glee. They held up their cookies, ready to break them apart.

"Okay, on the count of three," Cassie said. "One . . . two . . . *three!*"

15

The shoes on display at Styler's Footwear called out to Cassie with their sling-backed, peep-toed siren songs. She indulged her shoe passion mostly by trying on pairs and parading around the mall store. Today, however, would be different. The combination of her grandmother Evie's birthday present—fifty dollars, all in fives—and a sale at Styler's meant Cassie could actually buy a pair.

"Do you have these in a seven?" Cassie asked, holding up a strappy sandal for the store clerk. The young woman nodded and then disappeared into the back. Cassie took a seat to wait for the clerk's return, knowing it would be a while as the store was packed.

Browsing the area, Cassie watched various dramas unfold before her: a mother argued with her tween-aged daughter about the height of a heel, an elderly woman struggled to tie laces with knobby fingers, a trio of freshmen from George Washington collectively ogled a pair of pink satin pumps.

As she enjoyed each mini reality show, Cassie heard a laugh that made her smile. No sooner had she started to look around for the source of the giggle than her search was cut short by the store clerk.

"I've got a seven in the tan but not the black," the girl said as she opened a shoebox. "Want to try them on?"

"If I like the fit, can I order the seven in the black?"

The girl nodded. "It'll take a couple of months to get them in." She sat on a small bench ready to help Cassie into the shoes.

"I can do that," Cassie said. "Go help somebody else—it's pretty crazy in here."

The girl gave Cassie a look of frazzled appreciation. "This is my first Saturday sale. They said it would be busy, but this is ridiculous." And with that, the girl left, only to be snagged by a young woman waving a ballet flat in her face.

Cassie pulled a tan sandal from the box. As she slipped it on, she heard the chuckle again, this time as if the little girl were standing right behind her. Cassie turned around—women and girls of all ages crowded the store, but none were young enough to lay claim to the giggle.

That's so weird, Cassie remarked to herself. *I could have sworn I heard a kid.*

She smiled at her own foolishness, then returned to the sandal. Bending down to fasten the buckle, Cassie heard the chuckle once more. A jolt of recognition caught her by surprise—*that laugh sounds just like Cody!*

A dream Cassie had the night before appeared in her mind. She and Cody were playing hide-and-run, the game they'd made up that combined hide-and-seek with tag. The rules were simple: one player hid while the other searched. Just before being found out, the hiding person would bolt from his or her secret spot, becoming 'it' only when tagged by the searcher.

In the dream, Cassie opened the door to her mother's closet. Like a slingshot, Cody flew past her, running out of the bedroom and down the stairs. Following peals of laughter, Cassie chased her brother into the living room, through the kitchen, and down the stairs into the basement; he was always one step ahead of her, just out of sight.

Shaking off the mist of the dream, Cassie searched the store again but found no little girl. Then the blur of a small figure darted past the freshmen girls. Wearing a sandal and a sneaker, Cassie worked her way through the shoppers.

I know it's not Cody, she told herself, the laughter still echoing in her ears. *I just want to see the little girl who sounds so much like him.*

Cassie continued her search, darting her head around the crowded store. Out of the corner of her eye, she glimpsed a fuzzy figure dashing out of the store. The giggling grew faint.

Cody! Wait!

Cassie ran into the hall. She stopped and pivoted full circle— except for two mall walkers and a knot of teenagers, the hall was empty.

***

By the third day of the trip, Sam was weaving in and out of consciousness. His body had become a battleground between burning heat and shivery chills. The thought of food made him gag. His mouth was dry and metallic. Thirst made him long for cool water, yet when he drank, the liquid made a nauseating puddle in his stomach.

Sam opened his eyes to a four-lane highway cutting through an urban landscape. In a daze, he saw Hilda trying to read highway signs and a tattered road map at the same time.

"I need help," Hilda grunted, squinting at the map.

"Where are we?"

"The Columbia Sector. I'm not too good at city driving. Here, find the address."

A car honked as it swerved to avoid the lane-drifting Cadillac. Sam tried to sit up but was knocked down by the pain. His shoulder was on fire. He lifted himself again, this time using the pain to stay conscious. Sam looked at the map but couldn't focus on the blur of lines and symbols. His eyes rolled back.

"No, stay awake!" Hilda shouted, pounding Sam with her open hand. But it was no use—he was out cold. The old woman cut in front of a Suburban, then took the exit marked Pentagon City Mall.

Rows of cars expanded in front of the mall, yet Hilda wasn't concerned about the lack of an empty space—she had no intention of parking. "Wake up!" she yelled, slapping Sam in the face. He didn't stir.

Hilda stopped in front of a light pole and put the car into park. She got out and opened the passenger side door; Sam slid out half way. With a dirty thumb, Hilda lifted one of Sam's eyelids, revealing a rolled-back oyster eye.

"You're not going to die on me, girlie," Hilda muttered. "That wasn't part of the deal." She dragged Sam's drooping shape out of the car. When he hit the pavement, Sam momentarily came to.

"What? Are we there?"

"Yes, we are," Hilda said, her voice as rough as gravel. "This is the end of the line." She grabbed Sam's backpack from the front seat and rifled through the main compartment. After stuffing the wallet into her pants pocket, Hilda pulled out the gun.

I could get a pretty penny for this at a pawn shop, she thought, admiring the weapon. Then she put the gun back into the main compartment and tossed the backpack onto the passenger seat.

Sam lifted himself only to flop against the light pole. He rubbed his eyes to clear his head, yet the fever had burned away any chance at clarity. The only thing he saw was Hilda's hazy form getting into the car.

"No, wait!" Sam croaked.

"You're on your own, girlie. I'm not getting stuck with your dead body."

Hilda slammed the door and gunned the engine. As the old woman raced the car out of the parking lot, Sam fought to stay conscious; his feverish brain, however, had other plans, deciding instead to send him spiraling down a dark well.

16

Cassie walked back to her car, wondering whether to tell her mother that she thought she heard Cody in the shoe store. The more she mulled over the events, the more ridiculous they sounded in her head. *Yeah, Mom, Cody was right behind me, giggling . . . I thought I saw him, too. What's that you say? Time for a little vacay at the local looney bin?* Eventually, Cassie decided to keep the episode to herself, choosing instead to add the incident to the ever-expanding list of strange things happening in her life.

Ahead, Cassie noticed a figure leaning against a light pole. *Somebody's well into their day drunk*, she surmised, taking note of the curved form's disheveled appearance. Cassie moved to the right, giving the girl a wide berth; when the slouching shape slid to the pavement, Cassie stopped. She waited for something, a cough, a toe twitch, anything to let her know the girl was still alive.

Nothing.

Moving closer, Cassie braced herself for the smell of alcohol but was instead assaulted by the acrid tang of body odor, topped off with the fermenting overtones of a sick room. Brushing aside strands of greasy hair, Cassie examined the girl's sallow face.

She's not much older than I am.

Suddenly, the girl shot her eyes open, causing Cassie to jerk back in surprise. The girl tried to lift herself only to fall back onto the asphalt, her face contorting in pain.

"I'm calling security," Cassie announced as she rose to her feet.

"No, don't," whispered a feeble voice.

"You need help."

"Please, no . . ."

Cassie's thoughts raced: *What if this girl is running away from an abusive mother? Or is strung out on drugs?* Cassie knew the girl wasn't her problem. She also knew she couldn't just leave her. She looked at the pathetic figure.

"I'm going to bring my car around."

***

The girl slumped in the passenger seat, groaning as the Mini Cooper jostled over a pothole. Her hair was a tangled mess, her crumpled clothing making her look like a pile of dirty laundry.

Sick and alone, Cassie thought, feeling sorry for the bedraggled girl. *I guess the Black Years haven't ended for everyone.*

Cassie's plan was simple: get the girl home, nurse her back to health—hopefully in a day or two—and then send her on her way. Cassie knew her mother would balk at first. During the Black Years, Cassie rescued dogs and cats, healing the sick ones and saving the healthy ones from becoming someone's dinner. At first, Amanda protested. She relented only after seeing how diligently Cassie cared for the animals. Her mother had only one stipulation: the pets had to go to good homes as soon as possible.

Cassie turned to see the girl's eyes open in slits.

"Water." The word barely crept out of her mouth.

"We're almost there. I'll get you some soon."

As Cassie pulled into the driveway, she frowned when she saw that her mother's Volvo was not parked in its usual spot.

Darn, Cassie thought, hoping her mother would have finished running her errands. It had been difficult dragging the girl into the car—getting her up the front steps and into the house would pose an even greater challenge. Cassie put the Mini Cooper into park. "We're here," she announced.

The girl didn't respond.

"Hey," Cassie said as she shook the girl's shoulder; she came to with a strangled cry, then fell unconscious again. Cassie got out of the car, opened the passenger side door, and drew her arms around the sagging form. "If you want some water, you'll have to help me get you inside."

Again, the girl opened her eyes and, with a great effort, lifted herself into Cassie's arms. They inched their way toward the front door and then up the steps. Once inside, Cassie led the girl into the living room and flopped her on the couch. The girl let out a sigh, as if lying on something soft had been worth the struggle. "I need water," she whispered.

"It's coming. I'm going to take your temperature first, then give you some water and Motrin."

Cassie left and returned with a digital thermometer, a glass of water, and the medicine bottle. She lifted the girl's feet onto the couch and then slid the thermometer past parched lips. Drained of energy, the girl couldn't keep her mouth closed; Cassie held up her chin for a reliable reading.

The thermometer beeped.

105.7.

Cassie looked at the number in panic, hoping there was something wrong with the read-out. A year ago, she'd come down with the flu; her fever of 103.2 had sent her mother into full maternal meltdown.

If 103.2 was bad, what did that make 105.7—life threatening?

When the same number came up on the second try, Cassie grabbed the bottle of Motrin and scanned the label for the highest dose. After tapping out three red pills, Cassie nudged the girl and held out the glass of water. "You've got to sit up so I can give you something for your fever."

The girl looked up with bloodshot brown eyes. Cassie shivered at the sight of those eyes, seeing something raw, something frightening in her wide black pupils. After barely sitting up, the girl latched onto the glass with both hands and gulped furiously, spilling all over her front.

"Hey, easy does it!" Cassie exclaimed. She put the pills into the girl's mouth to make sure they went down with the rest of the water. Slumping back onto the couch, the girl exhaled and closed her eyes.

As Cassie took off the girl's boots, she heard a low moan. The girl jerked upright, her torso undulating in waves. A guttural sound heralded the rush of water that jumped from the girl's mouth, drenching Cassie in a yellow-tinged liquid; three red pills stuck to her shirt.

Gross.

Cassie picked off the pills and scooped up the medicine bottle, hoping the second set of pills would stay down. The girl hurled more fluid—this time, Cassie dodged the shower that ended up on the rug.

Just then, Cassie heard the creak of the back door and the crackle of grocery bags. Sprinting into the kitchen, she found her mother sniffing the garbage.

"Something smells rotten, but I emptied the trash yesterday. I hope we don't have a dead raccoon somewhere."

"It isn't a raccoon," Cassie murmured. "It's, well, I'll show you." They had just crossed into the living room when Cassie turned to block her mother. "Now, before you get mad, Mom, just remember, you always said the only way everyone got through the Black Years was by helping each other, right?"

Amanda looked sideways at her daughter, wondering how much she would regret her answer. "Yes, I did. What's going on?"

Cassie stepped aside. Amanda entered the living room to find the girl sprawled on the couch. "Our raccoon, I suppose."

"I found her in the mall parking lot. I was going to call security, but she begged me not to."

Amanda shook her head. "So you brought her home?"

"I had to. She's sick. See, she's burning up. I tried to give her some Motrin, but she threw it up."

Amanda sidestepped the dark patch on the rug and leaned over to inspect the girl. "We'll try the Motrin again, only this time she'll drink through a straw—that will limit how much water she can get down." Amanda touched the girl's arm. "Hello?" When there was no response, she pressed her hand to the girl's forehead. "You're right, she definitely has a high fever. Let's get her to my bathroom. She needs a bath to cool her down."

Amanda slid her arms under the girl's shoulders while Cassie took hold of the girl by the ankles. They carried her up the stairs, stopping occasionally to rest from the dead weight. After entering the bathroom, mother and daughter carefully laid the girl in the tub.

"Get some scissors," Amanda said as she took off the girl's socks. Cassie left; when she returned, she passed off the scissors to her mother who used them to cut through the sleeves of the jacket.

The girl groaned and tried to sit up, her face misshapen by fever and fear; Amanda gently pressed her back into the tub. "Relax, we're trying to help you." Despite Amanda's reassuring tone, the girl started to mumble and thrash.

"Take it easy!" Cassie declared. She held down the girl's legs, barely able to keep her steady. "She's strong!"

"And delirious. I'm almost done."

Amanda continued to cut through the girl's jacket and shirt; in time, a pile of fabric pieces materialized on the bathroom floor. Cassie concentrated on not getting a knee to the chin while Amanda pulled away the last fragment. Then she stopped.

"Cassie, look."

Amanda slowly peeled away a blood-soaked bandage on the girl's left shoulder, revealing a red, swollen hole oozing pus. "She's been shot, and it's infected."

Cassie looked at the girl's naked front. "Make that a *he*."

With her focus on the bullet hole, Amanda had overlooked the fact that the girl didn't have breasts.

"She's an illegal mec," Cassie stated. "That's why she—I mean *he*—didn't want security."

The girl—now the mec—had fallen unconscious again. Amanda cut through his blue jeans, and then Cassie and Amanda lifted him to pull away the remaining pieces. Cassie braced herself—botched surgery pictures on the Internet were bad enough. She wasn't sure if she could stomach the real thing. They both stared at his genitals.

"So that's it?" Cassie asked, trying to wrap her head around the fact that it had once been a vagina. Amanda moved in closer with knitted brows.

"What's wrong?" Cassie asked. "Did they mutilate him?"

"No, they didn't," Amanda replied as she flopped his penis from side to side. "In fact, they did *too* good a job. There aren't any suture marks, any scars."

Cassie wasn't sure what her mother was saying.

Amanda looked up. "He's *male*."

Cassie stared, first at her mother, then at the slumped figure in the tub. "How's that possible?"

"I don't know—what I *do* know is that we need to call Dr. Stanton."

Cassie narrowed her eyes, thinking her mother's obsession with finding the cure for XY had finally pushed her off the deep end. "Mom, are you sure it's not that you just *want* him to be male?"

Amanda rose and then paused in the doorway. "Cassie, some things you don't forget." She nodded toward the boy. "And that's one of them."

17

The boy lay beneath the covers, cleaned up, and in Cassie's pajamas. An IV bag hung from the coat tree that Cassie had dragged up the stairs. Clear liquid dripped into a blue vein that traced up the boy's forearm.

Dr. Stanton put her stethoscope and thermometer back into a leather bag. With salt and pepper hair and rimless glasses, she was the kind of woman who did not offer nor tolerate any nonsense. When she heard the urgency in Amanda's voice, Dr. Stanton, now retired but still volunteering at a free clinic, recalled the day when she'd examined a sick boy in a secret room many years before.

Now she looked at the sleeping boy, his face as white as the pillow, wondering if she would lose him, too. After placing vials of blood into her bag, Dr. Stanton turned to Amanda and Cassie.

"I removed the bullet and sterilized the wound, but the blood infection is the real problem. He's on Vancomycin, the strongest antibiotic available. I'll have the results from the lab in a few days." She put on her coat and stopped at the door. "Where did you find him?"

"In the parking lot at the mall," Cassie answered. "And that's pretty much all I know about him."

"Well, we do know one thing," the doctor added. "He *is* immune."

"Do you know why?" Amanda asked.

Dr. Stanton shook her head, wishing she could have answered the question. "The next 24 hours will be crucial."

***

Later that evening, Cassie and Amanda stood next to the bed, watching the sleeping boy's chest move in shallow breaths.

"Now all we can do is wait," Amanda said, her voice calm, measured. Yet Cassie heard something bubble beneath the even tone—she knew her mother was working hard to contain her excitement.

"Mom, you can say it—finding this boy might be the key to the cure."

"Let's not get ahead of ourselves," Amanda chided. She then examined Cassie with concern. "You look tired. Why don't you go to sleep in Cody's room. I'll keep watch over the boy."

Cassie barely suppressed a yawn. *Mom's right. I am tired—exhausted, really. But I don't think I could sleep knowing the boy might not make it through the night.* "No, I'll do that. I want to stay with him."

Amanda gave her daughter a dubious look. "Are you sure? You'll have to watch him all night—we don't want him waking up and pulling out the IV. And the bag needs to be changed every three hours."

"Mom, I can do it," Cassie said, settling into the chair next to the bed. "I'll be fine. If I need you for anything, I'll come and get you."

Amanda nodded, cast one more glance at the boy, and then slipped out of the room. Luka padded over to the bedside. She cocked her head, first at the boy, then at Cassie, her doggy brain trying to figure out the strange arrangement.

"It's all good, Luka. Go to sleep."

***

Several hours into the night, Cassie shifted in the chair, trying to bring her numb legs back to life. When she gazed at the hypnotic *drip, drip, drip* of the IV, fatigue washed over her.

Yet her head became clear when she looked at the boy's face in the glow of the nightlight. His nose was large and had a bump like it had been broken. His lips, though parched, were full; high cheekbones protruded under taut skin. A faint cleft marked his chin. Lying on the bed, his long hair splayed on the pillow, the boy looked like a marble figure on a crypt, his features captured for all time.

Please don't die, Cassie pleaded silently as she gazed at his ashen face. Then she thought of the blood coursing in his veins, the blood that might hold the secret to the cure for XY. Her spirits lifted when she thought of Jamie walking out of his small room into the sunlight.

Yet Cassie didn't want the boy to survive just to save Jamie—and the world—from the viral scourge. She also longed to know everything about the stranger in her bed, starting with his name.

***

The next morning, Cassie awoke to the coat tree crashing down on her head. She jerked her eyes open to see the boy struggling to get out of bed.

"You're up!" she exclaimed, fumbling to stand the coat tree upright.

The boy examined his arm as if trying to figure out why a tube was coming out of it. He grabbed the long piece of plastic.

"Don't!" Cassie yelled before he could yank. "You need that."

The boy responded with only one word: "Pee."

Cassie unhooked the IV bag from the coat rack. "I'll carry this. The bathroom's over there."

The boy rose to his feet and wobbled. Cassie steadied him with a firm grip, then ushered him to the bathroom. Once inside, she let go of the boy only to have him buckle. She caught him, and they sidled up to the toilet. Cassie tried to turn him around to sit, but he gave her a baffled look. He pulled down his pajama pants and let loose a stream that sounded liked a bucket being poured.

"Ah," the boy moaned.

Cassie turned her head in a vain attempt to give him some privacy. They stood there for what seemed to be an eternity.

Is his bladder the size of a basketball? Cassie wondered as the rushing sound stretched on and on. When he was finally done, the boy gave a quick shake and then pulled up his pants. Cassie waited for him to flush. He didn't, so she did.

Once back in bed, the boy looked around at the room. "Where . . . ?"

"You're at my house. You're safe."

"Safe," the boy echoed. His eyes glazed over. "My mother . . . my sister?" He fell back onto the pillow. "No!"

"I'm sure they're looking for you," Cassie said in her most reassuring tone. "Why don't you tell me where I can find them."

The boy didn't answer. Instead, he turned his back to Cassie and was out within seconds.

18

The wind whipped down Harrison Street, causing Brandon to turn up his jacket collar. He stood in front of Al's Corner Store, smoking a cigarette and scanning the streets. Two girls, one dressed in a grey sweatshirt, the other in a faded parka, hustled toward him.

"You're late," Brandon spat. He took a long pull on the cigarette; smoke came out of his nostrils, making him look like a dragon.

The girls, both of them no more than thirteen years old, panted heavy breaths. The one in the sweatshirt spoke: "The bus broke down—we had to run the rest of the way."

"That's not my problem. Tell me what you know."

"Last week a couple of women were selling T down by the Huntington Metro," Parka Girl said. "They weren't from around here."

"And how do you know that?"

"Because we *know* everyone around here," the girl answered with pride.

Brandon paused, not reacting to the information. "Anything else?"

"My cousin bought their stuff," Sweatshirt Girl replied. "She said it was good, you know, clean." She lowered her head.

"And?"

"And they said they'd be back."

Brandon acknowledged the comment. If the Sisterhood's testosterone was as pure as the girl said, Brandon knew his regular buyers would leave him in droves. He had a habit of diluting his T with water, squeezing the most profit from his product. And in the shadow world of illicit drugs, brand loyalty consisted of the best hit for the cheapest price.

His older customers took testosterone to stave off flappy, bat-wing arms and flagging libidos. The younger women, those too squeamish to actually turn, told him testosterone made them think clearer, act bolder—and made them horny as hell. And the teenagers? Who knew why they did anything.

Brandon could always tell who was overdosing—the hot tempers, the acne, the facial hair—all telltale signs of an addict. He told the women to back off the needle, to find the sweet spot of the optimal dose. His motives, however, like his T, were less than pure—he'd lost several of his best customers to knife fights or late night car crashes or bullets from the Columbia police. The trick was to keep as many users alive as possible.

Brandon pulled out his wallet, grabbed two tens, and handed one to each girl.

"Hey," Parka Girl huffed. "You said it would be $20 each!"

Brandon dropped the cigarette, crushed it, and then started off down the street. "Next time, don't be late."

***

Rain pelted the windshield as Brandon turned down Grover Boulevard. The beat of the wipers drummed a single thought into his head:

A war is coming.

Even if he survived the first wave from the Sisterhood, Brandon knew the syndicate wouldn't give up until Columbia was under its control. Tires splashed as Brandon drove past the White House.

Since the end of the Black Years, the presidency had been mostly ceremonial. The once most powerful person in the country now presided over the smallest sector with only minimal influence over the other sectors.

Still, the country clung to the idea of the presidency—the concept of a single leader was deeply ingrained in the hearts and minds of those who had survived the epidemic. Women still wanted the illusion of a unified country if not the day-to-day logistics of it.

The five branches of the military—having been mostly male—had been decimated by XY. With no strong central government, the armed forces were never reinstated. Each sector relied on police units and security squads to keep the peace. In the post-plague world, simple survival took precedence over fighting enemies, both foreign and domestic.

As Brandon turned right onto Avenue G, an idea crystalized in his mind, one as outrageous as it was brilliant: *I need to defend my territory against the Sisterhood—that means I need to build an army.* He stopped at a red light. *And if I have an army, why not take over the Columbia Sector?*

The phone rang, jarring Brandon from his reverie. The caller ID read: Margaret. He pressed the Answer button. "What?"

"I've got bad news and good news," Margaret said, trying to hide the apprehension in her voice. When Dana failed to return his phone calls, Brandon sent Margaret to investigate. He waited for her to speak, as if uttering one word was too much concession.

"Dana's dead," she continued. "I found her body, or what was left of it, scattered at the back of some cabin. There was also a shallow grave—judging by the markers, I'd say someone buried an adult and a child."

After recovering from the disappointment of losing his most useful employee, Brandon realized the good news. "And no sign of the authentic?"

"None."

"And Dana's car?"

"Gone."

Brandon contemplated the information. "Get back here as soon as you can," he ordered, ending the call. He turned right onto Pennsylvania Avenue, his thoughts electric with possibilities. *A live male—and even better, an immune male.*

Brandon's excitement made it difficult for him to concentrate on the road. *And a soon-to-be-captured male!* It didn't matter where the authentic had gone—Brandon knew he could find him through Dana's license plate number.

The price of an immune male on the black market will be staggering, Brandon thought, *enough to pay ten times over the cost of arming a militia.* He took the news as a sign that his plan wasn't just a desperate fantasy—it was, in fact, his destiny.

Create an assault unit, assassinate the president, establish martial law over Columbia. Then no one will control me—ever again.

Brandon hit the brakes at a red light. As he glanced through the rain-streaked window, he saw his reflection, the ghostly image of a man in his thirties with thin lips and coarse hair. As he looked deeper, he saw the face of a fifteen-year-old girl, her nose crooked and swollen, her cheeks bruised. Blood, warm and acrid, trickled from the corner of her mouth; her left eye was puffy and purple. The sound of punches and grunts echoed in her ears.

You taught me well, Father. You always said 'hurt or be hurt.' Now I'm going to take charge.

The car behind Brandon honked. He snapped out of his daze and drove through the intersection.

***

Since that rainy day, Brandon's attention had been focused on his master plan. He let Margaret take over the street-level sale of T, a duty she accepted with equal parts pride and apprehension. Margaret knew if she did well, she would fill Dana's position as right-hand. If she failed, she would be punished in ways she didn't want to imagine.

What Margaret didn't know was that Brandon no longer considered the black market sale of testosterone to be worthy of his attention. He had his sights on bigger revenue sources: the sale of the authentic and the eventual control of Columbia commerce, both legal and illicit.

But he was a long way from imposing his will on the city. First, he had to recruit and arm a militia. And for that, he needed cash. The only place he could get a large enough stash of it was from the Vandovers, the crime family that ran Baltimore.

***

During the hour-long drive to Baltimore, Brandon mentally rehearsed his pitch to Ingrid Vandover, the head of the clan. She had a reputation as a ruthless negotiator, although Brandon knew it wasn't a negotiation at all—Vandover held all the cards. She could shut him down on the slightest whim. Still, Brandon didn't want to come across as groveling. He hated to see weakness in people; he assumed Vandover felt the same way.

Brandon pulled up to a two-story house in a middle-class neighborhood. He checked his phone. *This is the right address*, he confirmed. *Not what I was expecting.*

The house was unassuming—white clapboard siding with grey shutters—until Brandon spotted two women standing near the front door, one with a sawed-off shotgun tucked under her arm. As Brandon got out of the Lexus, the woman raised her weapon.

"I'm here to see Ingrid Vandover," he called out, holding up his palms. "I have an appointment."

"What's your name?" the woman without the weapon asked.

"Brandon Davies."

"Come forward."

Brandon mounted the steps to the porch. The woman frisked him, leaving no body part uninspected.

"Wait here."

The woman disappeared into the house, leaving the three of them: Brandon, the guard, and the shotgun. After a minute, the woman returned. "Follow me."

They entered the house. Brandon couldn't tell if the décor was a collection of antiques or just a bunch of old crap. The smell of baking bread filled the foyer.

They walked through the living room, Brandon finally deciding *Old crap, definitely*. The woman swung open a door to reveal the avocado green linoleum and yellow lace curtains of a small kitchen. An elderly woman stood at the counter in a ruffled apron. She was petite with glasses perched at the end of her nose. A Labrador retriever with cloudy eyes and a muzzle as white as the matron's bun lay sprawled at her feet.

"Thank you, Danielle," the woman said. Danielle nodded and disappeared through the door.

Brandon grimaced as he surveyed the kitchen: a large bowl containing a mound of dough sat on the counter; several loaves cooled on racks. *I'm not here to deal with some bread-making grandma*, he thought, yet before he could speak, the woman cut him off.

"I know you were expecting my eldest," she said as she spread flour on the counter. Then she grabbed the mound from the bowl and plopped it dead center in the white dusting. "And you will see her. But first, I wanted us to have a little chat. My name is Agatha. I'd shake your hand, but I'm covered in dough." She raised gnarled hands in evidence.

"I'm Brandon. I've come here—"

Agatha interrupted with a plate of golden-brown pastries. "Scone? I baked them this morning."

"No, I'm not hungry. I think there's been some kind of mistake . . ."

Agatha smiled, causing lines to fan out from the corners of her eyes. "No, there's no mistake. Are you sure you don't want one? They're very tasty."

Brandon relented. After the first bite, he raised his eyebrows in appreciation.

"See, I told you they were good," Agatha responded, glowing with satisfaction. "It was my grandmother's recipe." She glanced around the kitchen. "This was her house, then my mother's—now it's mine. Money can buy a lot of things, but it can't buy family history." The elderly woman's face creased into a smile, one as smug as it was serene. "Have a seat."

"No, I'll stand."

"I insist. What kind of hostess would I be if I let my guest eat a scone like he was loitering at a hotdog stand?"

Brandon sat at the kitchen table, wondering if their conversation was some kind of joke, if Ingrid Vandover had no intention of loaning him the money.

Agatha returned to her bread dough, kneading it with vigor. "What doctor did your surgery?" she asked, nodding her head slightly toward Brandon's private parts. "I'm assuming you did it with us. You don't strike me as someone who goes the traditional route, filling out forms, waiting on lists."

Ordinarily, Brandon would have flatly ignored such an invasive question. But he knew why she'd asked: the Vandover family controlled the illegal medical market, including but not limited to turning. Any woman in need of a new heart, kidney, liver, or lung could get one for a price. It was also wise not to ask questions about the original owner of the body part.

"It was Dr. Rose."

Agatha nodded. "You were lucky—she's one of our best employees. We try to hire competent people, but quality control is always a problem." She rolled over the dough, pushing on the elastic mass. "More and more women are choosing to become male. What do the kids call it?"

"Turning."

"That's it . . . *turning*. I can't for the life of me imagine why anyone would want to do that—I think being a woman is a blessing." Agatha punched the center of the dough ball. "Still, it's good for business. And as always, women will do just about anything to have a second chance at life. Ruin your lungs with smoking? Just get a new pair. Destroy your liver with alcohol? A fresh one can be yours," Agatha noted as she placed the dough into a bread pan, "if you have the cash."

What little patience Brandon had was ebbing away. "The reason I'm here—"

"Yes, to get a loan. I'm aware of that, quite a sizable one over a short period of time, I might add."

"That's right. I can pay you back in a month."

"Then why not just wait the month? Why take out a loan? Our interest rates are steep—it tends to keep away the amateurs."

"I can't wait a month. I need the funds now."

Agatha chuckled. "You young people, in such a hurry. You should learn to bake bread . . . that will teach you patience."

"I'll pay you back. You don't have to worry about that."

Agatha brushed egg white on the loaf. "Oh, I'm not worried. You'll repay the loan, one way or the other."

Heat rolled over Brandon as Agatha opened the oven door and slid the pan onto the rack. "Either you settle your debt in full by the deadline," she said as she closed the door, "or we'll take your body—every organ, every inch of skin, every drop of blood—as payment. We'll even grind up your muscle and bone and feed it to our dogs."

Agatha looked down at the retriever who lifted its head and weakly thumped its tail. "It's good for their coats." She wiped her hands on the apron. "And hiding from us would be foolish and futile."

Brandon looked at Agatha, realizing that he was, in fact, talking with the true leader of the notorious Vandover crime family.

The old woman turned to the wall. "Danielle, our guest can see Ingrid now to work out the details." Danielle appeared in the doorway and motioned for Brandon to follow. As he moved toward the door, Agatha once again lifted the plate of scones.

"Sure you won't have one more?"

19

The boy flinched when Amanda poked him with the needle. Cassie looked on, glad that he was reasonably awake.

Please stay conscious for more than a few minutes, she thought as the boy relaxed into the pillow. During the last three days, he'd woken up five times; each time, he'd eaten a little, gotten poked or prodded by her mother or Dr. Stanton, or taken a leak. Yet Cassie only knew that because of her mother's updates: every time the boy had been awake, she'd been stuck at school.

Amanda drew up the syringe, filling the chamber with dark blood. "My name is Amanda," she said to the boy. "I'm a scientist who studies viruses." Even though she knew the boy was still too groggy—or too reluctant—to respond, she continued: "I'm trying to figure out why you're immune to SN-146."

The boy nodded slightly.

Amanda pulled out the needle and transferred the blood into a blue-topped vial. After putting a Band-Aid on the stick site, she felt the boy's forehead.

"You're still warm," she noted as she slid the digital thermometer under the boy's tongue. After it beeped, Amanda read the result: "102.8. Well, that's better than 105.7."

The boy tugged on the IV like a dog on a chain. Amanda placed her hand on his arm. "The doctor says we can stop the IV and start oral antibiotics as soon as your fever gets to below 101. Hopefully, that'll only be a few more days."

"I'll get a cool washcloth," Cassie said. After returning from the bathroom, she placed the wrung-out cloth on the boy's forehead.

"There's good news," Amanda announced. "We got the results from your blood work—the medicine you're taking is very effective against the kind of infection you have."

Cassie perked up at the news, but the boy was too zoned to appreciate it. He flipped over the damp washcloth, then rubbed it on his face and neck.

Amanda rose from the bed. "Remember, if you need anything, we're both just down the hall."

Before Amanda slipped out of the room, Cassie caught her in the doorway. "He was doing better yesterday," she whispered. "His fever was only 101.7. If the antibiotic is so great, why is his temperature back up to 102.8?"

Amanda looked at her daughter, deciding to address her real question: "Cassie, he doesn't have SN-146. I've tested him for that. Dr. Stanton said his recovery would be like this—two steps forward, one step back. I know it's hard, but we're just going to have to be patient."

Cassie nodded reluctantly. *Patience isn't my strong suit*, she thought as she returned to the boy's side. She took the washcloth that was warm and almost dry and once again headed for the bathroom. Under the flow of cold water, Cassie rinsed the terry cloth, then returned to the bed, parking herself in the indentation left by her mother.

Too bad I can't just draw blood like my mom to find out what I want to know, Cassie thought as she placed the washcloth on the boy's forehead. *Like who shot you—and why?*

The boy peered at her with bleary eyes. He took the cool cloth and rubbed his face and neck. Then he unbuttoned the pajama top and pressed the white square to his chest.

"Careful," Cassie warned, trying to keep the boy's hand away from the bandage that covered his bullet wound.

The boy closed his eyes, giving Cassie the chance to sneak a glimpse at his chest. A nest of hairs sprouted between his nipples. Even though she'd seen pictures of shirtless men, Cassie still found the look of a flat chest—with hair—to be odd. The boy opened his eyes; Cassie quickly brought hers to meet his.

"This feels good," he murmured, holding the cloth to his skin.

"Tell me when you want it cooled down again."

After making several circles on his chest, the boy handed the cloth to Cassie. Once again, she entered the bathroom; when she returned, she found that the boy had taken off his pajama top and flipped over.

"My back."

"Okay," Cassie mumbled. She stroked the cloth down his spine, prompting a groan of relief to float from the boy's lips. His back, wide at the shoulders, narrowed to a slim waist. The muscles in his arms were defined and rounded, even if they were slack from lying down. At the sight of the boy's nakedness, which seemed at once so foreign yet completely natural, Cassie felt her own heat rising, as if his fever had somehow found its way to her core.

"My name's Cassie. What's yours?"

The boy turned his head to the side and closed his eyes; soft snuffling let Cassie know he was fast asleep. She put the cloth on the bedside table and covered him with the sheet.

Oh well, it was worth a shot.

***

The green light flashed in the chamber. After the door opened, Cassie saw Jamie dressed in blue jeans and a white T-shirt. It had been six days since her last visit—she hoped he hadn't noticed. His expression told her otherwise.

"First of all, I know it's been a while," Cassie said, easing into the conversation.

"One hundred forty-four hours, fifty minutes and change," Jamie responded, trying for lighthearted but not succeeding. "But who's counting."

"There's a good reason why I haven't been to see you," Cassie went on. "And it affects you, so when you hear it, you'll understand."

No look of agreement crossed Jamie's face.

Cassie continued: "To make a long story short, I found a guy, a real guy like you, only he's immune to XY." She stopped to assess the impact of her statement, hoping to see a softening in Jamie's demeanor—whatever he was thinking didn't register on his face. "Mom's been taking his blood to figure out why he's immune. This is a big step to finding the cure—he may be the key."

Jamie's expression relaxed at Cassie hopeful pronouncement. "So where's this guy now?"

"He's at our house. He was really sick, but he's better now, thanks to a boatload of antibiotics."

"Where did he come from?"

"I have no idea—we don't know anything about him. He wakes up every so often, then crashes."

Jamie studied Cassie's face. "Why do you blush when you talk about him?"

"I do not!" Cassie shot back, bristling at the interrogation. "Why would you say that?"

"Because it's true. Look, you're still doing it."

"I'm flushed because you're giving me the third degree."

"It isn't the third degree—it's just a question."

Cassie sensed the smallness of the room. "Listen, these last few weeks have been crazy, finding out about you, learning that Cody died only a few years ago, finding this guy. I haven't slept much, so if I'm blushing, it's because I'm tired."

"Okay, that's an answer," Jamie conceded. They stared at each other. Cassie didn't want to use her trump card—she could leave, but he couldn't—because she knew it would be cruel. Finally, Jamie said, "Maybe not an honest one, but still an answer."

Deciding that Jamie wasn't going to let it go, Cassie stepped into the decontamination chamber. "I'll come back when you're in a better mood."

Jamie snagged her by the arm and gently pulled her back into the room. "Don't go. I was just disappointed—I usually don't count time in here because I have so little to look forward to. I just wanted to see you again." And with that, the chill between them evaporated.

***

After several rousing games of Speed—a card game Jamie picked up quickly—Cassie and Jamie relaxed into the afternoon. Jamie described his online differential calculus course, mentioning his plans to take internal calculus during the summer. He clicked his fingers on the keyboard, pulling up his homework.

"It took me a while, but I understand it now," Jamie said, a satisfied look settling on his face.

Cassie looked at the screen filled with Martian equations. *Well, that makes one of us*, she thought, wondering how the bizarre markings made sense to anyone. Then she curled up in the overstuffed chair and ran her fingers over the threadbare upholstery.

"You know, Manfred could use a makeover. If my mom snuck him in, she could sneak him out." Cassie stroked the armrest. "What do you think, Manny? Nothing flashy, maybe a nice blue-green paisley?"

Jamie half-smiled, not sure if Cassie was making fun of him for naming the furniture. If she was, he didn't care—he was happy just to have her there.

When did she get so pretty? he asked himself, trying not to stare. The sound of her voice, the way her hair fell on her shoulders, the soft curve of her blouse gave him a strange feeling in the pit of his stomach. *Exhilaration, maybe? Excruciation? Was that even a word?* To Jamie, words had always taken a back seat to numbers. If he were to quantify the experience, he would say being with Cassie was like infinity. The hundred-plus hours she hadn't come to see him? That was easy, too—negative infinity.

"Hello, Earth to Jamie," Cassie said, singsonging her mock chagrin. "Anybody home?"

Jamie snapped out of his mental side trip. "Sorry, got a little drifty there. Yeah, a Manfred upgrade . . . sounds like a plan." He watched as Cassie's expression turned serious.

"What was it like when my mom put you in here with Cody?"

Jamie shifted in the chair—talking about the past just reminded him of his waiting game with XY. He considered changing the subject. "It was tough. At six years old, I didn't understand why I couldn't play outside anymore. I was glad Cody was with me, although we had plenty of fights."

"Fights? Really? I don't remember arguing with Cody."

"No, this wasn't arguing. It was fighting—as in hitting, kicking . . . it wasn't pretty."

Cassie's jaw dropped slightly.

"Remember, we were left alone for long periods of time," Jamie said. "And we were scared and confused about what was going on. One time, we went after each other so hard, the room looked like it had been hit by a tornado. Actually, make that *two* tornados. Your mom was not amused."

"I can imagine. But I can't imagine fighting with Cody. We were just on the same wavelength. I guess it was the whole twin thing." A distant look shrouded her face. "I'm scared I'm forgetting him and my dad. And if I can't remember them, then it's like they've died all over again—or worse, like they never even existed." Cassie lowered her head, casting around for anything to shake her out of her funk. "What was the tornado fight about?"

"Something only a kid would get bent out of shape about—I wanted to play with Robot Dude, but Cody wouldn't let me. As the years went by, we got over the fighting. I guess we realized how lucky we were to have each other. What I wouldn't give to see him again."

The catch in Jamie's voice saddened Cassie, yet it was a sadness filled with something warm, something comforting. She looked into his eyes.

"I know what you mean."

20

It was Saturday afternoon after the lunch rush at Gail's Deli, Gail being Terry's mom. Cleanup fell to Terry while her mother made chicken salad, coleslaw, and pasta primavera.

Terry always put off cleaning the meat slicer for last. She swore the monstrous contraption, with its razor sharp blade and too many parts, had a personal vendetta against her. After unhooking the blade, Terry pulled off the heavy arm of the slicer.

"Shit!" she spat as a red line of blood appeared on her finger.

"You okay?" Gail called out from across the kitchen. "And language!" She came up to Terry. "I'll get a Band-Aid."

"No, Mom, I can do it," Terry responded as she pulled a box of bandages from a cabinet. "I'm not five anymore. You don't have to kiss my owies."

"I have no desire to kiss your owies," Gail answered, a sly smile curving on her lips. "My goal is to keep you from bleeding all over the place—the health inspector frowns on that kind of thing."

"I'll keep that in mind," Terry deadpanned as she cleaned the cut with soap and water.

"You've got to be more careful," Gail continued, her light-hearted lilt now eclipsed by concern. "If you're not paying attention when you clean that thing, it'll bite you every time."

Terry rolled her eyes and returned to her stainless steel adversary. She knew her mother was right—cleaning the evil slicer required concentration. But Terry had something on her mind. She glanced at the clock on the wall.

I need to leave by 2:15 to catch the crosstown bus, she thought, cleaning the blade with respect. After reassembling the now gleaming slicer, Terry grabbed her jacket.

"I've got to head out, Mom. I'll be back in time to finish the prep for dinner."

"Where are you going?"

"To meet a friend. I'll see you later."

And with that, Terry was out the door. She hustled down the street to the nearest bus stop. After boarding a bus, she found a seat at the back and settled in as the city rolled by in an endless loop of buildings, cars, and pedestrians.

After several stops, Terry got off at Tyler Street and headed north. She'd been instructed to meet Andrea—no last name—by the pond in Jackson Park. Terry pulled her wallet from her back pocket, needing to reassure herself that the money was still inside. Ten crisp fifty-dollar bills—the sum total of her earnings from the last three months—lay tucked in the billfold.

And this is just the down payment.

At the park, Terry hustled down a walkway that cut through a grassy area. Ahead she saw a girl biting her nails; she looked to be about seventeen.

"You waiting for Andrea?" Terry asked.

The girl gave her hand a rest and nodded. Terry wondered about the social protocol between two girls waiting to pay their first installment for turning. *Do we introduce ourselves? Do we chit chat about the weather?* "Hi, I'm Terry."

The girl smiled. "I'm Rachel, and I'm a little nervous." She laughed, not that anything was funny.

"Me too . . . it's not every day I hand over all of my savings so I can change into a different person."

After several minutes of silence, Rachel's twitchy ticks slid into annoyance. "For what we have to pay, you'd think this *Andrea* could be on time."

"You got that right," Terry responded. She scanned to see if anyone was approaching—the park was still empty.

Terry wanted to ask Rachel a question, one she knew was a far cry from small talk. "I know we don't know each other," Terry began slowly, "and if I'm being nosy, just tell me to butt out."

"I know what you want to ask," Rachel said, her shoulders slouching forward. "I'm doing this for my mother."

"Your mother? She asked you to turn?"

Rachel shook her head. "No. I had an older brother—Jack. He was the light of my mother's life. When XY got him, she just cratered. Even after ten years, she still sometimes cries herself to sleep." Rachel hesitated as if weighing how much to reveal to a complete stranger. "I thought becoming her son might get her to see that I'm still here."

Terry had no idea how to respond—Rachel's forlorn story made her wonder if turning for Cassie was just as sad and desperate.

"How about you?" Rachel asked.

"I guess I'm doing it for the same reason, to get closer to someone I care for."

The din of traffic filled the gap between them. Then Rachel asked, "Have you heard of girls waking up during the operation? Like they don't give you enough drugs to stay under and then *bam!* You're in crazy pain with your chest all carved up, and someone is throwing your boobs into a scrap bucket."

"No, I hadn't heard that."

Rachel shuddered. "That scares the hell out of me."

A woman came up the walkway. She was about forty with teased hair covering her head like a helmet. "Terry? Rachel?"

They nodded.

"I'm Andrea. You both have the money?"

Again, they nodded. Rachel pulled a large wad from her jacket pocket—it appeared to be all ones. "Waitressing money," she said sheepishly.

Terry brought out her wallet and took the bills from inside.

"The rest is due at the time of the surgery," Andrea said. "I'll let you know the time and place. You can't eat or drink anything before the procedure and plan on a ten-day recovery."

She pulled two paper bags from her purse and handed one to each girl. "Start injecting yourself four times a day. The instructions are inside. It might make you sick at first, but don't stop."

Rachel took a vial of clear liquid from the bag. "What's this?"

"Testosterone," Terry answered, noting that Rachel hadn't done her homework on becoming male.

Rachel held up a syringe with two fingers like it was a slimy toad. "Really?"

"Yes, really," Andrea said. "Four times a day for the rest of your life." She smirked with contempt and then glanced at the wad in Rachel's hand. "I'll take that," Andrea said, grabbing the rolled-up bills. She eyed the fifties in Terry's grasp.

So this is the beginning, Terry thought as she held out her hand. *Cassie will freak, but she'll get over it . . . eventually.*

Without warning, Terry was hit by a sucker punch of anxiety. It wasn't the fear of waking up on the table or the pain or the blood that made her feel woozy; it was the thought of Cassie's face lined with tears.

Terry snapped back her hand and stuffed the money into her pants pocket. "I'm going to think about this some more. I know how to get in touch with you—when I'm ready, I'll call." She gave the paper bag back to Andrea, then looked at Rachel. Not sure what to say, Terry kept it brief: "Good luck."

Rachel nodded a hesitant reply. As Terry walked away, Andrea called out, "Nobody likes the needle at first, but you get used to it."

"That's not it," Terry said, looking straight ahead. "I just can't do this right now."

21

Sam awoke to the sound of beeping and grinding machinery. He opened his eyes to an unfamiliar room.

Where am I?

He rose and walked over to the window to see if anything outside looked familiar—it didn't. Then he watched as two women in grungy jumpsuits dumped trash into the back of a large truck.

Sam searched his memory for clues as to how he ended up in the room. The last thing he clearly remembered was Hilda dragging him out of the car, although fuzzy images of a girl laying him on a couch, placing him in a tub, and putting him to bed floated in his head.

Sam turned from the window and studied the bedroom. Movie posters covered the walls; framed photographs of smiling faces stood on a dresser, pictures of family and friends, Sam assumed.

But whose family and friends?

Then Sam noticed a small black and white picture of a repeating design taped next to the bed. Before he could register that the picture seemed out of place, he looked up to see a girl entering the room carrying a stack of folded clothes; a dog loped in at her side. Sam froze—with its pointed ears and pale blue eyes, the animal looked just like a wolf.

"Welcome back," the girl said, looking surprised that he was out of bed. "You've been really sick, but the doctor said the worst is over."

Sam studied the girl, deciding she was the one from his hazy memories. Then he scrutinized the dog, feeling his fight-or-flight instinct kick in.

"I know she looks scary," the girl said, giving the dog a head scratch, "but really, she's just a big baby. Her name's Luka—it's Eskimo for 'likes to chew sneakers.' "

Sam knew it was a joke, yet the unnerving situation—waking up in a strange room, talking to a strange girl with a wolf-dog at her side—didn't make him feel like laughing.

The husky padded over. After sniffing, the dog seemed satisfied with Sam's scent enough to lift its head and pant into a smile.

Sam held out his hand; the dog responded by exploring with its nose. Then Sam touched the animal's head, cautiously at first, as though expecting to feel incisors sinking into his flesh. Then he stroked the husky's thick neck, seeing something of the woods in the dog's transparent eyes. Sam looked up.

"This is your home?"

"That's right, my bedroom as a matter of fact. Are you hungry?"

"Starving. How long was I sick?"

"I found you last Saturday, so it's been a week. But before that, I don't know. When I brought you here, you were already in pretty bad shape."

Sam noticed what he was wearing—snug blue pajamas with orange teddy bears. "I had this nightmare about pink hearts."

The girl responded with a small laugh. "That was no nightmare—that was my Grandma Evie. Every year for Christmas, she gives me pajamas: yellow flowers, blue puppies, red kitties, and my personal favorite, lavender unicorns. To her, I'll always be nine years old." The girl motioned to the clothes on the bed. "There are some jeans and a shirt. They were my dad's. I hope they fit better than the teddy bears."

"Where are my clothes?"

"We had to cut them off you. The pieces went in the trash."

"And my backpack?"

The girl shook her head. "There wasn't one."

Sam tried to hide his disappointment—the photo of his mother and sister, his money, the gun . . . all gone. He backed into the night table, knocking a scrapbook to the floor. The book flipped open to a picture of a young man with dark hair, topaz eyes, and pale, sparkling skin. Sam picked up the scrapbook, examining the photo. "What's with him?"

"He's a vampire."

Sam's jaw dropped. "They're *vampires* now? When did that happen?"

The girl unsuccessfully suppressed a snicker. "No, he's not a *real* vampire. He was an actor who played a vampire in some old movies, you know, from before."

Sam nodded, knowing he would have to work a little harder to avoid sounding like an idiot.

"What's your name?" the girl asked.

"Sam. Sam Harding"

"I'm Cassie O'Connell." They both paused, letting an awkward silence fill the air.

"There's a clean towel in the bathroom if you want to take a shower," Cassie said as she headed for the door. "Come on down when you're ready."

Sam could see Cassie working a no-big-deal attitude, but he knew a boy in her bedroom was anything but.

***

When Sam entered the kitchen, Cassie felt her chest tighten—seeing him in her dad's plaid shirt and blue jeans made her long to feel her father's arms around her.

"Never had a shower before," Sam announced, "or not one that I can remember." His wet hair was tied back with an elastic band.

Cassie placed a plate with a sandwich and potato chips on the table. "I hope grilled cheese is okay."

Sam nodded as he sat at the table.

"So, first time for a shower," Cassie started in. "Where you lived only had a tub?" Questions about the bullet hole would come later. Sam grabbed the sandwich and took a bite—nearly a quarter of it disappeared.

"No running water," he mumbled, working his way through the mouthful.

Cassie followed her reasoning to its logical conclusion: "That means no toilet?"

Sam nodded again and then swallowed. "An outhouse."

Cassie's eyebrows lifted in an *aha!* moment: *Mystery of the no-flushing—solved.*

Sam picked up and admired a potato chip. "I used to love these things. They were hard to get where I lived."

"And where was that?"

"Outside Sutter's Creek."

"And Sutter's Creek is . . . where?"

"Canada."

"Canada! How'd you get to Columbia?"

"Drove."

Impatience rose in Cassie like hot air. *Had the infection damaged the answer-with-more-than-one-word part of his brain?* "With who?"

"Hilda," Sam replied. "My turn—how'd I end up here?"

"Well, your pal Hilda dumped you off at the mall parking lot. You were half dead."

Sam shrugged, grateful that being sick was a blur. He could see that Cassie wanted to know more, yet the thought of telling her about his last night at the cabin brought the weight back to his chest.

"Do you know where 1302 Avenue B Apt. 4-C, Columbia Sector, is?" Sam asked. He'd memorized the address, knowing Hilda would take the cards at the end of their journey.

"Not specifically, but I can Google it."

A blank look fell over Sam's face.

"I'll look it up on the Internet."

Still no look of recognition.

"I'll search the computer to find out where it is. You know what a computer is, don't you?"

Sam's face twisted into an *I'm-not-a-moron* look. "Of course I do—it's the TV thing I used to play games on."

Cassie looked sideways at Sam, trying to decide if he was pulling her leg. His expression, one that radiated a confidence only the truly clueless could muster, told her he was not. "Do you know you're an authentic?" she asked.

"An authentic? What's that?"

"It means you're a real male—a *live* male. There aren't any of those left."

Sam put down his sandwich. "Oh yeah, I do know that," he said, thinking of his mother's never-ending struggle to keep him hidden. Then he remembered why he'd come to Columbia. "So, the address . . ."

"Why do you want to go there?"

"To take care of something."

"You mean *now*?"

"Yes."

"You're not strong enough to go out, and it's not safe for you. If you get picked up as an underage mec, they'll send you to some prison reform school."

"An underage *what*?"

"A mec," Cassie began, "is a woman who's changed into a man through hormones and surgery."

Sam tried not to look shocked. "They can do that?"

Cassie nodded.

"Okay," Sam said, taking control of the new information, "no vampires but half men/half women—got it."

Cassie suppressed a laugh, knowing Sam hadn't meant the comment to be funny—which it was . . . completely.

"You've got to get a permit and be at least 21 years old to have the surgery," Cassie said, distracting herself with facts. "Anyway, you're still recovering, so you're not going anywhere."

Sam could see her point, but that wasn't going to stop him. He used the only leverage he had: "If you take me there now, I'll tell you everything you want to know." He wasn't sure if he was telling the truth—what he did know was that it was the only way to convince her.

Cassie peered at Sam, deciding that the fever hadn't damaged his brain after all. "No questions off limits?"

"You ask, I'll answer."

"With more than one word at a time?"

"You won't be able to shut me up."

"I doubt that."

Cassie assessed Sam's clothes. Even though the lumberjack look was still around, Cassie decided a more feminine style was in order if they were going out in public.

"Follow me. You need a makeover."

***

When nothing fit from her own closet, Cassie brought in several of her mother's blouses and pants, flopping the armful on the bed. After various combinations, Cassie decided on a pair of pants that was too long for her mother—she had to roll up the cuffs—and a blouse with a stand-up collar that hid Sam's offending Adam's apple.

Cassie pulled the elastic (and too many hairs to Sam's liking) from Sam's ponytail and fluffed his hair around his shoulders. She gave him a pensive onceover.

"It's close, but something's not right." Then Cassie shook her head as if she'd been hit by a big *duh!*

"Just one more thing," she said as she opened the top drawer of her dresser. After rummaging through her underwear, Cassie pulled out a bra, a lacy little number with a bow between the cups. She dangled the bra in front of Sam like it was a worm on a hook. He wasn't biting.

"Is that absolutely necessary? It just seems wrong."

Cassie was not to be denied. "Yes, it is. And there's nothing wrong with breasts—every self-respecting girl has a pair, so you will too, at least in public. Time to get in touch with your feminine side, Samantha."

Sam shot her a look. "How'd you know that was my, you know, girl name?"

"Lucky guess," Cassie replied, taking no small delight in Sam's naiveté.

As Sam unbuttoned the blouse, Cassie fixed her eyes on his chest. *I've always been curious about guys*, she thought, trying to justify the stare. In truth, as Sam's muscles rolled beneath his skin, Cassie felt her knees wobble.

Sam threaded his arms through the loops of the bra. After a generous amount of tugging, Cassie hooked the clasp. Then she took out rolled-up socks from the drawer and, feeling the warmth of Sam's breath on her forehead, stuffed and smashed each cup into a breast-acceptable shape.

"That should do it," Cassie said in the most business-like tone she could muster. Sam put on the blouse and looked at himself in the mirror.

"Bras are uncomfortable."

Cassie smiled at his reflection. "Welcome to Girl World. Lucky for me, I can choose to go braless. If you want the girls, you can't."

"The girls?" Sam asked, looking perplexed. "What girls?"

"These are your *girls*," Cassie said, making a sweeping gesture in front of Sam's new acquisitions. "They're your badge of female honor."

Sam turned to the side, revealing the curve of his profile. "Maybe they're not so bad after all. They're like mini-torpedoes ready to be launched. You could put in more socks and go for the big guns."

"They're fine the size they are." Cassie responded, barely suppressing an eye roll. "The goal is to pass, not win a wet T-shirt contest."

Sam scrunched his face. "A wet T-shirt contest?" He said the phrase like it was a string of random words. "Why would I want to win that?"

"Never mind," she replied. Cassie took the laptop from her desk and sat crossed-legged on the bed. "Okay, let's find out where your mystery address is."

***

Sam grabbed the driver-side door handle to the Mini Cooper.

"Wrong side," Cassie called out.

Sam looked in the window to see the steering wheel on the right. "Why did they change that?"

"They didn't—it's a British car. The old Mini Coopers have the steering wheel on the right."

Sam stood back to take in the car. It was red and boxy with two black stripes running down the hood.

"You have a problem with my car?" Cassie asked. She was especially territorial about the Mini Cooper as it had been her father's car—she still thought of it as his. And anyone who dissed her car insulted her dad.

After the Black Years, the Cooper—as her dad had called it—sat in the garage, draped with a tarp like a shroud. Cassie's mother told her she wanted Cassie to drive it when she got her license, which was true enough.

Cassie also knew her mother kept the car because it was the embodiment of her father: goofy yet cool. The 1982 Mini Cooper was the love child of a race car and a clown car. When Cassie got behind the wheel, she could feel her father driving her and Cody to school or the grocery store or the local pool.

"No, I've just never seen a car like this before," Sam said. He looked at the square corners at the front, the small tires, the scaled-down appearance. "It looks like something out of a cartoon—it's awesome."

Cassie smiled as she and Sam got into the car. "You know, I'm breaking the law," she noted as she turned on the ignition.

"And how's that?"

"I'm not supposed to drive with anyone under eighteen until this summer . . . and I'm pretty sure that includes you."

Sam nodded and then squinted at Cassie. "Somehow I get the feeling this isn't the first time you've done something you're not supposed to do."

22

Brandon opened the passenger side door, letting a young woman swing her slender legs to the curb. She emerged from the car, straightened her skirt, and brushed a lock of stray hair from her forehead.

"How do I look?"

"Like a mother-to-be," Brandon replied. They entered the lobby of the building and approached a set of double doors; New Life Reproductive Services was etched in the glass in gold letters.

"Ready?" he asked, holding tight to the handle of a briefcase.

The young woman nodded, and they entered the waiting area. The receptionist sat at the front counter wearing a camel skirt and a peach blouse; she looked up with a professional smile. "May I help you?"

"We're James and Elizabeth Baum," Brandon replied. "We have an appointment with Dr. Richards."

The woman typed on a keyboard and searched the computer screen. "Have a seat—the nurse be with you in a minute."

The couple thanked the young woman and then sank into a plush sofa. Several women sat in the waiting area, their ages ranging from girls who looked too young for the responsibilities of motherhood to grey-haired matrons more suited to spending their golden years as doting grandmothers. Brandon leafed through a magazine yet hardly glanced at the pages. After fifteen minutes, a nurse in white approached.

"Mr. and Mrs. Baum? The doctor will see you now."

Brandon and Elizabeth followed the nurse into an office where a mec, dressed in a charcoal suit and burgundy tie, sat behind an imposing oak desk. The couple sat in chairs of polished cherrywood.

"Nice to see you again, Mr. and Mrs. Baum," Dr. Richards said as he rose and shook their hands. He settled back into his seat and brought up a screen on his laptop. "The results from your physical look good," the doctor said to Elizabeth. "You can start the hormone therapy we discussed during your initial evaluation. Refresh my memory," he said as he returned his attention to the screen, "this is your first daughter?"

"Yes," Elizabeth replied. "We're very excited." She placed her hand on Brandon's, giving it a light squeeze.

Nice touch, Brandon thought, admiring the performance unfolding before him. "Elizabeth" came highly recommended as an aspiring actress who could improvise and not ask questions. She also came cheap.

A photograph of a grinning toddler stood on the desk in a silver frame. "Is this your daughter?" Elizabeth asked.

"Yes—she's the light of my life. And my wife is pregnant with our second."

Elizabeth admired the toddler's dimpled face. "She looks like you."

"I had her before I turned," the doctor said as he glanced lovingly at the picture.

Brandon tried to hide his impatience with the small talk. "We've made our sperm donor selection. What's the next step?"

The doctor turned to address Elizabeth: "My nurse, Sophie, will review the hormone protocol with you, then after a month, we'll do blood work to see when you are ovulating. Once we've determined the optimal date, we'll schedule the insemination. After you become pregnant, you'll need to be tested in the first trimester to confirm the sex of the fetus."

"I thought your semen was free of the Y chromosome," Elizabeth commented.

"It is, but there have been rare but unfortunate instances where women carry male babies to term only to have them die within hours of birth—we want to make sure all babies are female." Dr. Richards rose and extended his hand. "We'll know if the insemination has been successful after about six weeks."

Elizabeth shook the doctor's hand, then furrowed her brow. "Is the sperm bank in this building?"

"Yes, it is."

"Can we take a look?"

"Unfortunately, the repository is for authorized personnel only."

Elizabeth pouted her disappointment. "We'd just like to see where it all starts. That way, when our daughter asks where she came from, we'll be able to describe everything in detail. We're planning on being very open with our children."

Dr. Richards looked one more time at the picture of his adorable daughter. "I suppose a brief visit wouldn't hurt. Follow me."

After an elevator ride, they exited on the sixth floor and approached a door where an eye reader confirmed the doctor's identity. As the door slid opened, a front of cold air rolled out of the room. Two large stainless steel tanks stood behind a counter where a woman wearing a white lab coat and latex gloves handled a vial of frozen sperm. A quiet hum permeated the room.

"The specimens can remain viable for hundreds of years if stored properly in liquid nitrogen," Dr. Richards noted in a hushed tone.

The technician pressed a button, causing the lid to lift slowly from the tank. Cold steam expanded upward. Brandon glanced over the woman's shoulder to see several layers of vials through the swirling mist. The technician placed a tray on the top rack.

"With over ten thousand samples, we're the largest repository in the Northeast/Columbia region," the doctor announced with pride. "Each specimen is rigorously tested for infectious agents, genetic anomalies, and, as I said, the Y chromosome."

Brandon surveyed the vials until the technician pushed a button, bringing down the cover. "It's like looking into the future," he said as he surreptitiously slid the briefcase behind the counter.

"Yes, that's a good way of putting it."

Brandon and Elizabeth thanked the doctor for the tour and made their farewells. They rode the elevator to the ground floor and then walked briskly through the lobby. Once across the street, Brandon took his cell phone from his shirt pocket.

"To the future," he muttered, then pressed the device. A fireball exploded from the sixth floor, raining down concrete, steel, and glass. Passers-by cried out or watched in horror as smoke billowed from the gaping hole. Alarms rang out from the building.

And that, Brandon thought, his ears muffled by the blast, *is the sound of the authentic doubling in price.* Although he hadn't actually secured the male, Brandon knew it was only a matter of time before he had him hidden away in the warehouse, chained to a pipe with duct tape over his mouth. Brandon smirked, thinking of the millions that would soon swell his private bank account. A warning for the authentic formed in his mind:

Ready or not, here I come.

Brandon pulled an envelope from his inside jacket pocket and handed it to Elizabeth. The explosion had lit up her eyes, first with shock, then excitement; she grazed his fingers in the transfer.

"If you ever need my services again, I'm available," the woman said, her touch lingering as she took the envelope. As Elizabeth approached the car, Brandon stepped in front of her.

"This concludes our business—find your own way home."

23

Cassie turned left onto Monroe Street, driving past a pawnshop, a chicken and waffles joint, and a liquor store. "There it is," she said, jerking her head toward an apartment building with crumbling tan brick and a decrepit fire escape that looked as dangerous as any building fire. She scanned the street for a place to park, eventually coaxing the Cooper into a space between an old truck and an even older station wagon. She turned to Sam. "Okay, we're here—time for some answers."

"Not quite," Sam responded. He opened the door and bolted across the street, dodging a sedan. The driver honked and then shot her hand out of the window in a middle-finger salute.

Cassie ran to catch up. "Who lives here—your grandmother? Your aunt?"

"First things first," Sam replied.

They entered the lobby. A "not working" sign taped to the elevator door forced them to take the stairs. At the end of a dimly lit hall, they found 4-C. Sam planted himself in front of the door, realizing that he hadn't thought through his plan.

If the person I'm looking for is here, will I be able to attack him in front of Cassie? He looked at the door. *Guess there's only one way to find out.*

Sam knocked.

No response.

He waited and knocked again.

Silence.

"Well, whoever she is," Cassie remarked, "she's not at home. We'll come back later."

Sam's doubts transformed into anger. *I haven't come this far to be stopped by a locked door.* He stepped back and kicked—the door didn't budge.

"What the heck are you doing?!" Cassie cried, pushing him back from the door. "Are you trying to get us arrested?"

"I need to get in."

"No, we need to get out of here before someone calls the cops!"

Just then, an elderly woman carrying bags of groceries shuffled down the hall, her frayed overcoat seeming to swallow her whole. She spotted the teenagers and then stopped in front of 4-B.

"Dana's out of town," the woman said as she fumbled in the grab bag of her purse. "Don't know when she'll be back."

"Let me help you," Cassie said, lifting a bag from the crook of the woman's arm.

"That's mighty kind of you." Finally, the woman pulled out a set of keys. "You Dana's sister?"

Cassie hesitated. "Yes, I am," she answered, not believing the words coming out of her own mouth. "I . . . I left something in her apartment." Cassie stopped, knowing a more elaborate story would find her out on a limb.

The woman inspected Cassie. "Funny . . . I pictured you different, maybe with dark hair like Dana's."

"I look like our Dad—he has chestnut hair."

The woman ambled over to 4-C, picked out a key on the ring, then unlocked the door. "When Dana goes out of town, I feed her cat." She walked back to 4-B. "I've got ice cream in here, so I've got to get it in the freezer. You lock up when you're done."

As she took the bag of groceries from Cassie, the woman added: "And don't let out Mr. Snuggles." Then she disappeared into her apartment.

Cassie and Sam looked at each other in silence as though uttering one word would jinx their good luck. They entered the apartment; it was a dreary place permeated by the tang of a full kitty litter box. Cassie poked her head around a corner, feeling like Little Red Riding Hood making her way in the spooky woods.

The compact living room featured a worn grey couch and a glass table with one leg bent out. A television and stereo stood against one wall. What passed for the kitchen occupied the far corner of the living room, complete with a small stove, an even smaller sink, and a half refrigerator.

Cassie looked around for the bedroom. Not finding one, she assumed the moldering couch was a pullout. A scrawny tabby lay in the room's only windowsill. As Cassie approached, the cat rose to its paws, arched its back, and hissed. Cassie backed off.

Mr. Snuggles?

She turned to Sam. "Okay, now I ask, and you answer—whose apartment is this?"

"It's your sister's, remember?" Sam answered as he rifled through papers on the coffee table. "Nice move, by the way."

"What are you looking for?"

"A name."

"Just any name?"

"The name of—what did you call it—a mec? An address would be good, too." Sam continued to inspect every drawer and cupboard in the apartment. Disappointed by his search, he turned his attention to counters and tabletops: cups with pens and pencils, photos, DVDs, knickknacks—nothing seemed unworthy of his scrutiny.

"All surgeries are recorded," Cassie offered. "With the Freedom of Information Act, we could look up to see who's turned."

"I doubt the person I'm looking for is registered."

"So the mec lives here?"

"No," Sam replied as he showed a photograph to Cassie. "She does, or did."

Cassie examined the image of a scowling woman obviously not happy with having her picture taken. A scar puckered her left cheek. "She left in a hurry and didn't take her stuff?"

Sam opened a closet door and, leaning over, threw items to the middle of the room. "She's not coming back." Boots, shoes, a broken tennis racquet, an ancient radio formed a pile at Cassie's feet. As he straightened up, Sam looked at Cassie with unblinking eyes: "I killed her."

The statement landed on Cassie like a sopping blanket; she dropped onto the couch from the weight of it. Then she gaped at Sam as he returned to cleaning out the closet.

Mystery Boy morphs into Scary Lunatic right before my eyes!

Metal clanged on metal as Sam dragged a duffel bag from the back of the closet. He unzipped the bag and pulled out an assault rifle and two handguns.

"What the hell . . . ?" Cassie said at the sight of the firepower. "What's she doing with all that?"

"Murdering people," Sam replied. He picked up a handgun, then pulled out boxes of shells. "Do you know which bullets this takes?"

"How would I know that?" Cassie retorted. "I've never been this close to a real gun." She eyed the firearm with apprehension. "What are you going to do with it?"

Sam stuffed the gun into his pants, grabbed boxes of ammunition, and then held up the photo. "See this woman? She killed my mother and sister. She was sent by some mec to kidnap me. So I'm going to find him . . . and I'm going to kill him."

***

After fifteen minutes, Cassie hauled Sam out of the apartment before he started tearing up the floorboards. They piled into the Mini Cooper. As she drove down Garfield Avenue, Cassie found it difficult to concentrate on the road—Sam's thirst for retribution had hijacked her thoughts.

Okay, so the boy I assumed was your average, everyday runaway—well, except for the bullet hole—turns out to be some vigilante hell-bent on revenge . . . no big deal. She glanced at the bulge of the gun under his shirt. "Do you know how to use that thing?"

"I've shot a gun," Sam replied. Seeing the fear in Cassie's eyes, he softened his approach. "Actually, I'm more of a bow and arrow kind of guy. I'm really good at it."

Cassie smiled at the good-natured brag. Then a wave of sorrow came over her. "Sorry to hear about your family—that must have been awful."

"I don't like to think about it."

Cassie accepted Sam's response, unable to imagine what it would be like to lose your entire family in one night. "The woman who did it—she's the one who shot you?"

Sam nodded. Cassie wondered how he'd killed her but decided against asking—she was still reeling from the revenge reveal. "How do you know the guy is a mec?"

"Because the woman said 'he.' *He* wants you—meaning me— alive. That means he's either a mec, or he's immune like me."

Cassie stopped at a red light. "I doubt he's immune. Do you even know if this mec lives in Columbia?"

Sam glanced out the window. "No. My only chance was to find something in that apartment."

When the light turned green, Cassie drove through the intersection and pulled into a McDonald's parking lot. "Maybe it's better that you didn't find anything."

Sam glared at her. "I'm supposed to forget the fact that this mec sent the woman who killed my mother and sister?"

"No, but if you find him, he could kill *you*."

"Like I said, he wanted me alive—the woman made that clear."

Cassie shook her head. "If you ask me, the farther you stay away from this dude, the better."

Sam opened the car door and gazed at the yellow M on the sign above the entrance. *The Golden Arches*, he thought, *something familiar in this crazy world*. "I need a Happy Meal . . . or three—that's assuming they still make them."

24

The convenience store clerk cowered as her boss, a stout woman with bushy hair and beady eyes, let loose a tirade that shot spittle from her mouth.

"Two hundred and sixty-three bucks! And you just handed it over! That's coming out of your paycheck!"

Brandon heard the woman's braying voice from the back of the store. He watched the drama unfold in the curve of the security mirror as he filled a to-go cup from the coffee machine.

A young woman dressed in a smock with Come 'N' Go stitched into the breast pocket gaped at the manager. "She had a gun! I'm not getting shot for some lousy job."

"Do you know how many women *want* your lousy job?" the boss snapped. "And that gun . . . I bet it was a toy—a toy that cost me $263!"

"It wasn't a toy! What was I supposed to do, get my head blown off?"

"What you were supposed to do was not crater the first time someone waved a popgun in your face. But I'll be reasonable—you won't have to pay back the money all at once. I'll take fifty bucks out of your paycheck until it's paid off."

Brandon wondered if the girl was going to cry or punch the boss in the nose. He stared at her steely reflection—*a fist to the face, definitely*.

"You can't do that!" the girl exclaimed. "It wasn't my fault!"

Brandon walked up to the counter. Both women fell silent; it was obvious they thought they were alone in the store.

The heavyset woman jabbed a finger at the clerk. "No more screw-ups," she snarled under her breath. Then she swung open the door and left.

Brandon set the coffee cup on the counter and asked for a pack of Marlboros. The clerk handed him the cigarettes, then rang him up, still steaming with anger.

"Ten dollars and ninety-cents."

Brandon handed her a twenty. "How'd you like to dump this for-shit job and be a part of something that's going to change this sector forever?"

The young woman snorted as she made change. "Sounds like a volunteer job, you know, save the world, blah, blah. What that tub of lard is paying me, I'm practically volunteering here anyway."

"Join me and there'll be money—lots of it. And, just as important, people will respect you, even fear you. You won't have to take crap from the likes of her ever again."

For the next few minutes, Brandon made his pitch, leaving out enough detail and adding enough exaggeration to entice the young woman. He wondered if the clerk would see through his lies; the gleam in her eyes, however, made it clear that she was blind to everything except her own fantasies of wealth and power.

"Think about it," Brandon said as he put the pack of cigarettes into his shirt pocket and headed for the door.

"Wait a minute," the young woman called out. She disappeared down an aisle and came back with two cans of spray cheese. Popping off a top, she proceeded to cover the candy display with a stringy, neon-orange mess. After emptying the first can, the girl opened the second and outlined letters on the floor.

Brandon looked at the message:

I QUIT.

The clerk tore off her smock and then turned off the lights.

"Sign me up."

***

Thanks to a crooked cop and a bribe, Brandon located Dana's car in Las Vegas. He readied the Lexus for the long car ride to the

Southwest Sector. The thought of taking a flight was tempting, yet he knew what he planned to return home with wouldn't fit in his suitcase.

With the help of a hypodermic syringe full of animal tranquilizer, lengths of rope, and the Lexus' roomy trunk, Brandon planned to secure his target and then drive cross-country back to the warehouse. On his way west, Brandon envisioned the authentic sitting at a blackjack table, not realizing that his luck was about to run out. For Brandon, however, Lady Luck had been dealing him all aces.

The bidding war for the authentic had taken on epic proportions, inflating Brandon's greed with each offer. Based in New York, the pharmaceutical company Pfizer offered 100 million to secure the male as a breeding tool. But the Saudis were not to be denied. They counter-offered with 125 million, and the Chinese, latecomers to the negotiations, floated a bid of 150 million. Pfizer's final offer—so they stated—was 175 million.

In Brandon's mind, the international bids served only one purpose: to force the Northeast Sector-based company to come in with the highest bid. So far, that purpose, assisted by the bombing at the sperm bank, had been spectacularly fulfilled.

Brandon's preference for Pfizer, however, wasn't rooted in a sense of patriotism. He wanted to sell the male to the local bidder solely due to logistics—transporting the authentic overseas ran too many risks. During the long journey, the boy might escape or be kidnapped by any number of rival factions.

Recruitment for the takeover of Columbia had proven to be surprisingly easy. Young women, like the convenience store clerk, were eager to dump their low-paying, mind-numbing jobs. All Brandon had to do was mention money, and the women lined up. He avoided drug addicts and the homeless, women who would end up being more trouble than they were worth. One trait he did look for was anger. It didn't matter at who or what their ire was directed—mothers, bosses, girlfriends, God—just as long as there was a wellspring of fury to be tapped.

Brandon bought weapons with the briefcase-full of cash he'd received from Ingrid Vandover. The recruits favored the semi-automatics as they were light, easy to aim, and fast at dispensing death. Still, Brandon made sure that "his girls" were trained on grenades, flamethrowers, and machine guns. The raw troops proved to be quick learners.

Brandon's diabolical plan was beginning to take shape. In two weeks, President Sanford would speak at the Capitol steps for Remembrance Day, the day designated to honor those who had died from SN-146. Being the tenth anniversary, the crowd would be especially large.

Good, Brandon thought. *I like a big audience.* He thought it fitting that, as President Sanford memorialized the departed, she would soon become one of them, courtesy of a well-aimed bullet.

With his soldiers in place at the Capitol, the White House, the Pentagon, and other installations of Columbia power, Brandon was confident the overthrow would be swift and irrevocable. Secret Service and the metro police would put up a fight, yet Brandon's army, with its superior firepower, would cut them down in a flood of red—the locals wouldn't know what hit them.

Brandon planned for the full-scale assault to begin only after he'd personally assassinated President Sanford. He wanted his enemies to know that he alone had taken down the president—the coup belonged to him.

Consider this a warning, Brandon thought, sending a mental message to the Sisterhood: *Attack me at your peril.*

***

In Las Vegas, Brandon tracked down Dana's car, finding the rusting vehicle at the Palace, a cheap motel that survived—barely—on the dregs of the gambling clientele. He waited until an old woman exited a room and got into the Cadillac. Just as the woman started the car, Brandon opened the passenger side door and slid in. Startled, she told him to get the hell out of her car. He told her it wasn't her car.

A country ballad about lost love whined on the radio. Brandon snapped it off and grabbed the woman by the front of her jacket; he hauled her out of the car, barking at her to open the motel room door, which she did with fumbling fingers.

The room was dark and smelled of decaying food and musty sheets. Beer cans and pizza boxes littered the area; the bed wasn't just unmade—it looked as if it had been the site of a wrestling match. The room was also empty—no male lounged on the bed watching some game show on cable.

Brandon dragged the woman to the bathroom, only to discover that it, too, was empty. Tightening his grip, he growled that he would ask only once where she was hiding the authentic. The woman blurted that she didn't know what he was talking about; when Brandon mentioned Dana Roberts, the car's true owner, the woman went pale, then started to babble about getting the Cadillac from some sick girl she'd dropped off at a mall in Columbia—Pentagon City she thought was the name of it.

Brandon exhaled a cold laugh. *How ironic! I travel over 2,000 miles to find that the male has delivered himself to my doorstep!*

When Brandon let up on his grip, the old woman tried to shake him off. Eyes flaring in anticipation, Brandon seized her by the throat, saying their conversation wasn't over. He locked his hands around her neck and began to squeeze; the woman beat her fists at Brandon's head and shoulders, sputtering and gurgling as her eyes bugged out. The more she flailed, the tighter Brandon gripped, his knuckles turning white against her ruddy skin.

She's putting up more of a fight than I expected, Brandon noticed with a certain admiration. *Too bad it's not enough to save her life.* In time, her body slumped; he unclenched his fingers, letting the dead weight fall to the floor.

Brandon straightened his shirt and glanced in the mirror, running stiff fingers through tousled hair. Then he took stock of the lifeless heap at his feet: it had been a while since he'd killed a person with his bare hands. Guns were noisy, knives messy—necessary tools to be sure but both lacking in style and grace. There was something

Stephanie Powell

satisfying about squeezing the life out of a living, breathing body. It was intimate, personal—everything a good death should be.

During the long car ride back to Columbia, Brandon had many hours to calculate his next move. He would determine which of the guards at the mall was the most vulnerable; from that guard, he would obtain footage from surveillance cameras for the afternoon in question.

If the male was as sick as the old bag said, Brandon reasoned, *someone must have helped him . . . and that person will lead me to my prize.*

25

Cassie was grateful the McDonald's wasn't crowded. She ordered at the counter while Sam slid onto a bench at a booth. Carrying a tray loaded with burgers, McNuggets, and fries, Cassie parked herself across from Sam, and the two of them descended on the meal.

Cassie washed down a bite of chicken with a gulp of Coke. She was still on information overload—Sam's desire to avenge the deaths of his mother and sister made her temples pound.

One more traumatizing tidbit, and my head is going to explode, she thought as she noticed a scar on Sam's forearm. It wasn't long but from the size of the raised mark, Cassie could tell the injury had been deep. *He probably got that in a knife fight. But I'm not going to ask because I don't want to know.* She trawled a french fry through a glob of ketchup, feeling something begin to gnaw on her like a determined rat.

Like hell, I don't, she sighed, giving in to her curiosity. "Where did you get the scar?"

"Rabbit."

Great, back to one-word answers. "I bet that hurt."

Sam took a huge bite of hamburger, his cheeks puffing out chipmunk-style. "It did, but I got the last laugh." He drained his drink, then added, "Flopsy was delicious."

Cassie and Sam finished lunch, threw away their trash, and piled back into the Mini Cooper. Riding in silence gave Cassie's imagination the room to run wild. *Maybe Sam killed that Dana person with a hatchet—that would be a woodsy way to knock somebody off.* An image popped into her head: it was of the woman with a blade buried in her skull, bad horror-movie style.

Yuck. Maybe talking is better. "Okay, what happens now?"

Sam's mood was as slouchy as his posture. "I don't know." He paused. "On second thought, I need to practice shooting the gun."

"Really? So you're going to just blow this guy away? And how are you going to find him, anyway?"

"I'm going to wait for him to show up at the apartment," Sam replied, recalling the first lesson he'd learned from the forest: stalking prey takes patience.

"And if he doesn't show up, then you just sit there for the rest of your life? Or he does make an appearance, and you fill him full of lead. Then you get caught and rot in prison, but not before you're discovered as a real male and flattened by a bunch of maniac women." Cassie took a deep breath; Sam's unyielding expression made it clear the blunt approach wasn't working. But she couldn't help herself. "Killing this mec won't bring back your mother and sister."

"No, it won't," Sam muttered, "but it's the only thing that makes sense."

Staring into traffic, Cassie relented with a sigh. She turned the Mini Cooper to the exit that took Route 1 out of the sector. "You don't seem to realize how important you are. My mom's been working for ten years trying to figure out why boy babies still die from XY. Your blood could have the answer."

"Your mom can have all of my blood she wants—she just has to leave me enough so I have the strength to pull the trigger."

Cassie considered telling Sam about Jamie. *Maybe it would make a difference if Sam knew he wasn't the last male on the planet.*

They fell back into silence as Columbia receded behind them. Skyscrapers gave way to gated communities that turned into rolling hills. Wildflowers dotted the countryside with reds, yellows, and purples; trees swayed in the spring breeze. After not seeing a house for several miles, Cassie turned down a dirt road that ended at a pasture. Several cows grazed in the distance.

"This looks like a good place for target practice," Cassie said as she put the car into park.

Sam pulled out the gun and examined the boxes of shells. After figuring out how to eject the clip, he tried all the bullets until size .45 slid neatly into the magazine. Sam got out of the car and started nosing around.

"What are you looking for?"

"If this is target practice, then I need a target."

Cassie rummaged around the back of her car, eventually pulling out a crumpled brown bag from a long-ago lunch. Sam put in some rocks for ballast and placed the bag on top of a wooden fence post. He strode back a distance, pivoted, and raised the gun toward the bag. He wasn't sure how to aim the weapon but had a box of bullets to work it out. Cassie steeled herself for the blast.

Sam pulled the trigger—it didn't budge. He looked at the weapon as if it had personally insulted him. "What the . . . ?"

Cassie walked over and took the gun. Inspecting it, she found a small button labeled **s**. She pushed it to the side until it read **f**. "It was on safety. Now try it."

Sam raised the gun and squeezed—no shot fired.

"Try pulling back that top part," Cassie suggested.

Sam did so; the gun made a sliding metallic sound. He narrowed his eyes. "I thought you said you didn't know anything about guns."

"I don't—I just watch a lot of movies."

Cassie put her fingers in her ears. For the third time, Sam looked down the barrel at the paper bag. He squeezed the trigger. A sharp roar split the air, scattering a flock of crows from a nearby tree. The kick from the gun rocked Sam back on his heels.

The paper bag remained on the post. Sam steadied himself and then once again lifted the gun toward the target.

Crack!

Still, the bag sat unfazed.

"I thought you said you'd fired a gun," Cassie commented.

"I did," Sam replied as he raised the gun one more time. "Didn't say anything about *aiming*."

Cassie gave him a sidelong glance. "Try lining up the notch with the bead on the front, then firing."

Sam looked at the gun and held it out to her. "Give it a shot."

Cassie leaned back, holding up her hands. "I'm not the one with a score to settle." She looked at the gun, wondering if she would have the nerve to shoot to kill.

"Go on," Sam taunted. "Take a shot—just like in the movies."

Not one to back down from a dare, Cassie took the gun; it felt cold and heavy in her palm. She planted her feet and raised the gun with both hands, trying to channel every shoot-out she'd ever witnessed on screen. Finding the bag in the sights, Cassie held her breath and squeezed. The recoil knocked her back as the bag exploded into pieces that fluttered to the ground.

Cassie held out the gun to Sam who looked both impressed and annoyed with the shot. He picked up a rock, put it on top of the fence post, and took the gun from Cassie.

"You couldn't hit the bag," she remarked, "but you're going to hit that little rock?"

"You got it. Bead in the notch?"

Cassie nodded.

Sam raised the gun and, pausing for the right moment, pulled the trigger. The rock shattered into a spray of chips. "Good tip."

After a few more shots, Sam felt comfortable with the firearm. He reloaded the magazine, slid on the safety, and then tucked the weapon into his pants. He knew the next time he fired the gun would be at the mec. He hoped he wouldn't have to wait long.

26

The sun cast long shadows across the winding road. Cassie was sure she'd retraced the same route, yet as she drove, nothing looked familiar. She pulled out her phone—it read: no service.

"Lost?" Sam asked as he rolled down the window, letting in the evening air.

"Temporarily unaware of our location."

Sam cocked his head like a dog hearing a whistle. "What's that sound?"

Cassie paused to hear faint music wafting over the treetops. "It's civilization—someone can tell us how to get back to Route 1." Sam hung out the window—again, like a dog—and guided them toward the source of the music.

As the Mini Cooper crested a hill, a carnival, the third-rate kind that traveled to small towns, came into view. Cassie parked in a field rutted with tire tracks. A Ferris wheel, colored lights flashing like a Christmas tree, loomed over various tents and booths. Families, teenagers in packs, and couples on dates milled about the grounds; silly circus music blared over the scene.

"We're just going to get directions, then we're on the road," Cassie warned as they approached the ticket booth.

Sam stopped and grabbed her arm. "Are you kidding me? The last time I went to something like this, I was *five*. We're going."

"We need to get home before my mother does. If she finds out I took you on this little field trip, she'll kill me. You're like the Holy Grail to her." Cassie could tell from Sam's blank face that he had no idea what that meant, but she let it slide.

"How about we stay until dark," Sam offered.

Cassie considered the suggestion. *Mom has been putting in long hours at the lab. If we arrive home around nine, it just might work.*

"Deal," Cassie stated. She paid two admissions to a fleshy woman in an unflattering tank top, then she and Sam strolled the midway, trying their luck at toss the ring, bop the gopher, and dunk the ducky. Dinner consisted of cotton candy, roasted peanuts, and lemonade. Cassie checked out Sam's chest, making sure that his sock-breasts were holding up.

They came up to a booth with moving targets; a line of buffalo streamed from left to right, disappearing as they turned under. A girl about Cassie's age stood in the booth. She wore braids, a fake buckskin dress, and a look of complete boredom.

"Welcome to the Great Plains," she muttered. "Kill three buffalo and take home any prize of your choosing." She waved a limp hand at a row of stuffed animals and cheap jewelry hanging from the front of the booth.

"How many tries do I get?" Sam asked.

"Five." The girl perked up a little. "If you hit two, I'll give you one more—it's harder than it looks."

Sam inspected the plastic weapon, as if trying to figure out its finer points.

"Lots of buffalo are getting away . . ." Cassie remarked.

Sam raised the bow and arrow, aimed, and released. *Ding!* A buffalo folded back and disappeared.

"Not bad," the girl said, impressed with the shot. Sam turned to Cassie. "Pick a buffalo."

Cassie squinted at the charging bison and pointed. "The black one, there!"

Sam tracked the gliding animal and shot. *Ding!* The black buffalo vanished to the happy hunting grounds. "Told you I was good," he said.

Cassie arched an eyebrow, all the while concocting a plan. She turned to the faux Indian maiden: "Can you make the buffalo go faster?"

The girl nodded. "There are three speeds—this is the slowest."

"Well then, crank it up," Cassie said, glaring at Sam. "I want a stampede."

The girl leaned to the back of the machinery and flipped a switch, making the bison whip around the track. Cassie smiled as she watched Sam's face fall.

Did I just see his head deflate?

"We never use this speed," the girl commented. "It's just too fast. I'll give you two more tries."

Sam raised the bow and arrow for the third time. "That's okay—it's all good."

Cassie touched Sam's arm. "And I want to pick the buffalo."

Sam held his position. He figured he had half a second to aim and let go. "I'm ready."

Cassie paused, hoping to unnerve Sam with the delay, then announced her choice. Sam pivoted and released, sending the buffalo down with a ding.

Booth Girl's eyes widened with delight. "Cool! Where did you learn to do that?"

"Hunting rabbits. They're much faster—"

"Okay, Chief, pick a prize," Cassie said, cutting Sam off before he could incriminate himself. He examined all the choices. Cassie assumed he'd go for the largest stuffed animal, a stoned-looking teddy bear. Instead, he took down a necklace of multicolored beads and small plastic fruit. He offered the necklace to Cassie, but she put up her palm. "I appreciate the thought, but it's all yours."

Sam shrugged and draped the goofy loop around his neck. Booth Girl, grateful for a break from the monotony, sized up Sam.

"It's a good look on you."

"Thanks."

***

At the back of the carnival, Cassie and Sam discovered a ride with a large globe at the center. The faster the Earth turned, the higher up the riders flew, swinging out like balls on strings. Sam approached the sign that announced: Circle the globe in the Apollo!

"We are doing this!" he proclaimed. "Apollo is my favorite Greek god." Then he scrutinized the sign. "But why is that the Earth at the center? Apollo rode his chariot around the sun."

"This Apollo was part of NASA," Cassie replied. "You know, the old space program, rockets, astronauts—it's ancient history." She pointed to the image of a large grey object on the sign. "That's a space capsule."

Sam accepted Cassie's answer with indifference. They entered the ride, jumped on their swings, and then held on as the centrifugal force lifted them high into the air. Sam's hair whipped behind him, his grin seeming to take up most of his face. Cassie wasn't sure why, but she took great pleasure in seeing Sam in good spirits. His smile made her feel like the ride itself, dizzy and far above the ground.

***

On the way home, Cassie pressed the gas pedal, working the fine line between speeding and watching for cops. She knew they'd stayed too long at the carnival, but the change in Sam's mood had been worth it. Now if she could beat her mother home, all would be well.

Sam looked ahead at the converging lines of the highway. "Thanks."

"For what?"

"For everything—the carnival, taking me to the apartment." Sam paused, his voice lowered. "Saving my life."

"Sure," Cassie responded, figuring it was a good time for a reality check. "You know I can't take you back to the apartment, not now, anyway. If we're caught hanging around there, it'll seem pretty suspicious, even to that old lady."

"You're right. And I get that you want to help me. It wasn't until today that I realized I could ever feel like this again."

"Like what?"

"Like . . . happy."

Sam's comment gave Cassie a slight thrill, along with an odd sense of embarrassment. Now it was her turn to change the subject. "So Apollo is your favorite Greek god . . . why is that?"

"Because he's the Sun God. He's the god of healing . . . and of plagues—that means he's both good and bad." Sam shifted in his seat. "I guess I can relate to him."

"Apollo does sound pretty human," Cassie noted, "except for the whole *Sun God* thing."

Sam chuckled and continued: "When I was little, my mom tried to teach me to read with those stupid first reader books. I hated them, so she brought home this huge book, *The Greek Myths*. It was the only thing I wanted to read. Go ahead, ask me anything about a Greek god or goddess."

Cassie knew exactly whom she wanted to pick. "Okay, she wasn't a goddess, but how about my namesake, Cassandra."

Sam looked dumbfounded. "Cassie is short for Cassandra?"

"No, actually, my real name is Casserole. Of course, it's short for Cassandra!"

Sam stared at her, making it difficult for Cassie to keep her eyes on the road. "Cassandra was Apollo's . . ."

Cassie wasn't sure whether to chime in. "Lover?"

"I was going to go with girlfriend," Sam responded. "She was very beautiful, so naturally Apollo fell in love with her. He gave her the gift of prophecy. Cassandra loved Apollo but, in the end, she rejected him. He got really mad and placed a curse on her, making it so that no one believed what she saw in the future."

"There's that pesky dark side."

Sam looked at the night sky through the open car window. "The story never explained why Cassandra left Apollo if she loved him. It really doesn't make sense."

Cassie shrugged. "Don't ask me—I'm not too experienced in the romance department."

"Me neither," Sam said with a slightly bemused smile. "Anyway, Apollo ended up with a lot of other women—nymphs, sprites, queens, you name it. A few guys, too."

"Considering the world I've grown up in, that doesn't seem so weird. So Apollo got around."

"But he never got over Cassandra. I'm sure of that."

"I don't know," Cassie countered, "sounds like he was having a good time."

Sam shook his head. "She was his first love—you never get over that."

Cassie took her eyes off the road just long enough to give him a teasing glance. "I thought you said you didn't know much about romance . . ."

Sam leaned back as if to take in Cassie's comment. "I don't, but your first love has got to be something special. How could you get over it?"

The question hung in the air as Cassie turned the Mini Cooper to the exit for home.

***

Cassie's heart sank as she pulled in the driveway—her mother's Volvo was parked in its usual spot. She killed the engine and turned to Sam. "Okay, here's our story: we just went out for sushi, got it?"

Sam nodded and got out of the car. He stopped. "What's *sueshee?*"

Cassie wondered if she would get permanent googly eyes from all the rolling. "Okay, forget sushi. How about tacos? You *do* know what they are . . ."

"Of course."

When they entered through the kitchen door, Cassie and Sam found Amanda planted in the middle of the room, wearing a robe and a scowl.

"Cassie, where have you been? I've been calling, and you didn't pick up. And I told you not to take the boy out. You don't know how dangerous it is for him." Amanda anchored her hands on her hips, reminding Sam of his own mother.

"I know, Mom, but we were hungry, and my phone was dead. Sorry."

"*Sorry* isn't going to cut it. First of all, he's still recovering and second, if he'd been found out—"

"But I wasn't," Sam interrupted. He moved closer to Cassie as if to deflect her mother's wrath. "I know you want to keep me safe, and I want to thank you for everything you've done for me. I'll help you with your research as much as I can." Then Sam locked his eyes on Amanda. "But I'm not your prisoner. If I want to leave, I will." He paused. "And my name is Sam."

Amanda's shoulders dropped as if they no longer needed to hold up the weight of the world. "It's nice to meet you, Sam. I'm Amanda." Then she was struck by an unexpected realization—the research specimen that had fallen into her lap through outrageous luck was, in fact, just a teenage boy trying to live his own life. Her anger dissolved, leaving only a sense of relief. She was glad they were both home safe and sound.

"And you're right, Sam," Amanda added. "You aren't a prisoner—you are our guest." She looked him up and down. "That outfit looks better on you than it ever did on me."

Amanda kissed Cassie good night, then headed for the door. "In the future, just be careful," she said before disappearing into the hallway. Then she called out: "And Sam . . . nice boobage."

***

From the shadows across the street, Brandon watched from his car as a Mini Cooper parked next to a Volvo. Two figures exited the car and entered the house. In the dark, Brandon couldn't tell which one was his mark. He started the engine, planning to continue his stakeout the next day.

Brandon's offer to the security guard at the mall had been simple: hand over surveillance recordings from the afternoon in question or lay flowers on your daughter's grave. The woman complied the next day, passing off a plastic bag full of disks.

Several hours into the footage, Brandon came across the jumpy image of a young woman loading a sagging figure into a red Mini Cooper. After capturing a blurry screenshot of the license plate and enhancing the image, Brandon identified the car's owner with the help of a department of motor vehicles employee who had no qualms about trading T for classified information.

Amanda O'Connell, 204 Butler Street, Brandon thought, *you have something I want—and I'm coming to get it.*

With less than a week until Remembrance Day, Brandon planned a final meeting at the warehouse to confirm strategy and stoke the fires of insurrection. Displaying the soon-to-be-captured authentic would prove to his soldiers that nothing was beyond their grasp.

27

Cassie dumped her books and backpack on the kitchen table. Her grumbling stomach demanded to be fed, and only one thing would be quick and tasty enough: a mixing bowl of Frosted Mini-Wheats.

"Sam?" she called out.

Sam entered the kitchen, wearing the heart pajamas. After his initial hesitation, he'd grown quite fond of the pink PJ's.

"A lounging kind of day?" Cassie asked as she took out milk and cereal.

"I've got nowhere to go, so I don't see much point in getting dressed," he responded, first landing on a chair, then flipping open Cassie's history book. "What do you learn in school?"

"Not much," Cassie replied, too preoccupied with her first crunchy mouthful to give more of an answer.

Sam examined the stack of books. "All this, five days a week and not much?"

Cassie munched, wiping milk from her mouth. "Well, I guess computer class is useful and maybe English. History is interesting except for the law and government stuff. But algebra? Please."

"So teach me computer stuff. I'm a little behind—if I'm going to live in this world, I need to know more about it."

A little behind? Cassie thought with an internal snort. *How about a lot behind.* She decided instead to filter: "That's a good idea. I'll show you how to surf the Internet."

"Great. I love to swim."

Cassie slurped the last of the sweet milk, then grabbed Sam by the pink hearts. "Okay, first we'll start with some basic vocab—surfing the net doesn't have anything to do with water. C'mon, I'll show you."

They mounted the stairs and entered Cassie's bedroom. "This is a laptop," Cassie said as she sat at the desk.

"That means it only works if it's in your lap?" Sam asked as he sat next to her.

"No, just stay with me. A laptop is a computer you can do a lot of cool things on." Cassie clicked her fingers on the keyboard. "This is a site called Facebook. It's a great way to keep in touch with friends. You can write comments, share photos, and get news."

Cassie brought up her profile and showed Sam various pictures of her—one with Terry and Ashley, another playing volleyball, a third with her mother and grandmother at Thanksgiving. Then she brought up a recent text. "You can also send and get messages."

Sam leaned in: the screen read: gr8 game, u r the best cu l8r k? B :D. "What is that, code? What does it say?"

"Oh, yeah, it says 'great game, you're the best, see you later, okay? Bye.' " She pointed to the end of the line. "That little thing there is called an emoticon. It shows that the girl was happy when she sent the message. See, it's a smiley face."

Sam tilted his head to reveal two eyes and a grinning mouth. "You have to learn this code to use the top lap?"

"No and it's *laptop*. The code thing is just a quick way of texting and stuff." *Okay, this might be harder than I thought.* "Here, let's try this. Remember when I searched for the apartment address?"

Sam nodded.

"You can type in something here," Cassie said, pointing to the search box, "then hit Enter, and the computer will bring up information. You can also ask it a question."

"So it's like the Oracle?"

"What's that," Cassie asked, "some kind of app?"

Sam narrowed his eyes, then quickly dismissed his uncertainty. "And if by *app*, you mean high priestess at the temple of Apollo, well then, yeah, she was an app. Kings would consult her to find out if they should go to war, if there were plots against their lives, if there would be famine."

Cassie turned the laptop toward Sam. "Go ahead and type in a question."

"And it doesn't have to be in code?"

"Nope, just plain old English."

Sam pecked at the keyboard, pausing occasionally to find a letter. When he was done, he turned the computer so that Cassie could read the question: Why am I still alive?

Cassie's heart dropped. "It can't answer that."

"I didn't think it could, but I thought I'd ask anyway."

A knock interrupted their conversation. The door swung open, and Amanda entered the room. "Hey, you two."

"Hi, Mom. What are you doing home so early?"

"I've got to go back to the lab later on this evening, so I thought I'd come home for a few hours. How about Sloppy Joes for dinner?"

"Sounds great," Cassie replied. "Mom makes the best Sloppy Joes," she said to Sam. "It's a special recipe—no tomatoes, but they still taste great."

"Why no tomatoes? They still grow them, don't they?"

"Unfortunately. I'm really allergic to tomatoes. If I eat just one little piece, I'm puking my guts out."

Sam didn't want to think about Cassie hurling. Thinking about dinner, on the other hand, was a favorite pastime. He didn't know what Sloppy Joes were but figured any food with the word "sloppy" in its name had to be good.

"I know I haven't been around much lately," Amanda said, "but the work I'm doing with the samples from Sam is starting to pay off."

"Really?" Cassie asked. "Do you think you'll find the cure soon?"

"Things look promising, but it's too early to tell—I'll let you know after I've confirmed some tests." Amanda turned to assess Sam in the pink pajamas. "Cassie, why don't you and Sam take Luka to the park. She could use some exercise and Sam, well, you could take a break from the heart explosion."

Sam perked up at the thought of getting out of the house. Then he looked down at his chest and curled his hands into two cups. "Do I have to, you know . . . ?"

"No, just wear a loose jacket," Amanda answered. "You won't be there that long."

Cassie smiled at her mom, as if to say *Thanks for lightening up*.

Sam bounded from the chair. In the last few days, he and Luka had bonded over days spent lounging on the couch. "Luka! Where are you, you wolf in dog's clothing?" he called out. "Time to make a run for it!"

***

Cassie and Sam entered the garage. She got out her bike and then took down her mother's ten-speed from a rack on the wall. As Sam looked over the sleek cycle, he casually mentioned that the only bike he'd ever ridden had three wheels and a horn that went *toot-toot*. Without missing a beat, Cassie decided it was a nice day for a walk.

Cassie and Sam headed down the sidewalk, passing by houses dappled in sunlight. Luka strained on her leash, pulling Cassie like she was a sled bound for the frozen north.

"Take it easy, Luka!" Cassie cried out to the determined husky.

When they arrived at the park, Cassie and Sam found it empty except for a mother and daughter at a picnic table. Shaded by two spreading maples, the park had a soccer field, volleyball sand pit, and a water fountain that froze up in the winter. Cassie unhooked Luka from the leash; the dog bolted like a racehorse at the starting bell, Sam not far behind.

Two peas in a pod, Cassie thought as she watched them tear around. After chasing each other and roughhousing on the ground, Sam and Luka returned. Sam was winded, but Luka looked like she was just getting started. Cassie pulled a tennis ball from her jacket pocket and tossed it to Sam.

"She loves to chase though she's not much on retrieving."

Sam hurled the ball into the air. Luka tore across the soccer field and snagged the yellow target, taking her sweet time in returning. When she did, Cassie wrestled the slimy ball from her mouth.

In her puppy days, Luka had been a fluffy ball of destruction, chewing anything not made of stainless steel. Shoes, toys, books, even volleyballs fell prey to Luka's relentless need to gnaw. But with her floppy paws and boundless energy, Luka had been impossible to scold. Whenever Cassie felt sad or lonely, she would hug her beloved dog, finding comfort in soft fur.

Cassie threw the tennis ball, prompting Luka to shoot off like a bullet. Sam noticed a fat squirrel running up a nearby tree. He picked up a rock and drew back his arm.

"Hey, what are you doing?" Cassie asked.

"Have you ever had squirrel? It's tasty, and you can make slippers out of the pelts."

The image of Sam chowing down on squirrel burger, his feet nestled in furry grey moccasins, materialized in Cassie's head. She pressed down on his arm. "Let's leave the squirrel alone, okay? My mom's got dinner already planned, and I'm good for footwear."

After several more throws of the ball, Cassie and Sam headed for the swings while Luka chomped on a stick. They landed on the seats and pumped their legs to get as much altitude as possible. Soon they were swinging through the air in wide arcs.

A girl about nine years old ran up to the swings and plopped down on a seat. She had strawberry blonde ponytails and a space between her two front teeth. After kicking off the ground, the girl leaned back and forth, trying in vain to get up into the air. She frowned as she watched Cassie and Sam swoop on their swings.

"You want some help?" Sam asked.

"My mom says I'm not supposed to talk to strangers."

"No problem," Sam replied. "You should always do what your mom says."

After some contorted pumping, the girl looked again at Sam. "Well, maybe a little push, just to get me started."

Sam dragged his foot on the ground to slow himself. He jumped off the seat and began to push the girl, gently at first, then with gusto. She squealed with delight at the top of each swing.

"Melinda!" the girl's mother called from a car in the parking lot. "It's time to go!" Sam stopped pushing, and eventually the girl hopped off the swing.

"Thanks!" she hollered.

As Sam watched the girl race to the car, a familiar pressure bore down on his chest. "My mom made a swing for my sister and me out of a long rope and a piece of wood." Cassie slowed on her swing as Sam sat on the seat. "I fell off it so many times," he continued, "but Emily never did—not even once."

"What was Emily like?"

"She was funny. And smart. And a pain in the butt sometimes," Sam said with a laugh. "She had this doll my mom made out of scraps of fabric. *Lulu.* Emily was nuts about that doll. It had two button eyes, only one of the buttons was big and the other one tiny. It always looked like Lulu was giving you the evil eye."

Sam leaned toward Cassie, one eye opened wide; she playfully pushed him away. "Emily couldn't go to sleep without Lulu."

"And your mom?"

"My mom? I guess she was like Emily—funny and smart and definitely a pain in the butt. You couldn't get away with anything with her around. Believe me, I tried. She was strict." Sam kicked the dirt, raising a puff of dust. "Now I know she was just scared."

"What about your dad?"

"I didn't really know him. My parents split up when I was five. I don't remember much about him except that he used this soap that made him smell like licorice. Then XY hit."

After a moment of silence, Cassie said, "I had a brother. His name was Cody. We were twins."

"No kidding. Isn't that kind of rare?"

Cassie nodded. "We were really close. When he died," she went on, deciding not to go into the long version of the story, "I felt like a part of me was gone."

"I know what you mean," Sam commented. "Does it ever get easier?"

Cassie wanted to say something positive, uplifting. She also wanted to tell the truth: "It does, but it takes a long time—I'm definitely not there yet." Cassie could see Sam drift into his own thoughts. "You hungry?" she asked.

Sam snapped back to the present and grinned. "Hey, I'm breathing, aren't I?"

Cassie made a show out of sniffing the air. "C'mon. I can smell my mom's Sloppy Joes from here." She stood up and called out to Luka; the dog loped toward them, tongue flapping, tail waving.

"Let's head home."

***

The Sloppy Joes were delicious as promised. Sam wolfed down the first one, which barely made a dent in his appetite. Ripping into the second, he looked up to see Cassie gawking at him. He slowed, thinking chewing might be a good idea.

Amanda and Cassie chatted about everyday things: the warm spring, the house that needed repainting, the latest spy movie getting rave reviews. Sam enjoyed listening to them talk—two female voices at the dinner table brought back good memories.

"Sure I can't interest you in one more?" Amanda asked Sam as she nodded toward a bowl of spicy beef.

Sam shook his head and put up his palms, the international sign for "I'm stuffed." He wasn't but knew a gallon of mint chocolate chip waited patiently in the freezer.

"We've got to save room for ice cream," Cassie noted. "And besides, when it comes to Sloppy Joes, two is the recommended dose." She cast a playful glance at Sam; the look made his insides ache.

How does she do that? Sam wondered, lingering on Cassie's smile. *Sometimes the smallest thing she does makes me feel like my chest is caving in—and it's happening more and more.* He turned away, trying to ease the pang that only deepened when he looked back at her. Then he gave in to the unfamiliar sensation.

But here's the weird part, Sam concluded as he watched Cassie brush a lock of hair from her eyes: *Whatever this feeling is, I actually like it.*

After ice cream, Cassie and Sam did the dishes while Amanda gathered up work papers and left for the lab. When the last plate had been put away, Cassie dried her hands on a dishtowel and told Sam she had homework to finish. She headed upstairs while Sam parked himself on the living room couch with a book about ancient Greece.

Cassie entered Cody's room and flipped on the light. It hadn't changed since the night her mother had spirited him away to the secret room. Pictures of cars and trucks covered the walls. A ceramic Mickey Mouse lamp stood on the night table, crisscrossed with lines where it had been broken and glued back together. A toy box stood at the foot of the bed, overflowing with the spoils of long-ago birthdays and Christmases.

After Cody was gone, Cassie liked to play in her brother's room. All of his stuff made her feel like he was there with her, just out of sight. As the years slipped by, Cassie realized Cody wasn't coming back. His room became a painful reminder that his disappearance had frozen him at age six.

I get to celebrate my ninth birthday, I get to enter junior high, I get to earn my driver's license, Cassie would think at each successive milestone, *but you don't.*

Cassie changed into pajamas—yellow kitties on a purple background—and sat on the bed. She leaned against the headboard and opened her history book to the tenth chapter.

Wish I could read a book of my own choice, Cassie grumbled to herself, thinking of Sam engrossed in the adventures of his go-to god, Apollo. Her history text, as dry as the bones of the people it described, could hardly count as pleasure reading.

After forty minutes, Cassie's eyelids started to droop. Each word was like the swing of a hypnotist's pendulum, lulling her into a drowsy trance. *Mr. Watson likes to give pop quizzes*, Cassie thought, *and that last history test I took had crash and burn written all over it.* Taking a deep breath, Cassie renewed her focus. One page later, her eyelids, once again, headed south. A soft knock came at the door.

"I saw your light on," Sam said as he poked in his head.

Cassie closed the book and put it on the night table. "Come on in. If I read one more word, I'm going to fall into a coma."

"That interesting, huh?" he said, plunking himself on the bed, then looking around at the young-boy trappings. "So this is Cody's room." He picked up a mangy-looking stuffed dog from the toy box. "I'm surprised you and your mom didn't put me in here. I don't like the fact that I've kicked you out of your room."

"That's okay. I used to spend a lot of time in here. Then I couldn't." Her voice trailed off. "It's nice to be back. And there's a reason why you're in my room." She slipped down on the bed, her feet sticking over the edge. "This bed is small even for me. For you, it'd be like a crib."

Sam stretched out on the bed, his legs dangling over the edge. "Not so bad from the knees up." He looked around at the pictures on the walls. "I had a room like this once. All I can remember is a really scary T-Rex poster. I was a serious dinosaur freak."

"Hmm, dinosaurs and Greek gods," Cassie noted with an ironic lilt, "that's quite the combination . . ."

"Yeah, huge beasts and beings with crazy powers . . . what's not to like?"

Cassie smiled and then added, "For Cody, it was cars, trucks, motorcycles—anything with wheels."

"Wheels are good. I want to learn how to ride a real bike and how to drive a car. You're going to have to teach me."

"We'll start with the bike, how about that."

"Okay," Sam replied. "Then this summer, it'll be you and me and the funky little hot rod."

"You'll have to get a learner's permit first."

Sam narrowed his eyes at Cassie. "That's if I want a *license*."

"Well, yeah!"

"I just want to learn to drive. I can do without all the official stuff."

"If you're going to be on the road," Cassie said, "you're going to *need* the official stuff. But we have plenty of time to work it out."

The mental image of Sam speeding and swerving in all of his overconfident glory made Cassie both smile and shudder. "I'll get you behind the wheel. But, definitely, let's start with the bike."

Sam nodded. "Two wheels before four—that makes sense." He rose from the bed and headed for the door." Good night, Cassie." And with that, Sam slipped out of the room.

"Good night, Sam."

Cassie turned off the Mickey Mouse lamp and nestled under the covers, comforted by the fact that in two months' time, Sam would still be down the hall.

28

Cassie slouched in her chair as Mr. Watson handed back the latest test. She hoped for a miracle, although a curve would do.

Most of the time, I do pretty well in history, Cassie thought as the girl next to her broke into a smile at her grade. *Then again, most of the time, my life is pretty normal.* She watched as her teacher continued to pass out papers.

Normal . . . seems like I left that *a long time ago.*

Mr. Watson approached. He had settled into his new gender, the students along with him—only his floral ties brought to mind his days as a woman.

Cassie couldn't bring herself to look into her teacher's eyes. He slid the test on her desk—a big "F" dominated the top; red slashes covered the page. Even worse, the four words every student dreads to read were written at the bottom: See me after class.

***

The bell rang. Girls gathered up their books and backpacks and converged with the raucous current of bodies in the hallway.

"Chapter 33 for tomorrow," Mr. Watson called out above the commotion, "and don't forget your group work is due next Monday." Cassie hung back, waiting for the classroom to empty. In time, she approached the front, forcing herself to look up. Mr. Watson turned from the whiteboard.

"Cassie, I was surprised by your grade. You're usually at the top of the class. What's going on?"

Well, my best friend wants to turn for me, and I found out that my brother lived six years longer than I thought. I met two boys—that's right, I said boys—*one who's been locked away for ten years. And the other boy . . . did I mention he's immune to XY?*

"I just had an off day, that's all. I'll do better next time."

Mr. Watson looked at Cassie, not buying the line but respecting her right to say it. "If you ever want to talk about anything, my door is always open. A lot of people think that since the Black Years are over, everything is back to normal."

Cassie grimaced. *There's that word again!*

Mr. Watson continued: "But I know that's not true."

The second bell rang. Mr. Watson scribbled a note and handed it to Cassie. "Give this to your next teacher so you won't get a tardy."

Cassie took the paper. "Thanks," she said, holding up the note, "for this and for the offer."

***

Terry and Ashley sat at a table in the cafeteria, Ashley straining to see who was in the lunch line.

"This is the fifth lunch Cassie's missed," Ashley whined. "Where is she?"

Terry was silent. She'd inherited Ashley through her friendship with Cassie, a situation Terry could deal with most days. Today, however, was not one of those days.

"What's up with Cassie?" Ashley demanded, squinting at Terry. "Did you two have a fight? Because if you did, her problem is with *you*, not me."

Terry chewed in silence as Ashley blathered on about how she wasn't going to put up with Cassie if she didn't "get her act together."

Maybe that's the thing to do, Terry thought, *find something that will piss off Ashley enough to make her end their friendship.*

But Terry had no idea what that would be. And even though Ashley was a drama queen, Terry knew she wasn't a *stupid* drama queen—she wouldn't cut ties with the only person at school who tolerated her. Terry swallowed the last of her sandwich, gathered up her stuff, and left Ashley in mid-sentence.

***

Cassie glanced at the clock as the bell rang. She stuffed her books and papers into her backpack and then pushed through the library doors. Every period, even lunch, felt like a stone around her neck.

Two more classes today, two more months of being a junior, then senior year. Ugh.

Through the crowd of students, Cassie saw Terry waiting by the classroom door. Cassie was still trying to avoid Terry but not just because of their ongoing argument about turning. A new feeling had been added to the standbys of anger, frustration, and exasperation— and that feeling was guilt.

Ever since elementary school, Cassie and Terry had confided in each other about everything. Any secret, no matter how intimate or embarrassing, could be revealed, knowing it would never be told to another or used as a weapon. Cassie didn't want to lie to Terry about the boys, but she also didn't want to make a slip. Her mother had explained the point in no uncertain terms: telling anyone about Sam and Jamie put them both at great risk.

"Where have you been?" Terry asked, more accusation than question. "I've had lunch with Ashley every day this week. One more lunch and I'm going to break her glasses—while they're still on her face . . . so stop avoiding me."

Girls jostled into the classroom, pushing Cassie closer to Terry. "I'm not avoiding you," Cassie responded. "I've been doing home-work in the library. I tanked my last algebra test and my last history test, come to think of it." Cassie moved aside, making room for the incoming girls.

"You are such a crappy liar," Terry stated.

Cassie considered arguing the point—she could fudge the truth like a pro with her mother. Lying to Terry, however, was a different story. *Well, it wasn't a complete lie*, Cassie considered. *I may be ditching you because of Sam and Jamie and, yeah, the turning thing. But the failing part is unfortunately all too true.* "If I don't do well on the next history test, I'm going to have to ace the final so I don't flunk the class."

With the tardy bell only seconds away, Terry switched gears. "I know the whole girlfriend thing freaks you out, so I've decided to put turning on hold. I just want you to know, I'll wait for you as long as it takes."

"I'm glad to hear that," Cassie said, "I mean, the part that you're not going to do it."

"I'm not going to do it until you're okay with the idea," Terry clarified. She managed a smile, hoping Cassie would return the same. When she didn't, Terry pressed on. "Hopefully, that'll be soon. Can we meet this afternoon at The Diner?"

The bell rang. "I promised my mom I'd help out at the lab." *Okay, so that was a complete lie*, Cassie thought, hoping the fib wouldn't ping on Terry's radar.

Mrs. Duncan, the economics teacher, approached. "Wrap it up, girls. Terry, you're late for class."

29

Jamie sat at the computer, scrolling through the dense text. The treatise on inter-dimensional travel was making his head spin. He understood the words and the sentences made some sense. But the paragraphs might as well have been written in Sanskrit. Still, Jamie read on, teasing out what meaning he could from the article. He liked puzzles because solving them was so satisfying.

The sound of the chamber door opening rumbled in the small room. Jamie welcomed the distraction as it signaled the one thing he'd been waiting for: Cassie's return. When Amanda stepped into the room, Jamie couldn't keep his disappointment from clouding his face. Amanda returned the look with a knowing smile.

"Well, that's a first," she commented, carrying a bag of groceries and a gallon jug of water. "Usually you're happy to see me."

"Sorry," Jamie said, "I'm just really into this new physics paper. I *am* glad to see you."

Amanda put the food—cold cereal, powdered milk, apples, and cookies—into a large crate under the table. She raised an eyebrow. "Hoping for someone else?"

"Yeah, Dr. Stanton," Jamie answered with his most straight-faced delivery. "I'm really looking forward to my next check-up."

Amanda laughed. "I'll tell Cassie to come by. She's been trying to bring up her grades. This may be hard for you to understand, but she's not doing so great in algebra—not everyone's a math whiz like you."

Jamie perked up, not at the thought of Cassie struggling with equations and calculations but that he could do something about it. "It just needs to be explained in the right way. Tell her to bring her books so we can go over some stuff."

Amanda nodded, then pulled a package of Oreos from the bag. "I brought your favorite."

To Amanda, the end of the Black Years had been marked not by the advent of clear skies or safe drinking water or an ample food supply—it had been in the sweet, familiar scent from a just-opened Oreos package. After she'd split apart that first cookie and licked the white icing, Amanda knew the worst was over.

"You remembered . . . thanks, Mom." Jamie hesitated. "I can still call you *Mom*, can't I?"

"Of course. Why would you call me anything else?"

"I don't know. I guess seeing Cassie reminds me that you have your own family and that I'm really not your son."

"Well, I may not have given birth to you, but you're still my son—make no mistake about that." Amanda tore into the Oreos package and tossed him a cookie. Jamie caught it and immediately popped it into his mouth. Amanda leaned over to look at the computer screen.

"*The Einstein-Rosen Bridge and Its Implications for Parallel Dimensions,*" she read out loud. Several names expanded under the title, each one followed by an alphabet soup of advanced degrees. "And what, may I ask, is an Einstein-Rosen bridge?"

"It's a wormhole," Jamie answered. He glanced around the confines of his small room. "I like to think about space because I have so little of it."

"You'll get your space someday," Amanda said, "and an impressive set of letters after your name, too. I have no doubt about that."

Jamie sat at the computer. "And speaking of getting out of here, how's it going with the samples from that guy? What's his name?"

"Sam. It's going well. He definitely has characteristics that make him immune. Factors in his blood wrap themselves around the virus, containing it in some kind of casing. I need to identify those factors and isolate them. Then I can synthesize a treatment, either a vaccine or a cure. But that's still a long way off."

"And the guy . . . ?"

"Sam? What about him?"

"What's he like?"

Amanda paused, thinking how to sum up Sam in a few words. "He's a good kid. Considering what he's been through, he's remarkably normal." Then Amanda realized the same thing could be said about Jamie. "Actually, I know more about Sam's blood than I do about him. When Cassie comes to visit, ask her—she and Sam have been spending a lot of time together."

The casual remark made Jamie flinch, a reaction he hoped Amanda hadn't noticed. "I bet Cassie likes that, like she's got a brother again." He set his eyes on Amanda, watching intently for her response.

"She has enjoyed his company. And as to whether Sam is like a brother to Cassie?"—Amanda let the question hover—"You'll have to ask her about that."

Jamie didn't think it was possible for him to want to get out of his sanctuary/prison any more than he did. Yet the thought of Cassie spending time with some unknown guy pushed his desire for freedom to the breaking point.

30

Cassie spied the cop behind the bushes as Amanda slowed to 20 miles per hour in the school zone. The Mini Cooper was in the shop with a bad starter, a problem common to the older models. Having her mother drop her off at school made Cassie feel like she was back in the third grade.

Sam had been with them for three weeks. He was getting stronger every day, yet with his increased stamina came a growing restlessness. Cassie knew it wouldn't be long before he would ask to return to the apartment to lie in wait for the mec.

"How's it going with Sam?" Amanda asked. "Kind of nice to have a guy around, isn't it?"

Cassie shrugged, trying to act nonchalant. "Yeah, it's cool." She didn't want to tell her mother that the last three weeks had been the best—if not the weirdest—of her life. She was grateful her mother hadn't asked more about the night she and Sam had come in late. In order to stave off any prying, Cassie continued: "He's fun to be with, but he's also a little odd."

Amanda barely suppressed a smile. "Why do you say that?"

"Well, for starters, remember those cupcakes you brought home the other day? I offered one to him. And he said, 'No, thanks. I don't like cupcakes.' And I said, 'Okay.' Then he said, 'But I like cake.' And I said, 'But cupcakes and cake are the same thing.' And he said, 'No, they're not—one's a cake and one's a cupcake.' And I said, 'But the only difference is the *size*.' And he said, 'No, they *taste* different.' After that, I just gave up."

Amanda pulled into the line of cars dropping off students. "Okay, that's odd but hardly fatal."

"There's more," Cassie said, feeling her insides winding up. "I put on some makeup the other day, just eyeliner and mascara, and he laughed at me and said I looked like a raccoon. When I got mad, he got all, 'Why are you getting mad? It's not personal.' And I said, 'How is you telling me I look like a raccoon not *personal*?' "

"Since when are you interested in makeup?"

Cassie rolled her eyes. "You're missing the point, Mom! He was insulting me but was completely clueless about it. Was that just him, or were all guys like that?"

Amanda gently pressed the Volvo's brakes. "Growing up in an isolated cabin doesn't make for the best people skills. But you have a point—a lot of guys, your dad included, were light in that area." Amanda chuckled to herself. "There was an old saying: Boys will be boys."

Cassie looked unconvinced. "What did *that* mean? Boys could be rude, but it's okay because, well, they're *boys*?"

"Something like that."

"Well, it's annoying," Cassie grumbled.

Amanda looked at her daughter with raised eyebrows. "Annoying yet strangely intriguing?"

Cassie wasn't going to take the bait. *Sam might say and do strange things*, she thought as she opened the car door, *but that doesn't mean I still don't think about him all the time. But there's no way I'm going to tell that to my mom.*

"I'm staying for the game after school," Cassie said. "I'll catch a ride home with a friend. See you later, Mom." And with that, she shut the door and melded into the throng of girls filing through the high school's main doors.

***

The basketball game between George Washington and its archrival Monroe High was the big game of the year. Having lost for the last two years, George Washington was primed for payback. Cassie found a spot on the bleachers at mid-court and saved a seat for Ashley. Terry couldn't make the game because she had to work at her mom's deli.

Girls chatted and laughed, their voices up several notches due to the air of excitement and the music blaring from the PA. Many of Cassie's friends from volleyball also played basketball; every year, they tried to convince her to play basketball, telling her she would make a great point guard. Cassie was only five feet, five inches tall but was fast on her feet and knew how to handle a ball.

But Cassie's heart was in volleyball. As the team's leading setter, Cassie loved the feeling of sending the ball to just the right height, then watching her teammate slam down the spike.

Connie Forenza landed on a seat in front of Cassie. She sat next to Cassie in English; they'd done several projects together.

"Hi, Cassie. Hey, what did you get on your *Scarlet Letter* paper?"

"A B minus. Seriously, why do we have to read books like that? I know it's a classic"—Cassie put the word in air quotes—"but really, I just wanted to light the thing on fire."

"I know what you mean," Connie responded with a conspiratorial snort. "Everyone in that book deserved a good slapping." As they chuckled, Ashley came through the gym doors, waving at Cassie like a lunatic. Connie looked at Ashley and sighed.

"Honestly, Cassie, I don't know how you do it—if there's such a thing as *friendicide*, you know, no one would blame you."

A feeble smile appeared on Cassie's face as she remembered how she and Ashley had become friends. During the Black Years, their mothers had helped each other through hard times, forging a friendship that was still going strong; because of that friendship, Cassie and Ashley spent a lot of time together when they were young.

With Cody gone, Cassie felt like half of her body had disappeared—being a twin meant always having someone at your side. Ashley helped to fill that empty space. As a kid, she was funny and brave, qualities that reminded Cassie of Cody.

Yet as the years passed, Cassie began to appreciate her time alone. By her thirteenth birthday, Cassie realized the traits she'd once admired in Ashley had somehow taken a turn to the dark side. Her wit turned into making fun of anyone who didn't live up to some unknown standard of cool. And instead of being fearless, Ashley had just become mean. Her mouth was now a faucet of snide remarks, one that was on a constant drip. Cassie considered ditching Ashley, but she also didn't want to cause a rift between their mothers. So Cassie sucked it up, playing the part of dutiful daughter and friend.

"It's complicated," Cassie responded to Connie with a sigh. Ashley bulldozed her way up the bleacher stairs and then plopped down next to Cassie. "Couldn't you get better seats? I like to be right up close."

Connie shot lasers of contempt at Ashley. "I think the correct thing to say is 'Thanks for saving me a seat.'" And with that, Connie rose. "See you in English, Cassie." She gave one more *what's-your-problem?* look to Ashley, then joined some friends near the end of the court.

"She's so lame," Ashley clucked, letting Connie's words float over her like the wisps of a cloud. "I saw Heather Thurston in the bathroom. You won't believe it—"

"Ashley, I don't want to hear about it," Cassie said, hoping to derail the snark. The referee tossed the ball between the two centers, starting the game.

Ashley steamrolled on, undeterred by Cassie's deflection. "She got the runs and crapped all over herself. Ew."

Cassie knew it was best not to respond when Ashley started in. Suddenly, a voice called out, "Hey, Ashley . . ."

Ashley pivoted to get a big splash of Coke in the face. Girls in nearby seats snickered. Heather Thurston sat two rows back, holding an empty cup. Her eyes bore into Ashley.

"Next time you want to start a rumor," Heather began, "look around first. And not that it's any of your business, but I sat on a spill of brown paint in art class. So eff you!"

Ashley faced forward, too stunned by the hot words and cold liquid to respond. She wiped her dripping face with her sleeve. Laughter floated up from behind, punctuated by a single phrase— douche face!

Great, Cassie thought, *that's gonna stick.* She tried to concentrate on the players running up the court, but the splash attack had taken over her thoughts: *Either I live with the aggravation of being Ashley's friend or dump her and hurt my Mom—not much of a choice.*

"Bitch!" Ashley muttered under her breath. She rubbed her eyes. "That stung!"

"Just let it go," Cassie said, her voice tense and low. She leaned forward, making Ashley disappear from her peripheral vision.

I'm like Hester Prynne with that red "A" on my front—only this time, the "A" stands for Ashley.

31

Captain Underpants flew across the TV screen, looking like a bumblebee in tighty whities. It was Saturday morning, and Sam and Luka were lazing on the couch, Luka's head in Sam's lap.

Transfixed by the cartoon, Sam soaked up every exaggerated move, every outrageous expression. He couldn't remember much of his early years, yet cartoons, from Sponge Bob to Johnny Bravo, were favorite memories from that distant past. In no time, Sam had relapsed into his addiction, mainlining the endless supply from Cartoon Network.

A whole channel with nothing but cartoons, Sam marveled to himself. *This world does have its good points.* Captain Underpants socked the bad guy, sending stars and tweeting birds circling around the villain's head. Sam chuckled.

"It's really not funny," Cassie said as she walked by the living room.

"Sure it is . . . Captain Underpants is my hero."

"I thought you said Apollo was your hero."

Sam considered the comment. "He is. Captain Underpants can be his sidekick."

Cassie croaked a laugh, surveying Sam's lanky frame sprawled on the couch. *It's like having Big Foot in your living room, this long-haired creature that's not supposed to exist. But there he is—laughing at the antics of a fat kid with a thing for BVDs.*

"What?" Sam exclaimed, ungluing his eyes from the screen long enough take in Cassie's skeptical expression. "It's hilarious."

Cassie only shook her head and then disappeared into the kitchen.

"Sit with me," Sam called out. "I'll explain the finer points of the Captain."

Cassie returned with a piece of toast and landed on the couch. *If Captain Underpants keeps Sam's mind off of grief and revenge, I'm all for it.* Suddenly, the channel changed.

"Must have sat on the remote," Cassie said as she began to search the cushion cracks.

A jerky, taken-with-a-cell-phone video of women wearing black hooded robes and vacant expressions appeared on the screen. They chanted and carried candles.

"Who are they?" Sam asked.

"They're some cult called Those-Who-Wait," Cassie replied, giving up on her hunt for the remote to bite into her toast. "They're led by some nutcase who says all the men are coming back. Her followers promise to remain celibate until they do."

"Sell-a-bit?"

Cassie smiled. "It means they're not supposed to have sex."

Sam nodded in confirmation. "So *that's* got to be mental."

"Pretty much," Cassie replied. "And they think women getting it on and mecs are abominations."

Sam leaned over to chomp on Cassie's toast. "Well, it's a good thing I'm not a mec," he said with mock relief. He stood up and headed for the kitchen—the bite had been like a tripwire on his appetite. "We should check out a meeting."

"Now *you're* mental."

"Consider it part of my continuing education," Sam called out from the kitchen, "like the computer lesson." He returned to the couch with his hand stuck in a bag of Fritos. "See, don't they look like a fun crowd?"

Cassie gazed at the blank faces of the chanting women. "Yeah, they're real party animals."

"I'll ask the Oracle when the next meeting is," Sam said, proud of his newly acquired computer skills. He cupped a handful of corn chips to his mouth.

"Don't you remember the part where my mom chewed us out for our little escapade?"

"I remember she said, 'Just be careful.' "

"So . . . ?"

"So we'll be more careful—this time we won't get caught."

***

Cassie heard the start of the Volvo engine from the warmth of Cody's bed. She glanced at the clock on the bedside table.

Geez, Mom, it's seven on a Sunday morning—give it a rest. Her mother had always worked too many hours—now that Sam was in the picture, she seemed to live at the lab. Yet Cassie took comfort in the fact that the cure must be close at hand. As the sound of the car engine faded, Cassie rolled over and went back to sleep.

By ten o'clock, both Cassie and Sam were up and dressed and had scarfed down scrambled eggs and English muffins.

"I'm going to take a shower," Sam announced. "If you get the dishes now, I'll do them after dinner."

"You're on," Cassie answered, knowing she'd just made a good deal—cleaning up after dinner was always more labor intensive than doing the breakfast dishes.

Unless Mom brings home take-out, which means Sam will get out of dishes for the day. Hmm, Cassie wondered, *cagey sneak or naïve innocent—which one is he?* She decided Sam was both, serving only to fuel her interest.

Sam headed up the stairs while Cassie started in on the dishes. After she'd loaded the dishwasher, Cassie looked at the stack of textbooks on the kitchen table. *I can't put off studying any longer. If I don't pass algebra and history, I'm going to have to take summer school, and that's so not going to happen.*

Cassie sat at the table and cracked open her math book to the chapter on factoring polynomials. A light rapping came at the window; she looked up and immediately froze at the sight of Terry's face through the glass. Cassie got up and opened the back door, realizing she hadn't spoken to Terry since Mrs. Duncan's doorway.

"Hi. Can I come in?" Terry asked, like it was a real question and not just a formality.

"Sure."

Terry edged her way into the kitchen. "No lab work today?"

"No, not for me. My mom's there, but you know Amanda—she's obsessed."

"True that."

Terry looked at the spread of books and papers on the table. "Isn't there some law that makes studying illegal on Sunday?"

"I've got a test on Monday."

"Need any help?"

In an instant, Cassie saw her way out. "Yeah, that'd be great." She started to stuff notebooks and pencils into her backpack. "But I want to get out of the house—let's go to the library."

"It doesn't open until noon on Sundays."

"Then we'll go to Starbucks." As she shouldered her backpack, Cassie heard a voice coming from the stairs.

"The hot water ran out," Sam announced. He stopped in the doorway, clutching a towel around his waist.

Terry gaped at him in disbelief. "Who are *you?*" she asked, sizing up his dripping, half-naked body.

"Terry, I can explain," Cassie said, her voice shaking.

"No, I want him to explain . . . because you're a *him*, aren't you?" She stared at Sam's flat chest.

Sam peeked under the towel. "Yep, it's all still there."

Cassie groaned. "Terry, it's a long story—"

"No, it's not, Cassie. When I told you I wanted to turn for you, all you did was give me this big speech about how dangerous that would be. And all this time, you've had a mec right under my nose. God, what a fool I've been!"

Terry's shock escalated to anger. "And what a hypocrite you are! You didn't even have the decency to tell me you already *had* someone. No, you just had to string me along."

Sam moved forward. "Listen, I don't know what your prob—"

"I'll handle this, Sam," Cassie cut in, knowing anything he would say would only make it worse. Then she looked at her best friend, knowing she couldn't reveal that Sam was a real male. "I know what this looks like, but please, trust me, it's not what you think!"

"Oh yeah?" Terry shot back. "Then tell me, Cassie, what the hell *is* it?"

Cassie fought to keep from blurting out Sam's true identity: "I . . . I can't tell you!"

Terry leaned back, glaring daggers. "Right . . . because if you *do* tell me, then you'll just out yourself as a total bitch!" Terry grabbed the doorknob, looking at Cassie through watering eyes. "I thought I knew you . . . guess the joke's on me."

"Terry, wait!" Cassie cried, but it was too late. Terry had fled out the back door, leaving Cassie reeling from the deathblow to their already staggering friendship.

***

Sam leaned his ear to Cassie's bedroom door; soft sobs punctuated by heaving breaths emanated from within. He knocked and then tried the doorknob—it was locked.

"Cassie, I'm sorry. I thought the house was a safe zone."

Cassie didn't respond. She lay curled up on her bed, feeling like she was in freefall. *It's not what Terry thinks—I just can't tell her Sam's a real male!*

Yet a nagging thought wouldn't let her alone. Every time she tried to stuff it down, it only came back stronger.

Terry's right, Cassie relented, unable to fight anymore. *She saw right through me.* Cassie buried her head in the pillow that smelled like Sam, earthy yet slightly sweet. The lingering scent made her realize what she'd been trying to hide from herself:

I do feel that way about Sam.

Again, a knock came at the door. "Cassie, open up."

Dead air stretched between them until it ended with the sound of footfalls thudding down the stairs. Cassie got up and unlocked the door, then sat back down on the bed; quick thumps came up the steps.

"I don't know how I messed up," Sam began as he entered the room, "but I've got a talent for it." He sat next to Cassie on the bed. "My mom used to tell me all the time not to do stupid stuff. I just thought—"

"It's not your fault," Cassie said, wiping her eyes. She looked at his face in the muted morning light—it was the face she saw every time she closed her eyes. They sat, a faint unease rising between them.

Say something! Cassie scolded herself. *Tell him how you feel!* She tried to form a sentence from the jumbled thoughts in her head.

Sam, I like you. No, that sounds so dorky. She tried again. *Sam, I think you're—argh!* Cassie leaned back as if to clear her head.

Talking is so useless!

Then Sam smiled. It was that smile, the one that melted her insides. Cassie's mind went blank—the only thing left to do was to act on pure instinct. She leaned forward and kissed him, softly at first, then with urgency. Sam pulled back a bit, mostly from surprise.

Cassie continued to press against him. As she lingered, a tingling spread throughout her body, sending waves of heat to her fingers and toes. *I don't have a clue what I'm doing*, she thought, continuing to explore Sam's lips with hers, *except it's the one thing I've been thinking about ever since I met him.* Sam broke off the kiss.

"I guess this means you're not mad at me anymore."

Cassie gave a small laugh. "That's right, but I never really was."

This time, Sam turned his head and leaned in. Cassie sat very still, savoring the anticipation as he drew closer. Yet instead of welcoming the warmth of his mouth, Cassie was distracted by the sound of the front door opening.

Sam stopped inches from her face, held in place as if by some magnetic attraction. Then Amanda's voice called out from downstairs: "Cassie? Sam? I'm home!"

They both leaned back with embarrassed smiles. "We're upstairs, Mom," Cassie answered. "We'll be down in a minute."

***

The time on the dashboard read 11:15. It was a cold evening for late March, hovering in the mid-thirties. Brandon shifted in the driver's seat, trying to relieve his soreness—even a luxury car was uncomfortable after so many hours of sitting.

He'd watched the comings and goings at the house, first the mother leaving early, then a teenage girl entering through the side door later that morning. She didn't stay long. The mother returned only to leave again in the afternoon. She came home well after dark. After that, Brandon saw only shadowy figures move across the windows.

Brandon cautioned himself to proceed with care. The authentic had been resourceful enough to eliminate Dana, a woman skilled in the art of dispensing death. Brandon considered then rejected the idea of entering the house and taking the male.

First, there's the dog. Second, the mother and girl know the layout of the house, putting me at a disadvantage. And a frying pan or fire extinguisher can be just as deadly as a gun.

The lights went out in an upstairs room. Brandon planned to resume his stakeout the next day, putting an end to what had become more effort than he'd anticipated. Monday was work for the mother and school for the daughter, leaving the male unattended.

That still leaves the dog—not the best scenario, but it will have to do as time is running out.

As Brandon started the car, he caught sight of two figures climbing out a second-story window. They scrambled across an overhang, climbed down a trellis, and then dropped to the ground. He killed the ignition, hoping the pair hadn't seen the flash of his headlights. The figures disappeared into a small car and drove off.

Sneaking out on a school night, Brandon thought, reveling in his stroke of luck. He waited enough time to follow without being spotted.

Somebody needs to be grounded.

32

Cassie drove down the deserted street, scanning for signs of the Those-Who-Wait meeting. She was unfamiliar with this part of the sector—the buildings seemed vacant, as if a sharp wind had blown the life out of them. Broken streetlights cast swaths of darkness.

"The cult always congregates at midnight," Cassie told Sam, "but I have no idea why."

Sam picked up Cassie's phone. "Well, it's 11:50 . . . we need to find the place pretty quick." The red dot on the small screen came to a stop, then pulsed like a tiny beacon. "It's around here somewhere."

Cassie pulled to the curb and put the car into park. "So tell me again why we're out here freezing our butts off in the middle of who-knows-where?"

"Like I said, it's research," Sam answered as they both got out of the car.

Cassie cast him a doubtful look, then sidestepped trash on the sidewalk. She knew this little excursion had been a bad idea, yet after the kiss, Sam could have said he wanted to go to the moon, and Cassie would have climbed into a rocket.

Sam stopped and fixed his gaze in the distance. "There," he stated, pointing into the shadows. They hustled down the street and into a dark alley. Garbage cans lined the passageway, some upright, some tipped over spewing rotting refuse. A trio of rats climbed over a mound, rooting and scratching for a meal. The remnants of a construction project—split boards, warped sheetrock, chipped concrete blocks—lay abandoned by the side of the building.

"What did you see?" Cassie asked, working hard to keep up with Sam's long strides.

"Somebody went down here," he replied, jerking his head toward steps that led below street level. They descended the stairs and opened the door with a long creak. Inside was black. Feeling his way along the wall, Sam stumbled over a broken crate. Light glinted ahead. They came upon a woman dressed in a black robe, a single candle flickering in her hand.

"Is it your first time?" she asked in a hushed tone.

"Yes," Cassie answered.

"And do you pledge to wait in purity until The Return?"

Cassie hesitated.

"Yes," Sam asserted. The woman handed them robes and lit candles, then pointed to a dark doorway. Cassie and Sam slipped on the robes as they made their way down the gloomy corridor; the sound of chanting grew louder with each step. In the candlelight, Sam saw Cassie's eyes widen with apprehension. He took her hand and squeezed it.

Cassie jerked it away, glaring at him with a hint of irony. "Purity, Samantha."

They entered the chamber. It had a low ceiling and smelled of mold, sweat, and melting wax. Women dressed in hooded robes rocked to and fro, holding candles that made traces of light as they swayed. Over and over, they intoned the same dirge: "We await your return, we remain chaste, we worship the Seer."

Above the hooded heads, Cassie saw a small stage that was empty except for a wooden chair placed at the center. She was content to stand at the back near the door.

Not so Sam.

He motioned toward the stage. Cassie shook her head. He scowled at her. Still, she refused to budge. Sam shot her a look of exasperation and then disappeared into the thicket of black robes, pushing his way through the wavering figures like a fan at a rock concert.

The chanting stopped as if to some unheard cue. Two towering figures—*guards?* Cassie wondered—mounted the platform and stood at the front corners. A woman walked onto the stage. She pulled the hood from her head, revealing a mass of silver hair.

"We gather as we have gathered and as we will gather until The Return," she proclaimed. "We have kept the covenant. We have remained pure. Sisters, prepare yourselves." The woman lifted the hood back over her head and stepped to the rear of the platform.

A girl, guided by an attendant, slowly climbed the steps. She was dressed in jeans and a blue blouse, her long, full hair tied back with a loose ribbon.

She can't be any older than fourteen, Cassie thought. Then it dawned on her—*she's the cult leader!*

The attendant settled the girl onto the chair and left the stage. The leader closed her eyes, her body softening as if her bones had turned to putty. The congregation started to hum, sending an eerie vibration throughout the chamber.

"They wait as we wait," the girl said as if in a trance. "All will be well. The time—" The girl halted. She shot her eyes open, her face seeming to radiate its own light.

"The postern is here!" the leader shouted. She rose to her feet. "It is time!"

The humming stopped; murmurings rippled through the crowd. Without warning, the girl jerked left, then right as if slapped by an unseen hand. Her once illuminated face transformed into a death mask. The faithful gasped at the sight of their convulsing leader.

Cassie looked above the heads of the bewildered women, seeing something but not believing her own eyes—a dark mass materialized as if from nowhere. Swirling and prismatic, the mass appeared to be a giant cloud of twisting glass shards.

What the hell?!

The mass floated toward the stage. Women shrieked at the strange, undulating presence, pushing and trampling their way to the door. Through the frantic crowd, Cassie caught a glimpse of Sam standing motionless, seemingly unaware of the menacing phantasm. Then her blood ran cold:

That horrible black thing is heading straight for him!

"Sam!" Cassie yelled above the screams as she fought her way through the crush of oncoming bodies. Dropped candles littered the floor, igniting the robes of several women who screeched at the licking flames.

In the midst of the chaos, Sam stood like a statue. *What is he doing?* Cassie screamed in her head. *Why isn't he running?* Within seconds, the black cloud came down on him.

"No!" Cassie roared, battling the gauntlet of bodies. She looked at the leader who seemed to have recovered from her seizure. The girl locked her eyes on Sam and the roiling menace, raising her arms toward them. The cloud stretched in her direction, a part of it still wrapped around Sam.

Cassie gasped in amazement. *The leader is pulling that thing off of him!*

The girl continued to hold out her arms, her body shaking from the strain. Suddenly, the cloud snapped from Sam. The turbulent mass broke apart into smudges yet reformed quickly and descended on the girl.

The guards lunged at the hostile cloud only to be thrown high into the air. They slammed against the ceiling and then plowed into the horde of stampeding women. Cassie looked to Sam; now freed, he wobbled on his feet and collapsed.

"Sam!" Cassie yelled.

"Remember the day!" the leader cried out, her voice muffled by the engulfing mass. A blinding light filled the room. Cassie blacked out before she hit the floor.

***

When Cassie came to, she found herself sprawled on the cold cement. The room, lit only by the dying flames of scattered, burning robes, was empty except for Sam who lay close to the stage. She crept over to him and turned his face toward her.

"Sam, wake up!"

He didn't respond. She lifted an eyelid—no life flickered in his pupil.

"Sam!"

A small groan escaped from his lips, causing Cassie to choke back a cry of relief. "It's me, Cassie."

"Cassandra," he murmured. It took several minutes for Sam to fully regain consciousness. When he did, he winced, putting his hand to his forehead. Cassie helped him up, yet Sam crumpled before he could get to his feet. She lifted off the black robe; the part of his shirt covering the bandage was soaked with blood. "We've got to get you home," she said, helping him up as she fought back her distress.

Sam leaned on Cassie, and the two of them stumbled down the dark corridor. Once outside, Sam flopped against the building, looking as spent as the pile of construction debris next to him.

"Can't go on," he said, exhaling the words.

"We'll rest here, but not for long." Cassie considered bringing the car around yet didn't want to let Sam out of her sight.

A gruff voice came from the shadows. "Move away from him."

Cassie spun around as a figure stepped forward. In the dim light, she could see that the person was a mec. Fear shot through her—the mec was holding a gun and a syringe.

"Cassie, run," Sam uttered, his voice faint and hoarse.

"Good advice, little girl," the mec said. "You'd better take it." He closed in.

With the last of his strength, Sam pushed Cassie away and then doubled over. "Run!"

Yet Cassie only stumbled back from the shove, too terrified to think or move or cry out. The mec raised his arm above Sam—the sight of the needle glinting in the streetlight transformed Cassie's fear into something that burst within her: an anger so deep, so intense, it threatened to explode from her chest.

"No!"

Cassie grabbed a rough board and swung, slamming the wood against the attacker's face with a *crack!* Howling in pain, the mec dropped the gun and syringe. He fell to his knees, his face in his hands. When the attacker looked up, Cassie gasped: blood poured from his left eye socket, gushing down his face into his open, screaming mouth.

Cassie grabbed the gun and hurled it into the mound of garbage. Then she pulled Sam down the alley as fast as she could.

33

"That was the mec!" Cassie blurted as she jerked the Mini Cooper from the curb. "It had to be!"

Sam nodded, then flinched at the stab of pain in his shoulder. "But how'd he find me?"

"I have no idea."

"What does he *want* with me?"

Cassie gave him an incredulous look. "You're kidding, of course."

"I know, I get it—I'm *special*," Sam said, spitting the word like it was a mouthful of sour milk. "My mother drilled that into me." His face turned pensive. "But if the mec got me, what would he *do* with me?"

"I don't know—find the cure with your blood, then hold the world hostage with it? Or just use you as a live sperm donor?" Cassie held back, not wanting to consider any more possibilities. "One thing's for sure: whatever he's got in mind, it's no good." She watched as Sam grimaced. "How's your shoulder?"

When Sam shrugged his reply—again, causing him to flinch—Cassie decided to put the conversation on hold. They rode the rest of the way home in silence.

Cassie pulled into the driveway and parked next to her mother's Volvo. She knew Sam's shoulder needed immediate attention, but she had a question that couldn't wait: "Why didn't you run from that horrible black thing?"

Sam gave her an all-too-familiar blank look. "What horrible black thing?"

"That weird fog thing that went after you. It was like a cloud of flashing black knives."

Sam shook his head. "I have no idea what you're talking about. I remember the girl—next thing I knew, you were waking me up."

Cassie's mind swirled as she tried to piece together the strange events. *How can Sam not remember being attacked by that thing?* Then she was struck by an equally disturbing thought: *The black cloud was off-the-charts bizarre . . . so why did it seem kind of familiar?*

Cassie put aside the nagging question, knowing she had to focus on getting help for Sam's shoulder. She drew Sam's arm around her and, in a lumbering, three-legged-race hobble, the two of them made their way to the back door.

Before sneaking out, Cassie had put Luka in the kitchen so she and Sam could climb back through her bedroom window without tripping the canine alarm. Scaling the trellis, however, was no longer an option. Cassie opened the door slowly as if she were defusing a bomb; Luka let out a protective howl.

"Hush, Luka!" Cassie scolded as they entered the kitchen. She settled Sam into a chair and then examined the bloodstain, now a large, red splotch. "Hold this," she said as she put a clean dishtowel over the wound. "I'll be right back."

"Where are you going?"

"To get my mom. I know she's up, thanks to Luka. You need stitches."

"No, there must be another way."

Cassie shook her head. "The bullet hole needs to be closed up again."

She disappeared through the doorway, though she didn't have to go far—Amanda stood at the top of the stairs, her eyes squinting in the light.

"Cassie, what are you doing up?"

"Sam needs Dr. Stanton. His wound's opened up, and it's bleeding pretty bad."

The news hit Amanda like a jolt of caffeine. She vaulted down the stairs and into the kitchen where she found Sam slumped, holding a bright red dishtowel to his shoulder. Amanda washed her hands and unbuttoned Sam's shirt to inspect the wound.

"What happened?" she asked, wiping off blood to assess the damage. "You know what? I don't want to know, not now at least." Amanda washed her hands again. "I need your phone."

Cassie handed the phone to her mother, all the while formulating a cover-up. *Sam slipped on the way to the bathroom,* she thought, trying on an excuse. *Or maybe he fell out of bed.*

Yet Cassie was tired of lying—tap dancing to avoid her mother's wrath now just seemed like cowardice. And although her anger had been born out of fear, Cassie hadn't felt like a coward when she felled Sam's attacker.

***

Dr. Stanton laid out suturing materials and a sterile bandage on the kitchen counter. The once-healing bullet wound in Sam's shoulder had turned into a large gash. Dr. Stanton sewed with care; in time, a jagged line of black stitches appeared in Sam's skin.

As she taped on white gauze, Dr. Stanton shook her head in stony silence. "You need to be more careful," she said, knowing she was stating the obvious. Sam winced as he started to slip his arm back into the sleeve.

"I'll get you a clean shirt," Cassie said as she headed for the stairs.

"Hold on," Dr. Stanton declared. Cassie halted, thinking the doctor was talking to her. But she wasn't. Dr. Stanton leaned toward Sam, her nose only a fraction from his chest.

"What is it?" Amanda asked. Cassie returned to the kitchen.

"I don't know," Dr. Stanton replied. "Do you have a flashlight?"

Amanda took one from the utility drawer and handed it to the doctor. Once again, Dr. Stanton peered at Sam's skin, this time in the light of the bright beam.

"What's going on?" Sam asked, squirming at the doctor's bug-under-a-magnifying-glass inspection.

"Your chest is marked with lacerations—thousands of them."

Dr. Stanton gave the flashlight to Amanda, and she and Cassie examined Sam's chest. It was covered by a patchwork of cuts, some deep, some barely having broken the skin.

"I've never seen anything like it," the doctor remarked. She examined Sam's hands, arms, and face. "They appear to be all over your body."

"What are they from?" Amanda asked.

"I have no idea," Dr. Stanton murmured, holding her eyes on Sam.

"No, I didn't do this to myself," Sam said, answering her unspoken question.

"I didn't think so. I don't see how you could even manage this. The cuts themselves appear to be harmless—even the deeper ones have started to heal over." Dr. Stanton shook her head in bewilderment. "But I have no idea what *caused* them."

Cassie sighed. *Only one thing could have done this to Sam—the slicing cloud. But if I tell Dr. Stanton and Mom about the attack, they'll think I'm nuts—and I wouldn't blame them.*

Sam examined his forearm as if trying to wrap his head around the crisscrossing marks. He looked up at Cassie. "I could use that shirt . . ."

Cassie nodded and headed for the stairs.

***

At the front door, Amanda thanked Dr. Stanton profusely and, once again, apologized for the late night call. Dr. Stanton impressed upon Amanda that she could contact her anytime.

Cassie returned to the kitchen, clean shirt in hand. She helped Sam thread his arms through the sleeves. "So what's the cover-up?" Sam asked as Cassie buttoned.

"I'm going to try something different this time."

While retrieving the shirt, Cassie had tried and failed to concoct a plausible story. Most of the time, she found it easy to lie her way out of getting punished. But this time was different. Cassie realized she didn't want to fool her mother—she wanted her mother's help.

"We're going to tell the truth," Cassie stated, "about everything—the woman who killed your mother and sister, the apartment, the Those-Who-Wait meeting." Then Cassie paused, not wanting to say the words out loud: "And the mec who's trying to kidnap you."

Before Sam could reply, Amanda entered the kitchen. She sat with Cassie and Sam at the table, not saying a word. After a long silence, Sam began to recount his story. At first, it was difficult reliving the horror of the night that had changed his life. As he went on, he felt a burden lift as though his words had managed to carry away some small measure of his grief.

When exhaustion washed out Sam's voice, Cassie took over. She explained about the cult meeting, her mother's eyes narrowing at the sneaking-out part. Then Cassie took a deep breath, knowing she had to tell her mother about the knife-cloud. After stumbling through the explanation, Cassie kept on talking—she didn't want to give her mother the chance to dismiss the unbelievable story.

"I know it sounds crazy, Mom, but that's what happened! I think that's how Sam got all those cuts. I don't know what happened after the light flashed, but I'm pretty sure the cult leader saved Sam's life."

Amanda turned to Sam. "And you don't remember this black mass at all?"

Sam shook his head. "I was standing there one minute, then Cassie was waking me up on the floor."

"Cassie," Amanda said, "I'm sure you thought you saw something strange. In times of stress, the mind can make imaginary things seem very real."

"I know what I saw, Mom! And the cuts—how do you explain them?"

"There has to be a simple, logical explanation. Hallucinations can't cause physical damage."

"It wasn't a hallucination!"

Amanda let out a frustrated sigh, knowing the situation was well beyond reprimanding teenagers. Although she was concerned for her daughter's emotional state, Amanda realized there was a more urgent issue at hand: "Sam, how did this mec find you?"

"We were wondering the same thing," Sam replied. "Maybe he saw us coming out of the apartment and followed us back here."

"But we didn't go straight home," Cassie added. "We got home late that night—he wasn't following us."

"However he found you," Amanda said, "we have to assume he knows where we live. We have to leave immediately."

Cassie choked back fear—the thought of her house not being a safe place made her feel lost. "Do we call the police?"

Amanda rummaged through cupboards, throwing crackers, peanut butter, and canned peaches into a paper bag. "No. If word gets out there's a live male under police protection, it'll be chaos."

"Can we bring Luka?" Cassie asked.

Amanda shook her head. "It'll be too crowded. We'll drop her off at Harriet's." Harriet lived three houses down and had two Chihuahuas that played with Luka like she was a big, furry chew toy.

Amanda continued to fill the sack. "Don't worry, Sam. I have a safe place for you."

34

By the time Amanda, Cassie, and Sam had arrived at the lab, dawn was breaking. They crammed into the decontamination chamber; when the light blinked green and the door slid open, they found Jamie at the table working on a pen and ink drawing. He looked up, startled by the sight of the three visitors.

"Jamie, this is Sam," Amanda announced as she put a rolled-up sleeping bag in a corner. "He's going to be staying with you for a while. Sam, meet Jamie."

"Hi," Sam said, casting a wary glance at the walls. Jamie returned the greeting and then looked at Cassie. His expression needed no words—again, she'd let days slip by without visiting him.

"Hi, Jamie," Cassie said, her tentative tone part apology, part olive branch.

"Hi," he replied gruffly, accepting neither her remorse nor the peace offering. He turned back to Sam and sized him up. "So you're the guy . . ."

"Yes, that's me," Sam declared, making no attempt to hide his irritation, "the last male on the planet, the only hope for the future of mankind." He stressed the "man" in mankind. Cassie was taken aback. She hadn't heard Sam be sarcastic—she didn't like it.

"Not the last male on the planet," Jamie corrected. "The second to last."

Sam eyeballed Jamie. When he was young, Sam wondered what it would be like to have a brother. One look at the skinny kid before him gave Sam his answer: it would be annoying.

"Okay, off to a good start," Amanda said dryly. "I'll be back in a few hours."

"Wait, where are you going?" Cassie asked.

Amanda stepped into the decontamination chamber. "I'm going to talk with a friend who's a lawyer. We're going to figure out how to place Sam under police protection without him becoming a prisoner."

The comment gave Sam a chill—he wondered if bolting were a better option.

"I'll be back soon," Amanda said as she hit the button to close the door.

Cassie pulled out her cell phone and pressed Terry's number on speed dial. *There's no reason not to tell Terry about Sam, now that he's already in danger from the mec.* The phone rang several times. *Damn caller ID.* She texted a message: know ur pissed meet me moms lab parking lot will explain everything pls. Then Cassie slid the phone into her pocket.

"I'm going up to wait for my friend."

"The girl from yesterday?" Sam asked.

Cassie nodded. "She probably won't show."

"I'll come with you."

"Thanks, but if by some miracle she does make it, I need to talk with her alone."

Jamie looked at Cassie as she slipped into the decontamination chamber. "We'll be here when you get back," he called out. Then he glanced at Sam. "Well, I'll be here, anyway."

Cassie negotiated the secret corridor, entered the lab, and headed for the door. She glimpsed the picture of XY on the whiteboard, then stopped in her tracks—recognition mixed with shock hit her like a hammer.

No, it can't be, she thought, shaking off the ridiculous notion. *That would just be too strange.* She reached for the doorknob yet hesitated. *But it does look like it.*

Cassie walked over to the whiteboard and examined the picture. She imagined the image not as a photograph but as a video, the crisscrossing lines at the center of the virus morphing into black, cutting edges.

XY looks like the black cloud!

Cassie blinked her eyes, not knowing what to do with the crazy idea. She tried to convince herself that it was just a coincidence.

How could XY be the black cloud? she wondered as she paced down the hallway to elevator. *That makes no sense at all—not that much is doing* that *these days.*

***

Cassie sat on the steps in front of the Taft Building; she checked the time on her phone—twenty-five minutes had passed since she'd sent the text. There was no reply, but Cassie still hoped Terry would show.

It's early, Cassie thought. *Maybe she didn't get the message.* She stared at her phone, willing it to chime with a reply. When it didn't, Cassie looked away. *Or maybe Terry just hates my guts and never wants to see me again.*

A Honda Civic pulled into the parking lot—it was Terry. Cassie stood up and walked toward the car, her stomach starting to tighten. Terry rolled down the window.

"Hi," Cassie said.

"Hi."

"You going to get out of the car?"

Terry shook her head. "I'm good. You said you had an explanation? So let's have it."

Cassie took a *here-goes-nothing* breath and started her tale with finding Jamie in the isolation chamber. Her voice wavered as she talked about Cody and the six years of his life that had been lost to her.

She went on to describe finding Sam at the mall, then explained about the mec who was after him. Cassie ended with the cult meeting, trying to come up with a reasonable description of the black cloud. She made a point to keep the story short yet give enough detail to make it all fit together—the one part she did leave out was about the kiss.

Terry listened in silence, too dumbstruck by the unfolding drama to interrupt. At the story's conclusion, she got out of the car and gave Cassie a big hug.

"I can't believe what you've been through!" Terry declared. "So Sam is an authentic—didn't see *that* coming! And holy crap—the *black cloud?* What is *that* all about?!" Terry relaxed her arms with a smile of impressed disbelief. "Leave it to you to find two guys!"

Cassie let out a breath, relieved that Terry had believed her incredible story. "That day you came over . . . I wanted to explain to you about Sam, but my mom told me not to tell anyone about the boys."

"So why tell me now?"

"Because he's already in danger," Cassie replied. She held a beat. "But it's more than that. I guess it comes down to the fact that I trust you. If I ask you not to tell anyone about Sam and Jamie, then I know you won't. And I couldn't stand the fact that you weren't my friend anymore."

Terry's eyes began to mist. "You'll always be my friend, Cassie, that's a promise." Terry started to walk toward the building. "So, c'mon. I've already met Sam—I'm assuming he has clothes on now." She walked up the concrete steps. "And I want to meet Jamie. If they're your friends, I want to be friends with them, too."

***

Sam stared at the walls, sensing a pressure like he was diving too deep in the lake. Jamie turned from the computer. "It may feel like it but, no, they're not closing in on you."

"How do you do it? I'd go bonkers—I'm *going* bonkers."

Jamie pushed away from the desk. He had gone nuts several times, willing to succumb to XY just to breathe fresh air or to see a real tree. During those times, Amanda had to talk him back from the edge. Jamie returned to the computer screen, not about to tell Sam about his breakdowns. "It takes some toughing out."

Sam examined the fractal drawings on the walls. "You did these?"

Jamie nodded. "I have time on my hands."

"So you drew the picture Cassie has taped next to her bed." An expression of satisfaction spread on Jamie's face; Sam wanted to wipe away the look for good.

"Why did my mom put you in here?" Jamie asked. "Have you lost your immunity to XY?" On the one hand, Jamie hoped it were true, just so he and Sam would be on an equal footing. Then Jamie was struck by an alarming thought: *If this stringy-haired goofball isn't immune anymore, that means we'll become roommates.* Jamie scrutinized Sam as he perused the drawings. *Then how long will it take before we beat each other to a pulp?*

"No, some guy, some mec is after me," Sam replied.

"Because you're immune?"

"I guess so." His voice hardened. "He sent someone to kidnap me—my mother and sister ended up dead."

Not knowing what to say, Jamie blurted the first thing that came into his head: "That sucks." Sam acknowledged the remark and sat in the upholstered chair.

"So where were you when the mec tried to grab you?" Jamie continued.

"Cassie and I were at this weird cult thing . . ."

"A Those-Who-Wait meeting?" Jamie asked. He was familiar with the group from the Internet. "Why did you go there?"

Sam shrugged. "It seemed like a good idea at the time."

Jamie tried not to get sidetracked. "Okay, then what happened?"

"It's all kind of a blur," Sam said, becoming somewhat irritated by Jamie's inquisition. "I don't remember a lot. There were a bunch of women in robes, and this girl was on the stage. Next thing I knew, I was waking up on the floor. Cassie dragged me outside, and the mec was there, waiting for me."

"That's when he tried to abduct you?"

Sam nodded. "He was about to stab me with a needle when Cassie hit him with a board. Later, Cassie and I told her mom about everything, so she put me in here for safekeeping."

Thinking about Sam's dead mother and sister compelled Jamie to state the obvious: "That means you put Cassie and her mom in danger just by being around them."

Sam locked his eyes on Jamie. At that moment, he hated this scrawny kid for having the nerve to tell him the truth. "Maybe it would be better if I just disappeared."

"So why don't you . . . just disappear?"

Sam knew the reason was that he would never see Cassie again. But he had no intention of sharing that information with Jamie. Before Sam could respond, the chamber door slid open; Cassie and Terry stepped into the room.

"Hey you two, this is Terry," Cassie announced. "Terry, this is Jamie," Cassie said, "and you've already met Sam."

Terry said hello to Jamie and then smiled at Sam. "Met but not formally introduced. I want to apologize for acting like a jerk the other day. Cassie told me about you and . . . everything. When I showed up, I didn't know what I was talking about."

Sam still hadn't understood why Terry had been so mad at Cassie. He remembered Terry's rant, with certain words like "turned" and "hypocrite" rising above the tirade. Yet something else had preoccupied his thoughts from that morning—and that something else was Cassie's kiss.

Terry sat on the bed. "So Jamie, ten years," she remarked, making note of the small room.

"That's right. Welcome to my world—it's either this or be worm food."

While riding the elevator, Cassie told Terry to steer clear of certain topics like Sam's family or the mec. Hearing Jamie's morose response, Terry mentally added the subject of XY to the list.

So what do we talk about? The weather? No, that will just remind Jamie he has only one forecast: gloomy with almost no chance of getting the hell out of here. Fortunately, Jamie bailed her out.

"How long have you and Cassie been friends?"

"About seven years. She took pity on me because I was the new kid in fifth grade."

"I did, a little," Cassie agreed. "You seemed so . . ."

"Terrified? Yeah, that's it."

Sam joined in. "Cassie tells me you don't learn much in school. Is that true?"

Terry smirked. "I don't know. Some of it might sink in and actually be useful someday."

Sam held back, his face more serious than Terry's flippant answer. "I would've liked to have gone to school."

"Me too," Jamie added. "I got my GED and am taking online college courses, but that doesn't mean I went to school."

A pregnant pause big enough to deliver twins filled the room. Cassie spied the deck of cards on the table. "Who wants to play cards?"

"That's a great idea," Terry added. "Five card stud, Texas hold'em . . ."

"I was thinking something a little more basic," Cassie said as she grabbed the deck. They all sat cross-legged on the floor, squished in by the furniture. "Sam, what card games do you know?"

"Go Fish and War and some matching game I can't remember the name of."

"How about you, Jamie? You know Speed, but that really isn't a four-person game."

"Go Fish and War are about it."

Cassie started to deal. "Go Fish, it is."

Terry fought the urge to groan. Thanks to her mother's Wednesday night poker sessions, Terry found it hard to imagine playing cards without betting and bluffing.

"Why don't we make it interesting," Jamie began as he fanned the cards in his hand. "If you get four-of-a-kind, you can ask anyone a question, and that person has to tell the truth."

"I like your thinking," Terry said, sizing up Jamie with a new respect. "Like a mash-up of Go Fish and Truth or Dare."

"I'm in," Sam said. "Who starts?"

"Left of the dealer," Terry noted. "That'd be you, Sam."

In the beginning, all the questions could have been found on a getting-to-know-you survey: What's your favorite color? What kind of ice cream do you like? What holiday do you like best? Jamie answered Einstein as the person he'd most like to meet, and Sam took way too long to figure out his favorite candy. As the game wound down, Jamie took a turn.

"Terry, do you have any sixes?"

Terry rolled her eyes as she forked over three of them. Jamie placed the small stack of cards in front of him. He looked at Cassie.

"Have you ever kissed anybody?"

Cassie, Sam, and Terry registered the same look of surprise like a slot machine hitting the jackpot. Terry jerked her head to see Cassie's reaction—her face was red, and although her mouth was open, no words came out.

"I don't know if that question—" Terry started in.

"The question is fine," Cassie replied, resuming her composure. "Yes, I've kissed plenty of people—my mom, my grandmother. Does kissing Luka count?" Cassie glared at Jamie, her face still flushed.

Terry glanced at Sam who also seemed embarrassed. Then it hit Terry—*the person Cassie kissed was Sam!*

As if a magician's scarf had been whisked away, Terry saw what she realized had been right in front of her the entire time: the way Cassie looked at Sam with what she thought were secretive glances, the way her face lit up when he spoke . . .

She does *like him.*

After the question, the game came quickly to an end. Terry stood up. "I've got to head out. I open at the deli today." It wasn't true, but Terry needed to escape—the cramped room had become unbearable. Terry said her goodbyes to the boys and declined Cassie's offer to walk her to her car.

Once outside, Terry inhaled deeply, the fresh air helping to clear her head. In her most quiet moments, she knew Cassie would only think of her as a friend, yet a shred of hope always lingered.

As she made her way to her car, Terry gazed at the ground, the sky. *Everything looks the same, but everything is different.* Then her heart sank. *I can't kid myself any longer—Cassie will never look at me the way she looks at Sam.* Terry came up to her car, but didn't open the door.

Not ever.

The realization made Terry wonder if she could keep her promise to always be Cassie's friend knowing she would never be more than that.

35

Sam studied the black and white pictures on the wall, trying to distract himself from the close quarters. Jamie sat at the table; he picked up a pen, but didn't start drawing.

"Sorry about the question," he mumbled to Cassie. "I didn't mean to embarrass you."

Sure you did, she mentally shot back, still flushed from her stumbling answer. Yet no sooner had the thought appeared in her head than her resentment began to fade. Cassie had a hard time bearing a grudge, something Terry had once told her was one of her finest qualities. "That's okay," Cassie said. "It was just a game."

Jamie paused, knowing it was time to change the subject. "So some mec is after Sam—how bizarre is that?"

"Tell me about it," Cassie agreed. Sam continued to examine the drawings in silence.

"I still don't get what happened at the Those-Who-Wait meeting," Jamie wondered out loud.

"That makes two of us," Cassie noted. "Everything seemed normal—well, normal for a wacked-out cult, anyway. The leader was talking . . ." Cassie hesitated, wondering how Jamie would react to her next comment: "Then this freaky black cloud thing showed up. It went after Sam."

"Freaky black cloud thing?" Jamie echoed, his eyes boring into Sam. "You left out *that* little detail."

"That's because I don't remember it," Sam said, holding his gaze on a drawing.

"What was the cloud like?" Jamie asked Cassie.

"It was big and dark, like a million swarming knives."

Jamie wanted to ask more questions—about a hundred of them—yet the terrified look on Cassie's face let him know it was best to switch gears. "You mentioned that the cult leader said something—what did she say?"

"She said . . ." Cassie replied, scrunching her eyebrows only to sigh in defeat. "I can't remember. The place turned into a madhouse pretty quick."

Sam had his nose to a drawing. "She said, 'The postern is here.'"

Cassie and Jamie looked at Sam. "Those were her exact words?" Jamie asked. Sam confirmed.

"What the heck is a postern?" Cassie asked, wishing the word had been on an English vocabulary list. After a quick Internet search, Jamie had the answer: "It's a back door."

"A back door?" Cassie asked. "To *what?*"

"I have no idea," Jamie replied. "The cult leader said the postern was there, at the meeting. So what was in the room?"

"Not much," Cassie replied. "A stage, a chair, some candles, and . . ."

"And?"

"And a bunch of people. Could the postern be a person?"

"Sure it could."

Cassie had a hard time grasping Jamie's casual response. "How can a person be a door?"

"Anything can be anything," Jamie answered, realizing his response wasn't much help. He tried again. "We're all made out of the same star stuff from the Big Bang. There isn't much difference between doors or chairs or people on a quantum level."

"English, please—on a *what* level?"

"On a sub-atomic level."

"Sub-atomic? Like really small?"

"Add a thousand more 'reallys' and, well, you get the idea."

Cassie regrouped. "Could the mec be the postern? I mean, he was there, outside."

"Maybe," Jamie replied. "Or maybe you're the postern."

Cassie arched an eyebrow. "I doubt it." She passed the hot potato to Sam. "Maybe it's you—*you're* the back door."

Sam spied Ritz crackers on a shelf. He grabbed the box, tore into it, and popped a cracker into his mouth. "I'm not a front door, back door, side door, or trap door," he said, spraying bits of cracker, "but I am starving."

Cassie snatched the box from Sam's hand and thumped it on the table. "Stop eating for two seconds and focus!" *He can be so irritating*, she thought. *I'm getting whiplash from either wanting to kiss him or slap him.* "Sam, this is serious. You've got something to do with all of this. That cloud thing tried to kill you. I'm sure that's how you got all those cuts."

"Cuts?" Jamie asked. "What cuts?" He looked at the Ritz box and then at Sam. "And sure, help yourself," he added with derision.

"Sam has these slash marks all over his body," Cassie said, trying to get the conversation back on track. "Go on, show him."

"They're all healed over," Sam said, shaking his head. "I'm fine—Dr. Stanton said so."

"That's only because the cult leader pulled that thing off of you before it *could* kill you."

Jamie leaned back in his seat and eyeballed Sam. "You piss off some bizarre black cloud, and it wants payback?"

"Not lately," Sam retorted. "And thanks," he said, once again snagging the cracker box, "don't mind if I do."

Jamie scowled and then powered through the Ritz showdown. "If the leader saved you from the black cloud, that means *you're* probably the postern."

"Makes sense to me," Cassie added. Sam ignored the comments.

Jamie turned to Cassie. "Did the leader say or do anything after she saved Sam?"

"Yeah, she *did* say something, just after the cloud came down on her." Cassie scoured her brain but came up empty. "All I remember is a big flash of light, then waking up on the floor."

Sam opened a jar of peanut butter and spread a fingerful on a cracker. "She said, 'Remember the day.' " He wondered why the girl's words had been burned into his brain while the seething black mass—a memorable occurrence if there ever was one—made no impression on him.

The three of them sat in silence. "Remember the day?" Cassie asked. "Remember *what* day? This whole thing is giving me a migraine." Then she jolted. "Wait a minute," Cassie stated, looking at Sam. "You blacked out before she said that. How could you *know* what she said?"

Sam only shrugged, continuing to munch.

A smug smile crept onto Jamie's face. "So you *fainted?*"

"Like Cassie said, I *blacked out.*" The two boys glared at each other, their eyes locked in mutual contempt.

"Okay, you two," Cassie huffed, making no attempt to hide her exasperation, "let's just stick to the subject."

After several scornful seconds, Jamie recapped the ever-evolving story: "So the cloud went after Sam and gave him the cuts. The leader dragged the cloud off of Sam, only to have it go after her. She shouted, 'Remember the day,' and it all ended in a big flash of light."

"That's about it," Cassie said, goosebumps flashing up her arms as she envisioned the girl's tortured face in the slicing mass. "The next thing I knew, I was waking up on the floor." She rubbed her temples. " 'Remember the day'—what could that mean?"

Jamie responded by typing on the keyboard; he leaned forward as the search list illuminated the screen. "Remember the day" brought up the title of an old movie with Claudette Colbert, along with various websites about Pearl Harbor, the assassination of John F. Kennedy, the attack on the Twin Towers, and the wedding of then Prince, now King William and Kate Middleton. Further down, he saw it.

"Remembrance Day—that's this Saturday," Jamie said. "Could that be it?"

"Seems more likely than some ancient movie with Claudette Colbert, whoever she was," Cassie responded.

"What's Remembrance Day?" Sam asked.

"It's the day honoring all those who died from XY," Cassie replied. "There's a big rally at the Capitol steps. My mom and I go every year." Cassie thought of the crowds, a large congregation making an easy target. Her heart sank. "Maybe something's going to happen at the ceremony . . ."

"Like what?" Jamie asked.

"Like, I don't know, some kind of attack?"

"You mean from the black cloud?"

Cassie shrugged. "I guess so."

"Let's say this cloud thing does show up at the rally," Jamie suggested. "How do you keep it from slicing and dicing?"

"I don't know. We could find the cult leader—she stopped it, at least from hurting Sam."

Jamie typed again at the computer. "That's weird."

"What?"

"All the websites about Those-Who-Wait have been taken down. Look."

Cassie leaned in—the screen read: Sorry, there are no listings for Those-Who-Wait.

"Well, that blows that," Cassie said as she dropped onto the bed. "I don't even know if the girl is still alive—she *was* trapped inside the cloud." Putting aside the chilling thought, Cassie pressed on: "If I'm at the rally with my mom, at least we could warn people." She slumped against the wall in frustration. "I don't know—we just have to do *something!*"

Sam listened, scarfing crackers and peanut butter as Jamie and Cassie talked. Their discussion had been focused, animated. Yet there was something that distracted Sam from the rally and the black cloud—something that made him simmer on a low boil.

Then it dawned on him: *Jamie's into Cassie!* Sam stared at Jamie: the way he looked at Cassie made Sam want to drag the kid outside so that XY could fry his brain cells. *Jamie and I might be the survivors of an extinct gender*, he decided, *but that doesn't mean I'm going to let him have Cassie.*

"I'm going to be there too, at this rally thing," Sam declared.

"Right," Cassie shot back, "so you can give the cloud one more chance to turn you into mincemeat—no way."

Sam put away the cracker box and peanut butter jar. "And what's to keep the cloud from going after *you?*"

Cassie paused. "If it was going to do that, it would have come after me at the cult meeting."

"Maybe," Sam replied, "or maybe not. You don't know anything about this black fog thing. I want to be there, just in case."

Cassie shook her head. "We can't take that chance. It's too dangerous for you."

"So it's okay for you to protect me," Sam said, his voice as sharp as flint, "but not for me to do the same for you?"

"You don't get it," Cassie groaned. "That thing tried to *kill* you! If you show up—and *it* shows up—there won't be any cult leader there to save your butt!"

"And if I *don't* show up, that means there's one less person to save you, if the cloud decides you're a better target."

Jamie had been silent during the back and forth of their argument. He looked at Cassie with raised eyebrows. "As much as I hate to say it, he's right."

"Okay," Cassie said on an exhale, "two against one—that's not fair."

"Fair isn't the point," Sam replied. "Keeping you safe is."

Cassie frowned, reluctantly giving in. Yet despite her annoyance, she felt a faint thrill at the thought of Sam as her protector.

36

During the Black Years, vagrants, runaways, and drug addicts turned the warehouse on Avenue F into an impromptu shelter. The first time Brandon strode into the building, his handgun in full view, the squatters disappeared into the cracks of the city. Brandon wanted a private place to do business—little did he know that, in time, the warehouse would house his own private army.

In the cavernous space, Brandon stood before his fighting force, fifty women trained and ready to advance on his command. It was the eve of Remembrance Day. He surveyed their expectant faces, each of them impatient to leave behind her old life, to be the hammer instead of the nail. The allegiance they swore to him let Brandon know that Columbia would soon be his.

Yet all had not gone according to plan: the male was still not in Brandon's possession. Instead, a black patch covered his left eye, courtesy of the three-inch flat head nail that had been driven into the socket by the girl he assumed had been no threat. Having lost the sight in his eye, Brandon vowed to punish the girl who had marked him for life. What he would do to her would pale in comparison to the loss of an eye.

Brandon put aside his plan for the male and the girl until after the takeover. When the two had been captured, he would focus on the sale of the authentic and the death of the girl. His debt to the Vandover family was coming due—the thought of not being able to repay it made his gouged eye throb.

One last time, Brandon outlined the assault strategy with his militia. Urgency charged the air like an approaching thunderstorm. Brandon's voice echoed in the drafty warehouse as if sent from on high; he sermonized of seizing power, of making Columbia bend to their will.

As he described the wealth that would soon be theirs, Brandon imagined a bullet ripping through a skull. The head, however, did not belong to his assassination target, the President of the United Sectors—it belonged to the girl with chestnut hair.

***

The first of April had been chosen as Remembrance Day because it marked the beginning of the plague. Many thought it disrespectful: April Fool's ran contrary to the solemnity of the day. Others thought the choice was perfect—God had played the ultimate trick on the human race.

In truth, it was that day ten years ago when Elmer Cusack became patient zero in the worldwide epidemic. The elderly man had been taken by ambulance to Seton Hospital in Great Falls, Montana. Coughing blood onto his polyester shirt, Mr. Cusack told the EMS worker he felt like his body was exploding; the technician barely registered the comment as he struggled to insert an IV needle into the old man's collapsed vein.

Just after Mr. Cusack had been wheeled into the emergency room, he bucked and jerked on the stretcher in the grips of a seizure. His eyes rolled back to white; his body went rigid. He was dead.

The ER staff went about the business of paperwork and notification. Death was part of the job, and by the looks of the old man's withered frame, probably welcome.

Yet in less than 24 hours, the ambulance crew that had delivered Mr. Cusack to his final destination showed up at the hospital with fever and seizures. The driver and emergency technician were cold within hours. Next it was the doctor who had treated the elderly man. In time, other ER doctors were added to the casualty list. The daisy chain of victims grew to include hospital administrators and visitors along with their families.

But only the men.

The only thing that spread faster than the virus was the panic that swept the nation.

***

On the morning of Remembrance Day, Amanda showed up at the isolation chamber, ready to head to the rally. The evening before, Amanda had told Cassie they would be spending the night at the home of a family friend. Cassie's response had been brief but unshakable: "No way—I'm staying with the boys."

After a short but intense argument, Amanda relented. Now she looked impatiently at her watch. "The president will be starting her speech soon," Amanda said to Cassie. "We need to leave if we're going to get a decent parking spot." When Sam headed for the door, Amanda glowered at him. "Where do you think you're going?"

"To the rally."

"No, you're not."

Sam returned her stare. "Yes, I am. We think the black cloud might show up . . . and if it does, it might go after Cassie this time."

Amanda clenched her jaw. "I don't want to hear anymore about this *cloud*! It isn't real. What *is* real is that the mec is after you. It's too risky for you to go to such a large gathering. You are staying here, and that's final!"

Amanda's harsh words startled Sam, but they didn't shock Cassie—she was used to her mother's bluntness. What did take Cassie aback was the fact that her mother still thought of her as a hallucinating freak-job. The only silver lining was that now Sam had to get past her mother in order to go to the rally.

"I agree," Cassie stated plainly. "You should stay here with Jamie." Sam looked away, too angry to meet her gaze.

"Sam," Amanda began, gearing up for damage control, "I know I said you weren't a prisoner, but the isolation chamber is the safest place for you until we can come up with a more permanent solution."

Sam's skin prickled with heat. "You want to keep me safe so you can drain my blood to find your precious cure!"

"You're right, I do want to find the cure," Amanda said quietly. "I also want to keep you safe because I care about you."

Sam hesitated and then looked at Cassie. "You're right," he said, his resolve weakening. "Two against one—it's not fair."

"We'll figure something out," Cassie offered in consolation. "You won't be in here long." As soon as she'd said the words, Cassie flinched. She stole a look at Jamie; his head was down. She only wished her encouraging words applied to him as well.

Sam let out a long breath. Facing off against two females reminded him of countless arguments he'd lost to his mother and sister. He also thought of that terrible night at the cabin—his mother and sister were dead because he'd ignored his mother's warnings. "Okay," Sam relented. "I'll stay."

"We'll be back after the rally," Amanda said as she stepped into the decontamination chamber.

Sam pulled Cassie aside. "Here, take this," he whispered, slipping the gun into her jacket pocket when her mother and Jamie weren't looking.

The weight of the weapon made her feel off kilter. "What am I supposed to do with that?" Cassie hissed under her breath. "And besides, it's probably useless against the cloud."

"Just take it," Sam said. "You never know . . ."

Cassie shook her head and then joined her mother in the decontamination chamber. After the door slid shut, Sam heard faint clicking sounds. He tried to open the door, but it wouldn't budge.

"Don't bother," Jamie said without looking up from the computer. "My mom has locked us in."

**

Cassie looked out at the expanse of female faces turned toward the podium like sunflowers to the light. Remembrance Day always drew a large audience at the Capitol steps; the multitude stretched all the way to First Avenue. Amanda and Cassie stood to the right of the podium at the edge of the crowd.

Looking through a pair of small black binoculars, Cassie scanned the skies for any sign of an undulating darkness. Two flags, the Stars and Stripes and the Columbia Sector colors, ruffled in the breeze. President Sanford approached the podium to thunderous applause. She raised her hands to quiet the roar.

"Thank you for your warm welcome," she said, her voice booming over the PA. "We come here today as we have done so for the last ten years to remember those who perished from the plague that changed our world forever."

Amanda looked at Cassie. "Why do you think this cloud is going to show up—not that I'm saying it actually exists."

"Something the Those-Who-Wait cult leader said made us think so," Cassie responded, still intent on her search. "Anyway, it's just a hunch."

As the president intoned about XY, the Black Years, and the recovery of the nation, Cassie felt her eyes glaze over. The longer the president spoke, the more Cassie sensed her hunch turning into a dead end.

I'm glad the cloud hasn't shown up—if it does, it'll be a complete disaster at a gathering this large.

Still, Cassie wanted to believe she could unravel the mystery that had tied up her life in knots. *What this really means is that I don't have a clue about what's going on.* She lowered the binoculars, feeling like a game piece that had just been moved back to square one.

***

After pulling on the locked door, Sam began to pace the room. Five minutes later, he was still walking from wall to wall.

Jamie turned from the computer screen. "Have a seat," he said in a monotone. "You're going to wear out my floor."

Sam ignored the comment, continuing to stride three steps forward and three steps back. "I have a bad feeling about this."

Jamie returned his gaze to the screen. "Yeah, I get it—the room is small."

Sam shook his head. "No, I don't mean that. I'm talking about Cassie at the rally. I shouldn't have given in." He looked at his forearms, the network of scars a fading reminder of an attack he couldn't remember. Yet Sam knew how dangerous the cloud was by the fear in Cassie's voice every time she spoke of it.

"Cassie did have a point," Jamie noted. "The cloud didn't attack her at the meeting."

Sam halted. "I just can't shake the feeling that something bad is going to happen." He raked his fingers through his hair, thinking about the shallow grave at the cabin—instead of his mother and sister, Sam imagined Cassie buried in the cold dirt. "If anything happens to her . . ."

"You really think Cassie is in danger?" Jamie asked.

"If that *thing* shows up? Yeah."

Jamie clicked on the computer and brought up a streaming video of the president at the podium. "President Sanford just started her speech. If you run, you can make it there in five minutes. It's not far from here."

"What are you talking about?"

"I'm talking about you making sure nothing happens to Cassie."

"But we're locked in."

"I figured out a long time ago how to deal with the lock," Jamie responded, "just so I wouldn't feel so trapped. Problem is, the real lock is the virus that's waiting for me on the outside." He reached under his bed and pulled out a contraption made of wire, aluminum foil, duct tape, and what appeared to be the elastic from a cut-up pair of underwear. Sam cast a dubious glance at the gizmo.

"I know," Jamie conceded, "it looks funky, but it works."

After attaching the science project, Jamie grappled with the door until it slid open. Then he returned to the computer, typed on the keyboard, and brought up a map of the downtown area.

"We're here," Jamie said, pointing to the screen. "You need to get there. Just head for the big dome."

***

The president was winding up her speech, one she would be giving at rallies throughout the Northeast Sector.

"Let's head out so we can beat the traffic," Amanda said.

Cassie looked one last time at the crowd—a flash of movement caught her eye. She spotted a tall figure weaving through the throng.

"Wait a minute," Cassie said, peering at the form through the binoculars. "It's Sam!" She turned to her mother. "But you locked him in—I saw you do it!"

Amanda simmered with anger. "Obviously, Jamie has a few tricks up his sleeve."

Cassie watched as Sam fought his way to the front. "We've got to get him out of here!" she uttered, terrified that some woman would recognize Sam for what he was—a real male. Racing down the steps, Cassie struggled to keep the swiftly moving boy in her sights.

***

Sam knocked a woman on the shoulder, startling the toddler in her arms.

"Hey!" the mother snapped. She shot him a dirty look, yet Sam was too preoccupied to apologize. He continued to search for Cassie, bumping into several more spectators.

There are so many people here, he thought. *I'll never find Cassie in this crowd.* He stopped, then bent over, gasping—the all-out sprint to the Capitol had taken its toll. After catching his breath, he rose upright.

Just ahead, Sam saw a figure in black pull out something from the inside of a jacket—a gun flashed in the sunlight. In an instant, Sam recognized the shooter:

It's the mec!

Sam shoved his way through the crowd, knocking over women like bowling pins. As the mec took aim, Sam tackled him from behind. The gun fired, flew into the air, and then crashed down on a woman's head.

Screams erupted as women fled in all directions. Sam and the mec fell to the concrete in a blur of swinging fists. They rolled down several steps, trading punches and body blows before hitting a landing. Sam squeezed his hands around the mec's neck, causing his uncovered eye to bulge.

The mec boxed Sam's ears, yet instead of letting go, Sam dragged the would-be assassin to his feet and slugged him; the turned male toppled into a clump of shrieking women. Dazed, the mec shook his head, then wiped blood from his mouth. Just as Sam was about to lunge, he felt two hands grab him from behind. He turned to see Cassie yanking him by the shirt.

"We've got to get out of here," she cried, "now!"

The mec stumbled to his feet and fled.

"He's getting away!" Sam yelled, fighting Cassie's grip. He tried to see where the mec had gone, but it was no use—the turned male had disappeared into the frenzy.

"C'mon!" Cassie shouted as she jerked on Sam's arm—all he could do was let her pull him through the swarm of frantic women.

37

Amanda peeled out of the parking space just as Cassie and Sam slammed the car doors.

"I *had* him!" Sam bellowed.

"And what would have happened if the cops grabbed you?" Cassie shot back.

"Why would they do that? I'm not the one trying to kill the president!"

"But they don't *know* that! All they see is two people fighting." Cassie held back, trying to calm herself with long, slow breaths. "A crowd of women isn't the place for you to be found out as an authentic."

Sam stared out the window. "Now we're no better off than we were before."

"Not true," Amanda responded, looking at Sam in the rearview mirror. "President Sanford is alive because of you."

Sam relaxed into the seat, conceding the point. Then the frustration of having his hands around the mec's throat without being able to finish him off made Sam want to ram his fist through the glass window. As Amanda pulled into the Taft parking lot, he groaned, "Back in the box?"

"We're not having this discussion again," Amanda said, her voice set in stone. She parked but didn't turn off the ignition. "You two stay here with Jamie. I've got some things to take care of."

"Like what?" Cassie asked.

"I need to go home to get some papers for the lawyer. Then I'm going to talk with the authorities about bringing Sam in with enough security."

"And what happens after that?" Sam asked, blaring the question. "I spend the rest of my life moving from cage to cage? Maybe I should just take off." He got out of the car and shut the door with a *thwack!* Cassie piled out after him.

"Promise me you won't do that," she said, waiting for the reply that never came.

Amanda rolled down the window. "Go on, you two. I won't be long."

As Amanda drove out of the parking lot, Cassie and Sam headed for the entrance. No words passed between them as they entered the building. After the metal doors of the elevator had clanged shut, Cassie pushed the Hold button.

"I know you're pissed off," she started in. "I get that. But if any of those women had found out you're a real guy . . ." She hesitated, then examined the bruise under his eye. "Does it hurt?"

"Not much," Sam replied, returning her concerned look with a scowl.

Undeterred by Sam's sullen expression, Cassie laced her fingers into his. "I couldn't stand the thought of something happening to you."

Sam grimaced. He wanted to stay mad at her—only a few more seconds and he would have had his justice. Yet his anger fell apart the moment he felt the warmth of her hand. "Turns out, it wasn't the cloud after all—it was the mec."

"Which is so bizarre."

"Why do you say that?"

"Well, because the cult leader wasn't there when the mec tried to kidnap you. So how did she know he'd try to assassinate the president?"

Sam shrugged. "I don't have a clue. But I do know one thing . . ."

"Yeah? What's that?"

"You took out his eye. He was wearing a patch like some kind of psycho pirate."

"Argh, matey!" Cassie said in an ironic growl, taking a sinister delight in making fun of the mec.

Sam chuckled as Cassie hit the button for the basement. He drew her toward him. "I'll get him next time."

Cassie's lighthearted mood vanished in an instant. "I don't want there to *be* a next time!"

Sam looked at her, wanting to erase the fear he saw clouding her hazel eyes. He kissed her, lightly at first and then deeply, as if searching for the relief from his longing for her. He lifted her off the ground, not knowing what to do with the energy coursing in his veins. A feeling welled inside, one that left him undeniably strong yet at the same time just as weak. The tighter he held Cassie, the more the feeling spread throughout his chest. He broke away to catch his breath.

After settling onto limp legs, Cassie lifted on tiptoes to kiss Sam back, only to halt when the elevator door dinged open, as if signaling the end to their embrace. They separated, yet not completely as Sam took Cassie by the hand; fingers entwined, they made their way down the dark hallway.

***

Jamie had been watching the streaming feed when the gunshot popped like a firecracker, transforming the crowd into a swirling maelstrom. The video jumped from scene to scene, capturing jerky images of women screaming, running, falling. Secret Service pulled President Sanford from the podium.

Jamie searched for Cassie in the chaos, but the picture was too fuzzy to make out faces. He was relieved when she walked through the door, even if Sam was at her side. He assumed the flush on their faces was from the frenzy of the assassination attempt.

"It's all over the net," Jamie announced. "Witnesses describe a woman with an eye patch and a tall blonde. They're not sure who the shooter is—there are a lot of conflicting stories."

"Terrific," Cassie sighed at Sam. "The mec's after you, *and* you're Public Enemy Number One."

"Where's Mom?" Jamie asked only to catch himself. "I mean—"

"You can call her that—I know she thinks of you as her son. She's going to come by later." Not having eaten all day, Cassie realized the grumbling in her belly was as much from hunger as stress. "I'm starving," she said to Jamie. "What do you have to eat?"

Jamie pulled out bread, sliced cheese, apple juice, and Oreos and spread the items on the table. The three of them ate until empty wrappers and bottles littered the tabletop. Cassie leaned back, as tired as she was full. She asked Jamie if she could lie down on his bed—*Jasper, was it?*

Jamie nodded, and Cassie stretched out on the mattress. As soon as her head hit the pillow, she closed her eyes.

Just a cat nap, she told herself, *to clear my head.* Within minutes, Cassie fell into a deep sleep.

***

The impenetrable black seemed to go on forever. Cassie searched for a light, a sound, anything that would orient her in the void. Suddenly, a spark appeared. Cassie couldn't tell if it was in the distance or right in front of her. Drawn to the flicker, she tried to move only to realize that she had no body—she was nowhere and everywhere at the same time.

The light grew larger, seeming to come alive as it arranged itself into what Cassie recognized as the figure of Sam. A wave of yearning swelled inside of her. She wanted to touch him, to hold him—he was so close yet still out of reach. His incandescent form radiated like the sun. Then Sam burst into a million points of light; the brilliance lit up Cassie from within, filling her with exhilaration.

The lights began to swirl. The faster they spun, the more they transformed into a blinding blaze. Cassie was drawn to the center of the vortex. A voice reached into her mind:

Open the door!

In an instant, Cassie knew—not from any way that made sense to her—who was calling her name:

It was Cody.

Joy burst through her at the sound of her brother's voice. Then Cassie's elation turned into horror as something came over her, something terrifying.

No, it can't be.
But it was.
The black cloud!
Razor-like edges roiled as Cassie tried in vain to defend herself. Even without a body, she could still feel the stinging pain of a thousand cuts slicing her to pieces. Cassie panicked as she realized soon there would be nothing left of her.
Cassie, open the door!
Cody! Cassie screamed in her mind just as the darkness swallowed what was left of what she had been.

***

Jamie sat at the computer, clicking through the latest news on the assassination attempt. President Sanford had cancelled the rest of her speeches; she was scheduled to make an announcement on all the media outlets at 5 p.m.

The search for the two suspects continued. Jamie pulled up two sketches, one of a brutish person with an eye patch, the other a reasonably accurate likeness of Sam.

Cassie slept on the bed while Sam dozed in the armchair, folded like human origami. As if to some unheard cue, both Cassie and Sam started to mumble and shake. Jamie turned from the computer, watching in disbelief as they jerked uncontrollably, their eyes darting beneath their lids.

"What the . . . ?"

Jamie rose and leaned over the bed. "Cassie?"

She didn't wake up. He wrestled her by the shoulders. "Cassie!"

When he couldn't rouse her, Jamie turned his attention to Sam who had fallen from the chair in a cascade of seizures. Jamie yelled his name, slapping him several times—the hits served only to redden his face.

Then Cassie stiffened, her skin turning the color of ash. Jamie returned to Cassie's side; he sat on the bed and held her clenched hands, unwilling to accept his helplessness.

"Cassie, wake up!"

Cassie shot her eyes open and gasped; at the same time, Sam emerged from his jerking fit, looking groggy and confused. The three of them gaped at each other in bewildered silence.

Jamie slumped to the floor. "*What* was *that?!*"

Cassie sat up and leaned against the wall, fighting back the remnants of her nightmare. "I have bad dreams. Really, it's just this one bad dream over and over. This time it seemed so real."

Jamie trained his eyes on Sam: "You had a nightmare, too?"

A puzzled look appeared on Cassie's face. "What does Sam have to do with it?"

"You *both* had this weird convulsion thing—scared the crap out of me."

Cassie turned to Sam. "You were dreaming?"

Sam climbed back into the armchair but said nothing.

"Any time you want to fill us in," Jamie spat, not trying to hide his anger.

Sam rubbed his face and grimaced. "Did you *hit* me?"

"I tried to wake you up," he replied, his voice barely masking the fact that he'd taken a certain perverse pleasure in slapping Sam. "So what's going on?"

Sam bowed his head. "It isn't a dream, not usually anyway. I've only had it twice. This is the first time I've had it while I was asleep."

"The first time you've had *what?*" Cassie asked.

Sam shifted uncomfortably. "I don't know. I go somewhere. It's dark and endless. Lights start to spin. I'm being pulled into this big, swirling thing, then it all goes black."

Cassie's pale face turned even whiter. "That's *my* dream! How could you know that?"

Sam shook his head. "I don't know. The first time it happened, I was six. I don't remember much, but my mother told me she found me lying at the bottom of a swimming pool. She jumped in and saved my life. I told her I went to a strange place."

"And the second time?" Jamie asked.

"It was the day my mother and sister were killed," Sam said, barely able to get out the words. "I dove deep into a lake and caught my foot in the branches of a sunken tree. I tried to free myself but couldn't. Then I blacked out—I went there, wherever *there* is. I was being sucked into this whirlpool of light. The next thing I knew, I was swimming to the surface for my life."

"Do you hear a voice?" Cassie asked.

Sam shook his head again.

"I do," Cassie continued. "It's Cody."

Jamie sat up. "Cody? How could it be Cody?"

"I don't know. He kept saying the same thing over and over: 'Open the door.'"

Cassie pulled her knees to her chest as if to shield herself from her mounting fear. "Then this thing comes over me—only this time, it wasn't just a *thing*."

Sam and Jamie kept their eyes on her, waiting for an explanation. When none came, Jamie asked, "Okay, then what *was* it?"

Cassie let out a long exhale. "It was the black cloud."

The boys sat in dumbfounded silence. "Are you sure?" Sam finally asked.

Cassie nodded. "It was cutting me up like I was in the cosmic blender from hell." She paused. "And there's more—I think the black cloud is XY!"

Jamie gawked in disbelief. "Putting aside the fact that viruses tend not to be black or flashing or *visible*, why do you think that?"

"Because my mom has this picture of XY in her lab, and I just can't shake the fact that it looks like the cloud!"

A crease formed between Jamie's eyebrows—he hated puzzles that didn't fit together. "Sam, was the cloud in your dream?"

Sam shook his head.

Jamie turned back to Cassie. "Well, whatever you were dreaming, you almost didn't wake up from it. So you and Sam basically had the same dream . . . how strange is that."

"I know!" Cassie replied. "But my dream *was* different this time. Sam, you were in it, kind of."

"What do you mean?" Sam asked.

"You were there, but you were made of light. I know it sounds crazy, but it was so real. Then you vanished into this whirlpool. Actually, you *became* the whirlpool."

Sam nodded. "In my dream, I want to go into the whirlpool, but I also want to live."

"So, this whirlpool," Jamie asked Sam. "If you'd actually gone into it, where do you think it would have taken you?"

"I don't know. Somewhere far away . . . like *really* far away."

Jamie sat at the computer and typed furiously, bringing up the article he'd read not days before. After a brief pause, he read out loud: "In order to withstand a journey at the speed of light, one would have to be transformed into pure energy, reorganizing into a physical structure at the destination."

"What's that?" Cassie asked. "What journey?"

"Through a wormhole."

Cassie stared at Jamie as if he'd just started talking in Russian.

"What the hell is a wormhole," Sam asked, "other than the thing a worm makes in the dirt."

"It's a tunnel, like a shortcut through space-time. Physicists theorize that wormholes connect the multiverse, linking the past, present and future—"

"Hang on," Sam interrupted. "The multi . . . *what?*"

"The multiverse. For centuries, we've thought of our universe as the only reality. Now there's evidence to support that we're just a small part of a multiverse, multiple universes, all connected but separate that make up all there is."

"And how do you *know* this stuff?" Sam asked.

Jamie straightened his posture. "I'm going to be a physicist when I get out of here. A lot of new math backs up some pretty radical theories."

Cassie joined in. "So what are the dreams trying to *tell* us?"

All of a sudden, Jamie felt a puzzle piece snap into place. "Maybe Sam's specific set of matter is the entrance way—the postern to another dimension."

"Back to that idea?" Sam groaned.

"I'm just following the evidence," Jamie replied. "You said you were six the first time you had your blackout experience?"

Sam nodded.

"And you're how old now?"

"Sixteen."

"So ten years ago," Jamie said as if to himself.

"That's right," Sam said. "And what does that have to do with anything?"

"XY hit ten years ago . . . maybe there's a connection."

Cassie didn't know where Jamie was going with the observation, but that didn't keep her from disliking it. "That's kind of a stretch."

"No, it's not," Jamie responded point-blank. "Sam had this spiraling portal experience ten years ago. Then XY hits, and *he's* the only immune male on the planet? There's got to be some kind of connection."

"Well, it still seems pretty farfetched," Cassie noted, hoping her disdainful tone would end the discussion.

Jamie met her dismissal head on. "A lot of things—the earth being round, the sun as the center of the solar system—seemed unbelievable before people had the means to understand them." He looked at Sam. "What month did you almost drown in the pool?"

"I don't know. I just remember it was the spring."

"XY hit in April ten years ago," Jamie said, "in the spring."

Cassie's impatience with Jamie playing junior detective finally boiled over. "This is all just a big coincidence!" She looked at Sam for some kind of agreement—what she saw took her breath away: the blood had drained from his face, making him look like a ghost. "Are you okay? You don't look so good!"

"I'm fine," Sam uttered. "But I think Jamie is right."

Cassie faltered, feeling somehow betrayed by Sam's comment. "No, he's not—he couldn't be!"

Sam started out slowly: "Listen, I don't understand what's going on. But when I was six, I saw the swirling light for the first time . . .

and I almost died. When I didn't, something happened—something changed."

Cassie got up from the bed. "Okay, that's it! Now *both* of you are talking demented!"

"No, he's onto something," Jamie responded. "Sam must have something to do with the virus that killed all the men. Scientists never figured out where it came from—you of all people should know that."

Cassie thought of her mother's ten-year struggle to defeat the contagion. "So you're saying Sam is to *blame* for XY? Tell me, Jamie, exactly how did he make *that* happen?"

"I don't know," Jamie replied, not wanting to become stuck on a question he knew he couldn't answer. "What I *do* know—pretty much anyway—is that Sam can tap into a portal. I also know Cody called out to you to open the door. So maybe Cody isn't really dead. Maybe he's trapped—along with all the men—in the dimension that Sam almost went to." Jamie pulled back, trying to rein in his galloping thoughts. "And maybe Sam is the way to bring them back."

"But the men are dead!" Cassie shouted, her strained voice bouncing off the close walls. "We saw the bodies! How can they be dead but trapped in some . . . *dimension?*"

"Maybe it's a paradox," Jamie replied calmly, trying not to get sucked into Cassie's panic.

"A pair a *what?*" Sam asked.

"A paradox—when something is both itself and its opposite at the same time."

"So what you're saying is that the men can be dead and alive *at the same time?*" Cassie asked, not believing the sanity of her question.

Jamie nodded. "And an atom can exist in two different *places* at the same time." He paused, giving time for the two concepts to sink in. "That means there could be other versions of us, living in worlds just like this one." Jamie pressed on, not giving Cassie the chance to gain steam. "The Those-Who-Wait leader said the men were coming back . . ."

"Exactly!" Cassie cried. "And she's *nuts!*"

"Maybe," Jamie replied, "but she also saved Sam from the black cloud. Could you have done that?"

Cassie rubbed her eyes, too exhausted to think. "Okay, say you're right, say Sam can bring back the men—how is he supposed to *do* that?"

Jamie held back, not wanting to answer the question.

"I think it's obvious," Sam said quietly.

"Not to me!" she blurted. "So?" Cassie glared at both boys.

Sam looked at her with apologetic eyes. "Well . . . by *dying.*"

The single word hit Cassie like a fist to her jaw. She reeled back, then shook it off, denying it, defying it. "Well, you're *not* going to do *that* any time soon so end of story!"

Silence once again blanketed the small room. Then Jamie gave Sam an odd look, one that, this time, landed a blow to Cassie's stomach. She turned to Sam, her eyes boring into him.

"What you really mean is if you *kill* yourself!" Heat rushed to Cassie's face. "No, I don't believe it!" The more Cassie tried to push the absurd notion out of her head, the more she could hear Cody's voice from her dream pleading for help. A knot formed in her throat. "You end your life to put the world right? And if you're wrong, then you've offed yourself for nothing!"

Sam sat in the upholstered chair, wondering why he felt calm. "I've always wanted to know why I survived XY . . . maybe this is it."

Cassie looked squarely at Sam, completely unnerved yet too stubborn to give in. "Okay, so what are we talking about here—a bullet to the brain? Too messy. A swan dive off a cliff? Too chancy it might not work. A knife . . . ?" She broke down but not before managing to get out one last statement: "This isn't just crazy—it's *batshit* crazy!"

A small voice inside Sam's head echoed Cassie's sentiment: *Killing myself? Really? Cassie's right—this is insane!*

Yet the more he thought about the relentless question of his life—*why did I survive?*—the more he knew there had to be a reason. And this outrageous idea felt like the right answer. Stillness came over him, making his voice low and even: "It has to be by drowning. If I go too fast, it won't work."

"You don't know that!" Cassie blared. She turned to Jamie, her anxiety expanding beyond her control. "You're a really smart guy, Jamie, but this whole idea is seriously *warped!*"

Cassie dug into her backpack and pulled out her phone. "I'm calling my mom." She looked at the black screen—the phone was dead from a drained battery.

"Piece of shit!"

In a fit of anger, Cassie hurled the phone against the wall, shattering it to pieces. "My mom will talk some sense into you," she barked at Sam. "We're leaving!"

38

The streets were deserted due to heightened security from the assassination attempt. Cassie hurried down the sidewalk; she spied the bus stop, a metal pole with a sign displaying the dates and times of service.

"Cassie, wait up," Sam called out, hustling after her.

Before Cassie and Sam had left, Jamie pulled up the sketch of Sam that had been circulating the Internet. Seeing the drawing made Cassie want to be with her mother even more. Her mother could always calm her down when she was upset—and she was way past that. She needed to hear her mother's reassuring voice, to see things from her grounded perspective.

As Cassie approached the bus stop, she spotted a black and white patrol car coming down First Avenue. She grabbed Sam, and they ducked behind a tall ash tree; Cassie hoped the trunk was wide enough to hide them both.

The police car cruised the street and then turned right, disappearing down Wilson Avenue. The Smithsonian Metro station was only four blocks away, but Cassie didn't want to chance it—she knew there would be more riders on the subway than the bus. And more people meant a greater chance that Sam would be recognized.

When the street was once again quiet, Cassie and Sam walked up to the bus stop. Cassie read the sign and moaned. "We just missed the bus—the next one isn't for another hour." She slumped against the pole. "We can't just stand here, waiting for a cop car to come by."

"Cassie, it's not like I *want* to do this," Sam said, ignoring her statement.

She, in turn, ignored his comment. "We'll hide at Tidal Basin until the bus comes. C'mon." Cassie took off in the direction of a large body of water, Sam once again at her heels.

Tidal Basin was a manmade inlet next to the Potomac River that drained the Washington Channel after high tide. Across the expanse of water, the dome of the Jefferson Memorial rose above the pastel pink cherry trees that encircled the shore.

When Cassie was little, her mother would take her down to West Potomac Park for kettle corn and a rowboat ride on the inlet. Now the concession stand was closed, the boathouse as still as the water's surface.

Sam stopped, gaping in wonder at the bursting foliage. "Are these for real?" he asked as if to himself. He took hold of a blossom, feeling the creamy texture between his fingertips. "I've never seen trees like this before."

"They're cherry blossoms, some gift of friendship from Japan," Cassie responded, putting her anxiety on hold long enough to marvel at the magnificent trees. "I've lived in Columbia my whole life, and every spring, they still amaze me."

They started down the walkway, the sun's slanting rays glowing through blush-colored petals. A light breeze carried the sweet scent of roses.

"They're like clouds on the ground," Sam said, still captivated by the breathtaking sight. He reached for a low-hanging branch and snapped off a cluster of blossoms.

"I hate to break it to you, but it's illegal to take the flowers—I think it's a life sentence." She knew it was a lame attempt at humor but was too traumatized to care.

Sam slipped the blossom behind Cassie's ear. He gazed at her; she stared back. If her words couldn't convince him of the insanity of his plan, maybe her eyes could.

"It's official," Sam said, admiring his handiwork.

"What's that?"

"The flowers have done the impossible—they've made you more beautiful than you already are."

Cassie felt a flush at Sam's words. They were not, however, the words she wanted to hear. She wanted him to say, *Cassie, you're right— it's a ridiculous idea. I could never go through with it—I could never* kill *myself.* She sat on a bench near the water's edge and took the blossom from behind her ear.

"I know you think this is the right thing to do. And who knows, it might work." Cassie faltered in the face of her own mounting panic. "But you could be wrong."

Sam sat next to her. "If you could do something to bring back your father and brother, wouldn't you do it, even if it was a long shot?"

Cassie looked out at the water, hoping to find an answer in the sparkling surface. "Yes, I would. But there's nothing noble in throwing your life away." She turned to him. "Okay, I'm being selfish. I don't want you to die—I want you to live so you can be with me. Is that so terrible?"

Sam drew his arms around Cassie and kissed her, his breath starting to deepen. She responded by falling headlong into the caress, slipping one hand around his neck, the other under his shirt to feel the smooth nap of his skin.

Cassie broke away, prompting Sam to give her a puzzled look. Then she stood up and, taking him by the hand, led him to a secluded spot under a stand of cherry trees. Scattered pink petals blurred the distinction between ground and sky.

Cassie stretched out beneath the spreading canopy, pulling Sam down with her. The more she felt him against her, the more her anguish faded until all she knew was the touch of his hand, the softness of his lips, the weight of his body. She held onto him as if he might disappear if she loosened her grasp, the want, the longing building inside of her until it burned like wildfire.

After a long, deep kiss, Sam pulled away. "I don't know what to do," he whispered.

Cassie brushed the hair out of his face with her fingertips. "Neither do I," she said breathlessly, "but let's keep doing it."

39

The sun had set, leaving only a hint of afterglow in the darkness. Cassie awoke nestled in the crook of Sam's arm. She shifted her weight to snuggle into his neck, ready to drift back to sleep. Suddenly, Cassie shot her eyes open:

"The bus!"

Sam awoke with a start. They rose to their feet, buttoned, zipped, and dusted petals from their clothing. The sound of squealing brakes rolled across the water; in the distance, Cassie spied a bus approaching the stop. She took off down the walkway, Sam right behind her. The teens sprinted across Maine Avenue, dodging cars that swerved and honked. The bus discharged a passenger and then lumbered back onto the street.

"Wait!" Cassie shouted as she ran alongside the vehicle. Once again, the bus wheezed to a halt; the door swung open.

"I'm not supposed to make unscheduled stops," the driver said in a gruff voice.

Cassie murmured a quick "thanks" as she and Sam scooted up the steps. After swiping her card twice in the reader, she strode with Sam to the back, both of them trying to keep their balance on the swaying bus. After landing on a plastic bench, they looked at the six passengers evenly spaced among the seats, each of them clearly uninterested in the out-of-breath teenagers.

Cassie and Sam got off at Avenue D, leaving a forty-five minute walk home through leafy neighborhoods. When they arrived, Cassie was glad to see her mother's Volvo parked in the driveway. They burst through the front door.

"Mom?" Cassie yelled, wondering why the house was dark. She turned on a light—the hallway table was turned over, the mirror lined with cracks. Cassie went into the kitchen.

"I'll check the living room," Sam said.

After confirming that the kitchen was empty, Cassie met Sam in the hallway. He shook his head.

"Mom!" Cassie called out again. She flew up the stairs, trying to ignore the stone of dread that was lodging itself in her stomach. As Sam ducked into her room, Cassie entered the master bedroom. Scanning the area, Cassie saw no sign of her mother. In the bathroom, she held her breath as she pulled back the shower curtain.

Nothing.

"She's not in here," Cassie said in a loud voice. Turning down the hall, she saw Sam standing in her bedroom doorway. His head was lowered. She tried to push past him, but he stood in her way.

"Cassie, I don't know what to say . . ."

Her fierce look defied his words. "Let me in."

After a long moment, Sam moved aside. Cassie entered the room; in the dim light of the bedside lamp, she saw her mother lying on the floor, her face ashen, her arms and legs at odd angles like she was a dropped marionette.

"Mom!" Cassie cried as she sank to her knees. She shook her mother by the shoulders—there was no response. Something dark was wrapped around her mother's neck. Cassie tilted the lampshade forward; in the light, she saw purple bruises around her mother's throat. Cassie bent down, putting her ear to her mother's chest—the only sound she heard was that of her own pounding heart.

"No!"

Cassie slid her arms around her lifeless mother and wept.

Sam knelt down and folded Cassie into his arms. He spoke softly: "We can't stay here. Your mom put up a good fight, but she might have told the mec about Jamie's place." He tried to pry Cassie loose, yet she only tightened her hold.

"She'd never do that!" Cassie fired back, her voice tight yet defiant.

"You're probably right. Still, we should head to the lab, just to make sure."

Even thought she knew Sam was right, Cassie felt incapable of letting go, as if her arms no longer belonged to her but instead had somehow become a part of her dead mother.

Sam held Cassie as she sobbed. Finally, Cassie let go of her mother. "She should be in her bedroom."

Sam nodded. He gathered Amanda in his arms and carried her down the hall. After entering the room, Cassie motioned in solemn silence toward the bed. Sam laid Amanda down with care, resting her head on the pillow. Cassie smoothed her mother's hair and straightened her blouse. Then she draped a blanket over her, making her mother look she wasn't dead, just in a dreamless sleep. Cassie leaned over and kissed her mother's cold forehead.

"I love you, Mom."

Before they left the house, Sam asked Cassie if she still had the gun. She nodded and gave it to him. Sam slipped the gun into his jacket pocket, imagining the death of the maniac who had caused so much misery.

***

"We're going to check on Jamie, then go back to the house and finish this," Sam stated as Cassie turned the Mini Cooper into the Taft parking lot. She barely heard his words—she was too numb from grief to make sense of anything.

Maybe this is some awful dream, she thought with faint hope. *I just need to wake up.*

As she made her way toward the building, Cassie realized she would have to tell Jamie the terrible news. A wave of dread washed away her dullness as she imagined Jamie's face when he heard that now he had two dead mothers.

Cassie and Sam climbed the steps to the entrance. Without warning, an explosion rocked the building, hurtling them backward as if they'd been shot out of a cannon. A volley of debris blew across the parking lot, raining down glass, metal, and splintered wood.

Pulverized concrete bloomed from the wreckage as alarms blared. Flames shot out from broken windows.

Dazed, Sam struggled to sit up. His ears buzzed; his back throbbed from the impact. Cassie lay a few feet from him, as still as death. He crawled toward her. A clear shard, like a shark fin, stuck out from her thigh.

"Cassie?"

She moaned.

"Don't move—you've got some glass in your leg."

Sam pulled off his belt and strapped it above the wound on Cassie's thigh. After tying a knot, he pulled out the shard. At first, blood gushed from the gash; after several seconds, the makeshift tourniquet stanched the flow.

"What happened?" Cassie asked, raising a hand to her aching head.

"An explosion."

It took several seconds for Cassie to register what Sam had said. Then she cried out, "Jamie!"

Cassie pulled herself to her feet and stumbled toward the gaping hole in the building. "We've got to save him!"

Sam grabbed her arm. "You can't go in there!"

"Let go of me!" she yelled. She tried to wrench herself loose, but Sam's grip was too strong. Knowing she wouldn't be able to break away, Cassie made a fist with her free hand and punched Sam in the face; stunned by the hit, he loosened his hold, letting Cassie shake him off. She staggered into the hot, billowing dust. Sam came up from behind, lifted her off her feet, and carried her out of the smoke. Cassie kicked her legs, at the same time trying to bash him with her balled fists.

"This is your fault!" she cried. "My mother, Jamie—you did this!"

Sam let Cassie drop to the ground. She spun around, seething with pure hatred. "I wish I'd never met you! I never want to see you again!" Then Cassie hobbled back into the roiling dust.

Sam fell to his knees, his head in his hands. He knew what Cassie had said was true—somehow he *was* to blame for all of this madness. Yet it was the loathing in her eyes that made him feel like he'd broken into a thousand pieces.

A shriek pieced the air, jolting Sam from his anguish. He jumped to his feet and ran into the smoke.

"Cassie!"

He stopped short. Through the swirling dust, Sam saw the mec holding Cassie in a viselike grip—he pressed the barrel of a gun to her throat. Cassie struggled, making him dig the gun deeper into her neck.

"You've got no idea what a pain in the ass you are," the mec snarled.

"It's *me* you want!" Sam shouted. "I'll do anything you say—just *let her go!*"

"You're right about that—you *will* do anything I say. But you're wrong about one thing—I want her, too. She took my eye, so I took her mother. Seemed like a fair trade, don't you think?"

Sam froze. He remembered the gun in his pocket, his only hope. He wondered if could he pull it out and fire before the lunatic killed Cassie.

The mec spotted the drag in Sam's jacket. "Whatever you have in your pocket, throw it over here."

Sam hesitated. Once again, the mec forced the gun into Cassie's neck; a choking sound sputtered from her lips. "Do it now," he growled, "or say goodbye."

Sam pulled out the gun and tossed it to the mec; he kicked it away and then dragged Cassie toward a black car. "If you don't want to see her brains all over the pavement, I suggest you get in the trunk."

Cassie freed herself enough to cry out, "No Sam, don't! Run!"

"Let her go, and I'll get in the trunk," Sam said through gritted teeth.

The mec's mouth curved into a menacing smirk. "Having some trust issues? I'll let her go *after* you get in."

"He's lying!" Cassie hissed. "Don't do it!"

Sam knew Cassie was right. Still, he had to chance that she might survive if he did as the madman said. Sam opened the trunk and crawled in.

"Good boy. Get comfortable," the mec said with satisfaction. "You're going to be in there a while. And you'll have this to keep you company—the sight of a bullet ripping through her skull."

"No!" Sam yelled.

Cassie fought the mec's grip, yet the maniac clamped down on her until she almost passed out from fear. As the barrel of the gun dug into her throat, Cassie saw Sam climb out of the trunk as if in slow motion. His terrified face told her what she already knew— he wouldn't reach her in time. Cassie clenched every muscle in her body, steeling for the blast.

But no blast came.

There was only silence.

The mec let go and collapsed. Cassie bent over, coughing violently. She put her hands to her throat, gasping for air through her crushed windpipe. Then she looked over her shoulder—there was Jamie, holding a block of concrete. He dropped the chunk. Cassie hugged him, crying into his neck.

"You're alive!"

Sam kicked over the mec who flopped like a rag doll.

"Is he dead?" Jamie asked.

Sam knelt down, confirming the rise and fall of the mec's chest. "No, just knocked out." He looked at the unconscious form, realizing the time had come—his harrowing quest had come to an end. Sam picked up the gun and pointed it at the mec's head, every part of him burning with rage.

"My mother, my sister, Cassie's mom," he spat, the words like acid in his mouth. "It's time you paid for what you've done."

Before Sam could fire, Cassie put her hand on his arm. "No. I've got a better idea."

"Better than blowing his brains out?"

Cassie turned to Jamie. "I've got something to tell you, something bad—really bad." Her voice grated on her dry throat. "My mom—our mom is dead." She looked at the mec sprawled on the ground. "He strangled her."

Jamie bent over slightly and grimaced as though he'd been socked in the stomach. Cassie put her arms around him, knowing the embrace would do little to lessen the pain.

The mec groaned.

"He's coming around," Sam said.

"Grab him and follow me," Cassie declared. Sam and Jamie dragged the mec behind Cassie until she stopped at a pile of burning rubble.

"A gunshot to the head while he's unconscious?" Cassie asked. "That's way too humane for this monster." She cocked her head toward the flames. "And it should be from all three of us."

Sam and Jamie looked at each other and nodded. With Sam at the mec's shoulders and Jamie and Cassie at his feet, the three of them swung the dead weight onto the blaze. They stood back and watched as he caught fire. A bloodcurdling scream let them know he'd regained consciousness.

The mec lurched to his feet, engulfed by flames. He held out his hand, his face contorting in agony. Black smoke wafted from his head, disappearing into the dark sky; the stench of burning flesh filled the air. The mec dropped to the ground, his charred legs no longer able to bear his weight; flames shot upward as they consumed the last of him. In the distance, sirens wailed as fire trucks raced toward the bombed building.

"We've got to go," Sam said. As the three of them approached the Mini Cooper, Cassie stopped and looked back at the sizzling remains. In a low, deliberate voice, she growled, "Burn. In. Hell."

40

Cassie steered toward home to the drone of the car's engine. She glanced at Sam—he was looking out the window, lost in his own thoughts. Then she checked on Jamie in the rearview mirror. "How did you survive the blast?"

"The room wasn't blown up. I had to wait for the dust to clear before I could climb my way out."

"Mom thought it had been a bomb shelter in the fifties . . . guess she was right."

Hearing the word *mom* made Jamie dizzy. But it wasn't just grief that made his head spin—for ten years, he'd seen the outside world only through the flat display of his computer screen. Now, as buildings and trees passed by in a three-dimensional blur, the sense of depth made him sick to his stomach.

"I always thought the day I got out of that room would be the happiest day of my life," Jamie uttered, more to himself than to Cassie and Sam. He closed his eyes, hoping to steady his wobbling head.

In the frenzy, Cassie had overlooked a crucial detail: the count-down on Jamie's life had begun. She gripped the steering wheel, wondering how much time he had, knowing he was thinking the same thing. In the rearview mirror, Cassie watched as beads of sweat formed on Jamie's brow; his eyes were glassy.

"How do you feel?" Cassie asked. Jamie's reflection shrugged. She pressed the gas pedal and, looking both ways, ran a red light.

After pulling into her driveway, Cassie shoved the car into park, jumped out, and leaned the driver's seat forward. Jamie was flushed and sweaty. She placed her hand on his forehead; his skin felt like it could burn her palm.

"Can you walk?" Cassie asked.

"I think so," Jamie replied as he crawled out of the car. As soon as he shifted his weight to his feet, his knees gave way. Cassie caught him before he ended up as a clump on the asphalt.

"It's started," Cassie told Sam under her breath. "First, the fever—when the seizures come, it doesn't take long after that." She and Sam helped Jamie walk across the driveway, his arms around their shoulders.

Jamie surveyed his childhood home. "It looks just the same," he said, trying to manage a smile. The three of them entered Cassie's house; Cassie and Sam helped Jamie into the living room where they laid him on the couch. Jamie grabbed Cassie by the hand.

"Don't go."

Sam pulled Cassie aside. "There's no time," he said in a forceful whisper. "Don't you see? If I die, it could save him."

Cassie didn't know if she had the will to fight Sam anymore. "Hasn't there been enough death tonight? I can't keep Jamie from dying of XY, but I can convince you not to kill yourself!"

The wound in Cassie's thigh started to throb. She looked at Sam, her eyes brimming with tears. "What I said back there, after the bomb went off . . . I didn't mean it." She slipped her arms around him and leaned her head on his shoulder. "Please don't leave me—I need you."

Sam held her close. "I don't want to go. But just maybe, if I do this, I can make the world right again. And I can keep you from being killed because of me."

"But the mec is dead!"

Sam shook his head. "All of this, it won't stop, not until I'm gone." His voice became faint. "I couldn't take it if anything happened to you." He tightened his embrace, wanting to hold onto her—and the moment—forever. But he knew he couldn't. "It's time," he said, letting his arms go slack.

As Sam slid away from her, Cassie felt an emptiness that stopped her heart. It was as though he'd set her adrift, leaving her alone and helpless. She tried to think of something that would change his mind yet was too overwhelmed to do anything but let Sam take her by the hand and lead her up the stairs. They walked through the bedroom, past Amanda who was still pale and silent on the bed. Sam flicked on the light in the bathroom, then turned on the tub's blue faucet full blast.

"Only the cold?" Cassie asked, forcing herself to speak.

Sam nodded. "I don't know why, but the colder, the better—the trick is to make it as slow as possible. You're going to have to help me."

"How?"

"You'll have to hold me down. My natural reflex will be to want to breathe. I'll try my best to fight it, but you'll have to keep me under if I can't."

Cassie nodded, not that she agreed with him, just that she'd heard what he'd said—the words themselves made no sense to her.

When the tub was full, Sam peeled off his shirt and pants, wearing only the fruit necklace from the carnival. The sight of it made Cassie want to laugh and cry at the same time. He took off the necklace and draped it around her.

"Who needs diamonds and rubies when you've got plastic bananas and apples?" Sam said in a vain attempt to lighten the mood. Cassie touched the necklace, knowing it was more precious to her than a fistful of gems.

Sam stepped into the tub and sat in the water. "Something's not right. It needs to be colder." He looked up at her. "We need ice."

In a daze, Cassie nodded. She hurried down the stairs and into the kitchen. After pulling out the large bin of ice from the freezer, Cassie hesitated. *What if I don't go back upstairs? Maybe Sam won't—or can't—go through with this by himself.*

Cassie shut the freezer door, then stepped into the hallway. She stopped to look in the living room, blindsided by grief as she watched Jamie shake in a feverish dream.

When he dies, he'll go to that horrible place in my nightmare with Dad and Cody and all the men. Trapped. Afraid. Hopeless.

Yet Cassie knew it wasn't hopeless. Their one chance for survival waited upstairs in a tub full of water. She climbed the stairs and entered the bathroom with the bin of ice.

"How much?" she asked.

"All of it."

Cassie dumped the cubes into the tub. As the ice floated, Sam's pallid skin stippled with goosebumps.

"Better," he said, his teeth chattering.

Cassie sat on the floor next to the tub. Sam leaned over and kissed her with cold lips. She broke away.

"Sam—"

He kissed her again, cutting her off. Finally, he pulled back. "We're past that now. Don't ask me how, but I know I have to do this."

Cassie looked at him, not believing what she was about to say: "I know."

Sam clasped Cassie's hand in both of his. "I once told you I didn't know much about romance," he said with a shy smile. "And I guess that's still true." Then he looked into her eyes as if the only thing he desired was to take refuge in their warmth. "But I am sure of one thing," he continued, his voice quiet yet determined. He hesitated, not from doubt but from wanting to fill himself up with the feeling that surged inside of him. "I love you, Cassandra."

Cassie fixed her gaze on Sam, tears welling. Her heart pounded in her chest, the same heart that was at once blossoming and breaking.

"I love you, Sam."

Sam pressed his lips to hers yet pulled away, as if the kiss might have the power to change his mind. Still, he focused on Cassie, knowing the only way he would make it through the unspeakable task would be to keep his eyes solely on her.

After several seconds, Sam took a deep breath and then slipped under the water. His hair waved like seaweed; small bubbles escaped from his mouth.

Seconds passed. A minute. Two minutes. For Cassie, time seemed to pull her in opposite directions, dragging her down yet speeding past her in a blur. Then it happened—Sam jerked, breaking his gaze. Cassie knew he was concentrating, trying to prolong the inevitable. Panic distorted his face.

"Look at me!" she cried as she rose to her knees. Sam snapped his eyes back to hers, his expression at once terrified and pleading.

But pleading for what? Cassie thought. She wanted to believe he was desperate to live, yet the ache in her heart told her it wasn't so.

Sam started to flail, great uncontrollable jerks that drenched Cassie with icy water. She plunged her hands into the tub, pushing down on him with all of her strength.

"Sam!" she cried out, but he was too strong. His back arched, his head fought to break through the water's surface. When Sam gripped the sides of the tub, Cassie knew he wasn't trying to pull himself up—he was trying desperately to keep himself down.

"This isn't going to work!" Cassie cried.

She continued to press Sam into the tub, all the while realizing she wouldn't be able to keep him submerged. A thought flashed in her mind, one as shocking as it was horrific. She pushed it away, wanting only erase the idea from her brain.

No, I can't do that. It would be too much!

Yet even as she struggled to keep Sam underwater, she knew what she had to do. Cassie crawled into the tub and knelt on Sam's chest. His eyes widened in fear, his face turning blue as he continued to writhe in a frenzy. Cassie struggled to keep herself upright, knowing Sam was fighting his own will to live as much as the weight of her body. Suddenly, she felt as if she'd slammed into a brick wall.

"I can't do this!" Cassie wailed, the battle within her tearing her apart. She wanted to yank Sam from the water, to save himself from his own reckless resolve. Sobbing, Cassie couldn't believe what she was doing:

I'm drowning Sam!

Yet she knew she had to bear down on his chest, to stay with him until the end. Deep inside, in a place she'd never known before, Cassie understood something with an agonizing clarity—loving Sam meant helping him do what he needed to do, even if it meant losing him forever.

Suddenly, Sam stopped thrashing. Through the choppy water, Cassie watched as he looked at her yet through her. Then he smiled.

It was a strange smile, one somewhere between terror and ecstasy. His body shuddered, his eyes rolled under their lids. He went limp.

"Sam!"

Cassie jumped out of the tub. She lifted Sam out of the water, sending a great splash against the floor tiles. His body was slack, his face lifeless. Then Cassie looked up—a swell of darkness descended, erasing the ceiling, the walls. It didn't blot out the light so much as consume it.

Terror gripped Cassie by the throat. The blackness poured down, obliterating everything—Sam, the room, the world. She howled in fear, yet the dark devoured her cries.

Without warning, flashes of light blazed into view. Countless tiny stars began to circle, slowly at first, then faster until they blurred into a blinding light. Cassie's eyes burned. She tried to shut them but couldn't look away from the white-hot radiance. A deafening roar reverberated in the once dead silence. The flaming circle threw off sparks, spinning until it reached a speed beyond comprehension.

Again, Cassie screamed, this time, her cry seeming to reverberate through space and time. In an instant, she burst into a fiery brilliance and then disappeared into the swirling vortex.

41

Cassie opened her eyes. She was wet and cold and face down in a puddle. Inhaling sharply, she drew water into her nose; a fit of coughing brought her fully conscious. She pushed herself from the floor, then turned toward the tub, not wanting but needing to see Sam's naked body, white from cold and death.

The tub was empty.

Cassie rose to her feet. She stared at the tub as if she could will Sam to appear in it, coughing and choking but still alive. Yet the tub remained empty, and Sam was still gone.

"Sam?" Cassie yelled as she ran out of the bathroom. The house was silent and dark. She flew down the stairs.

"Cassie?"

"Sam!" Cassie cried out. She entered the living room only to discover that it was Jamie who'd called her name. He sat up on the couch, looking worn out but clear-eyed. Cassie landed next to him and gave him a hug. "You're still alive!"

"Yeah, and you're all wet!" Jamie shot back, flinching at her soaked clothing. "What happened?"

"I don't know. Sam was in the tub. He . . . I . . . everything went dark. There was a bright light." Cassie let out a breath, knowing there were no words to describe what she'd just experienced. "I blacked out. When I came to, Sam wasn't there."

Cassie looked closely at Jamie—the color had returned to his cheeks. She felt his forehead, but her hand was too cold to tell if he still had a fever.

"It's gone," Jamie said. "I can feel it. Whatever Sam did, it worked—I'm no longer infected with XY." Jamie hugged Cassie, this time unfazed by her sopping clothes.

Cassie broke away. "I'm going to look for him." She raced upstairs to check her bedroom—it was empty. Down the hall, she poked her head into Cody's room—no life stirred within. Then she bolted down the stairs and into the kitchen.

"Sam?"

The kitchen was deserted. Cassie opened the door to the basement and ran down the stairs. Pulling on the chain for the light, she scanned the mountains of junk in the musty area: an artificial Christmas tree, boxes of old books, a broken bicycle, rows of suitcases.

But no Sam.

Cassie slumped to the floor. *Where is he?* she wondered, her heart seizing in a knot. Tears spilled down her cheeks at the thought of never seeing Sam again. Her breath hitched as she tried to weep and breathe at the same time. She sat under the glare of the bare bulb in a wretched heap, undone by her own agony. Then Cassie froze in mid-sob:

What was that?

She heard something. Cassie held her breath to hear above her thumping heart. It was faint, but it was there:

Cassie!

"Sam!" Cassie shouted as she leapt to her feet. "Where are you?!" She spun around, trying to pinpoint his voice that seemed to emanate from all over the room.

"I'm here, Sam! Keep talking!"

In a panic, she shoved aside boxes, sending blankets and books to the floor. She tore apart one corner of the basement. Not finding Sam, she continued to plow through the room, breaking a glass vase, tearing gauzy curtains. Then she stopped.

Cassie heard a moan coming from behind an old dresser. She pushed on a box of Christmas decorations, revealing a pair of feet that stuck out past the edge of the dresser.

Cassandra!

Sam's voice was fading.

"I'm coming!"

She leaned into the dresser and muscled it out of the way—an indistinct form lay curled up in the dark.

"Sam!" Cassie cried. She rolled over the figure only to stop cold. The face that turned into the light wasn't Sam's—it was the face of her father. Cassie stared at him, overcome by shock.

"*Dad?*"

Matt opened his eyes, struggling to focus. Cassie helped him to his feet and then threw her arms around him. He pushed her away.

"I know, I'm soaked," she said sheepishly.

Matt trained a steely gaze on her. "Who are you?"

"Dad, it's me, Cassie!"

Matt ignored the remark and looked around. "What am I doing in the basement? What's going on?" Just then, Cassie heard the snuffling of a small child.

"Cody!"

She pawed through boxes, following the sound until she found her six-year-old brother standing and whimpering, his fist rubbing an eye. Her first impulse was to scoop him up into her arms, but she held back. "Hi, Cody! I'm so happy to see you!"

Cody studied Cassie like she was an odd bug, then threw his arms around her in a big hug. "I knew you'd hear me! I was so scared!"

Cassie picked him up and squeezed, her heart bursting with joy.

"I can't breathe! Cody squeaked, prompting Cassie to ease up on her grasp. He leaned back to stare at her with wide eyes: "You got big!"

Cassie laughed, louder than she had in a long time. "I *did* get big—it's because I'm your big sister!"

Before Cassie could hug him again, Matt pulled Cody out of her arms. "I don't know what kind of sick game you're playing, but you've got to leave right now."

"Dad, it's Cassie!" Cody exclaimed. "Can't you see?"

"Don't be silly, Cody." He turned to Cassie. "What have you done with my daughter?"

"I *am* your daughter, only I'm sixteen now. I know it's beyond strange, but I can explain everything."

Matt shook his head and climbed the stairs carrying Cody. "If you don't leave right now, I'm calling the police."

Cassie followed him up the steps and into the kitchen. She halted as memories of her father and brother flooded in.

"Remember that day at the playground? Cody and I were climbing on the jungle gym, and he fell off. He got six stitches on his chin."

"That doesn't prove anything," Matt said curtly.

"When I was five, you took Cody and me to a baseball game. Cody ate too many hot dogs and threw up in the Cooper. You stopped off at the car wash before we went home and told us not to tell Mom. You said it would be our little secret."

Matt froze, as if all of his energy had been diverted to his brain. "How could you know that?"

The memories kept rushing in. "Every night, you'd tuck us in and say the same thing—you'd look at Cody and say 'good night, sun' and then to me and say 'good night, moon.' "

Matt let Cody slip to the floor. He searched Cassie's face—recognition shone in his eyes. "How is it possible?" he barely uttered as he wrapped his arms around Cassie; she sobbed into his chest.

"I've missed you both so much!"

Just then, Jamie walked into the kitchen. "Mr. O'Connell!"

Matt sized up Jamie. "I guess I should know who you are, but I don't."

"It's me, Jamie."

"Jamie? From next door?" Matt dropped onto a chair, hoping to steady his bewildered head. "You're sixteen, too?"

Jamie nodded. He turned to Cassie. "Did you find Sam?"

Cassie shook her head.

Matt looked confused. "Who's Sam?"

Cassie smiled as Sam's voice echoed in her head. *Just the boy who brought you and Cody back*, she thought, *the boy who means everything to me.* "I'll tell you about him later—it's kind of a long story."

"I'm going home to see if my dad is back," Jamie said. He looked around the kitchen, still amazed that he was out of his small room for good. Before he slipped out the door, Jamie turned to Cassie. "I still can't believe he did it."

"Me neither!"

Cody tugged on Cassie's wet shirt. "Where's Mom?"

Cassie took a deep breath and knelt down to Cody's eye level. "I have something to tell you, something very sad," she said, her voice wavering. "In fact, it's the saddest thing in the world."

At first, Matt seemed perplexed. Then a despondent look darkened his face; he knew Cassie's comment could only mean one thing. He bowed his head and closed his eyes—whatever strange events had taken place, Matt knew they would pale in comparison to the loss of his wife.

"I want to see Mom," Cody insisted.

"Okay, I'll take you to her."

Cassie picked up her brother. Then she took her father by the hand and led them both upstairs to the bedroom.

Epilogue

Cassie awoke the next day to the afternoon sun filling her bedroom. She'd slept fitfully, waking several times during the night to make sure Cody was still tucked beside her.

The night before, Cassie had struggled to tell Cody about their cold, ashen mother. "Mom is in a deep sleep, a sleep she'll never wake up from," she'd said, her voice quiet and soothing. Cassie wanted to rub off as many hard edges as possible. Yet she'd forgotten one thing: Cody was a child of the epidemic. He looked at his mother.

"She's dead, isn't she?"

Cassie nodded. No comforting words could disguise the bleak reality.

Cody started to cry. He wrapped his arms around his father's neck; the two of them held each other for a long time.

Cassie shook off the memory, not wanting to become mired in sorrow. She gazed at Cody—he was fast asleep, his chest rising and falling in a relaxed rhythm. The faint sound of the television came from downstairs.

Being careful not to wake her brother, Cassie rose from the bed and crept down the stairs. She found her father on the living room couch, coffee cup in hand. Cassie sat next to him; he put his arm around her and kissed her temple. Then he looked at the TV and shook his head.

"It's just so hard to believe."

Cassie responded with only a nod, still amazed that men all over the world had suddenly reappeared as if from the dead. She clicked through the channels; news of what the media dubbed The Return had taken over every station. On a talk show, several scientists argued about the reason for the earth-shattering event—a super collider malfunction, a magnetic pole shift, and solar flares were only some of the reasons offered in explanation.

The scene cut to a clip of Those-Who-Wait followers laughing and dancing, throwing off their robes and chanting incomprehensible phrases. The men had returned at the stroke of midnight, the time of the cult's secretive meetings. Yet the young girl, the leader of the strange group, was nowhere to be found in the media frenzy.

The Return had also brought out the fringe element, legions of kooks and nutcases who explained in lurid detail their versions of the shocking occurrence. One fact was clear: not all of the men had made it back, making Cassie even more thankful that her father and brother had survived the horrifying ordeal.

***

Jamie came over that evening and suggested a walk to the park. Cassie agreed, thinking the fresh air would do her good. She put Luka on a leash. The husky had been unusually calm since Cassie picked her up at the neighbor's house that morning. Cassie nuzzled soft fur, grateful that Luka hadn't been at home when the mec attacked.

Jamie and Cassie strolled with Luka in the cool evening. Twilight glowed behind the rooftops.

"My dad came back," Jamie said. "I found him in the laundry room. He was out of it."

"I can't imagine what they went through. How'd he take the news about your mother?"

"Probably pretty much the same as your dad when he found out about your—*our* mother. And having a now sixteen-year-old son doesn't make it any easier."

Cassie nodded. They strode along the sidewalk, content to be in each other's company.

"How's your leg?" Jamie asked, ending the lull.

"It's better. I've got about a million butterfly bandages on it, but it still hurts." Again, they fell silent.

Jamie watched as the sidewalk passed beneath his feet. "I think we should tell people what happened."

Cassie looked at the crescent moon rising above the treetops. "Do we even know what happened? Anyway, no one will believe us. They'll think we're one of the crackpots." Cassie crossed her arms in front of her, wishing she'd worn a jacket.

They arrived at the park and sat on a bench. Cassie unhooked Luka from the leash, yet instead of running off, the husky curled up at Cassie's feet—it was as though she knew the place to be was at Cassie's side.

Jamie looked straight ahead. "Sam gave up his life for me and for every male who made it back. I don't understand how he did it, but I wish I could thank him for it."

The sound of Sam's voice calling her name resonated in Cassie's mind. It was like a small treasure she'd wrapped in soft cloth for safekeeping. "He didn't give up his life."

"What do you mean?"

Then Cassie voiced the thought that had been keeping her on life support: "Sam's alive."

Jamie gaped at her in surprise. "You saw him?"

"No, he called my name when I was in the basement—twice."

"Cassie, that was probably your father."

"No, it was Sam," Cassie replied, digging in. "I'm sure of it. And my dad didn't even know who I was in the beginning."

Jamie hesitated. He knew Cassie was hurting. He also knew avoiding the truth would only prolong her grief. "I know you want Sam back, but he's gone."

"Yes," Cassie said with defiance. "Not dead, just gone."

Jamie shook his head. "I think you wanted Sam to be alive so much, you heard his voice—your mind played tricks on you."

The moon rose in the sky—night was drawing near. "You're right. I did want him to be alive. I still do, more than anything. He called out to me, just like Cody did." Cassie tucked the memory of Sam's voice in a private place in her heart, knowing she would rely on its promise in the coming days.

"So I'm going to look for him," Cassie said as she raised her head toward the vast, darkening sky. "And I'm going to find him."

Thanks for reading *Pink*. Please visit my website www.stephanie powellbooks.com to find out the latest news on *Puzzle*, the next book in *The Pink Trilogy*.

Made in the USA
San Bernardino, CA
09 May 2016